# THE WORRIED WIDOW

# GERALD HAMMOND
# THE WORRIED WIDOW

St. Martin's Press
New York

Library of Congress Cataloging-in-Publication Data

Hammond, Gerald.
    The worried widow.

    I. Title.
PR6058.A55456W67   1988      823'.914      87-28620
ISBN 0-312-01541-0

First published in Great Britain by Macmillan London Limited.

First U.S. Edition

10  9  8  7  6  5  4  3  2  1

# THE WORRIED WIDOW

# ONE

In the echoing emptiness of what, according to the estate agents, had once been a coach-house, Keith Calder was reloading his pressure-barrel when his wife, heralded by a flood of daylight, came through the door. He sighed and raised one muff of his ear-protectors.

'There's somebody on the phone,' Molly said.

Keith was both busy and absorbed. 'Tell them I'm dead,' he said shortly.

'I can't. I said I'd fetch you. And I wouldn't have said that if you really were dead, now would I?'

Keith thought that she very well might have done so. Sometimes he thought that it was Molly's mission in life to call him away from absorbing problems to take unwelcome phone-calls.

'I'm too busy. Say I'll call them back.'

'I'm not telling any more lies for you,' Molly said. 'Not after telling Mr Wilmington you'd gone to Lerwick and you bumping into him five minutes later. It's a lady, a Mrs Henderson,' she added temptingly and gave a quick gurgle of laughter. 'She asked if you were Keith Calder the private eye.'

'Well, I'm not.'

'You do investigate things,' Molly pointed out.

'I investigate things like burst gun-barrels,' Keith said, 'which is what I'm trying to do now to get your Mr Wilmington off my back. Anything else, she can go to one of the agencies.'

'She sounded a nice-like body,' Molly said. 'But she seemed very upset. It's about her husband's death. The sheriff called it suicide and she said that he'd never do a thing like that.'

Keith fitted a cartridge into the breech of his pressure-barrel. This was bolted to a heavy table and pointed towards a large,

5

steel plate which was angled to deflect the shot safely into a bed of sand. Keith had a dislike of small-shot ricochetting around in a confined space. 'I'm not investigating any more crimes, firearms or no. Whenever I take on anything like that,' he said, 'something nasty happens.' He turned his back and fitted a fresh lead 'crusher' pellet into the stirrup.

'You usually manage to stop something worse happening. Shall I say you'll come and see her?'

'No, no and no!' To emphasise his words, Keith slammed his hand down. The third smack caught the primitive trigger and the cartridge fired. Between stone walls, the crack of the discharge and the ring of the pellets against the steel plate were deafening. A fresh cloud of blue nitrocellulose smoke tainted the air. 'Now see what you've made me do.'

Molly had retreated hastily out of the door. She came back and cupped her ear. 'What?'

He raised his voice. 'You said Henderson. Did you mean Hendrickson? Would that be Sam Hendrickson's widow?'

Molly's hearing was beginning to return. 'I suppose so,' she said. 'I ought to have realised. What shall I tell her?'

'She'll have hung up by now.'

'I don't think so, she was too het up. Anyway, I have her number. I can call her back.'

'You do that,' Keith said. 'Tell her I wouldn't touch it with a barge pole. Shooting himself was the only good thing he ever did. But you needn't put it quite like that.'

'But suppose he really didn't do it?'

'Then I might find myself putting the finger on whichever public-spirited citizen knocked the bastard off. And I'd rather give him a medal.'

Keith's reaction came as no surprise to Molly. He usually jibbed at any attempt to lure him out of the tight circle of his immediate enthusiasms. She offered a compromise. 'I'll tell her to come and see you at three o'clock,' she said.

Keith threw up his hands. 'You haven't heard a bloody word I've said, have you?'

'How could I, with you shooting off guns in my ear?' Molly asked triumphantly. 'If you want to turn her down, at least you can hear her out first and then tell her to her face. You might even be able to give her some useful advice.'

6

'I'm seeing Wallace at the shop at three.'

'I'll phone Wal and make an excuse,' Molly said firmly. Keith was going to see the lady and to take her case. Molly loved her husband in all his moods. If she should ever lose him, she would not know how to live on. But far, far worse was the image of his being branded a suicide. That would be the last straw, the final denunciation of a failed wife. No woman should have to face that.

An hour later when Keith, summoned by three peals on an electric bell, crossed the small courtyard and joined her for lunch in the blue-and-white kitchen of Briesland House, Molly's dormant curiosity had had time to germinate.

'Why were you so much against Mr Hendrickson?' she asked. 'What did he ever do to get up your nose?'

'Nothing personal,' Keith said with his mouth full.

'He was quite a famous sort of person, wasn't he?'

'So was Hitler.' Keith decided that he would only get peace to eat his meal if he kept Molly talking. 'What do you know about him?' he asked.

Molly put down her fork. 'He was leader of one of the big Scottish unions,' she said. 'I've seen snippets about him in the papers now and again. And then there was a report of the Fatal Accident Enquiry in yesterday's paper. It said that they'd moved here from Edinburgh after he fell ill, only three months ago. I mean that they moved here three months ago – he'd been ill longer than that. The sheriff – it was Sheriff Walker, the nice old man who kept looking down the front of my dress at Sir Peter's Christmas party – decided that he'd taken down his shotgun and ... and done it while he was depressed over his illness. Mrs Hendrickson heard the shot and found him. That must have been awful for her,' Molly added breathlessly, visualising the scene and mentally embellishing it with a wealth of gory detail.

'Messy,' Keith agreed. He finished his plate and pushed it away. 'It was more than just an illness, though. He'd had a stroke and was pretty badly incapacitated, which would be enough to push anybody in the direction of suicide. The sheriff decided that he'd done it while the balance of his mind was disturbed, which is a gimmick to permit his burial in consecrated ground. Not that Sam Hendrickson would have given a fart where he was buried, from what I've heard of him, but buried he was in the kirkyard a few days ago. But the point is, nobody could blame the widow for his doing it, so why would she be taking it so personally?'

'Likely she'll tell you when you see her,' Molly said. 'But nothing we've said sounds like a good reason for you to despise him so. I know you don't like the unions, Keith, but it can't just be that.'

Keith toyed with his coffee cup. 'I've nothing against unions as such,' he said. 'I haven't had a whole lot to do with them after being a one-man band most of my life.'

'There's Wallace.'

'Wal's a partner. So're you and Janet. And although we do have the occasional, casual employee, the partners have never outnumbered the staff by less than two to one. From what little I know about unions,' Keith said, 'there are some very good and responsible ones. I just think it's time that some of the other kind forgot the Tolpuddle Martyrs and started acting in their members' interests instead of out of hatred and prejudice. Sam Hendrickson was a prime example of the sort of hypocrite I mean. I never knew him and I'm only putting together a hundred different bits and pieces that I've heard or read over the years. But he came from a good home and had a good schooling, yet he was an out-and-out Marxist, dedicated to serving the communist cause whenever he could, usually at his members' expense – and the more harm he did his own country's economy, the better he was pleased. He lived better than most capitalists, with a swanky home and a big car and his children at private schools. What's more, he didn't live like that on his salary as general secretary of a medium-sized union.'

'Yes. I can see why you and he might not have got on,' Molly said, nodding. Keith, when he thought about politics at all, was right-wing and a fervent patriot.

'There's more. I've been hearing whispers. There was some big scandal brewing and only his illness was keeping it at bay. You can't drag a man into court if his doctor certifies that he isn't fit. If somebody did knock him off,' Keith said, 'I'd guess that it was something political, which I'm not equipped to deal with. Even if I wanted to, which I don't. For that sort of thing,

8

you need dozens of men, months of time, power to compel answers and the status to get search warrants.'

On the upper floor of Briesland House two large rooms, formerly bedrooms, were given over to Keith's need for workshop space, storage and other overflow from the shop in Newton Lauder a mile or two away. A former dining room had also been made over into a study for his paperwork and occasional writings, but it was in the upstairs workshop, at a bench among the racks of antique guns, that Keith was gauging and tabulating the lead crushers from his morning's work when Molly again interrupted him.

'Mrs Hendrickson's here,' she said. 'And – guess what? – I know her. She was Jenny Kerr and we were at school together. She was my senior but I remember her well. I've put her in the study and the kettle's on. Are you coming?'

Keith put down his micrometer and noted a reading in his neat tabulation, but he made no move to get up. Instead, he swivelled his chair and looked out of the window, over the Borders scenery which reached to the town of Newton Lauder. Sunshine was settling warmth on to the bright greens of spring. Splashes of colour were appearing and he wished that he could get out with a gun and a dog. Such weather so early in the year could never be trusted to last until tomorrow. 'Tell me about her,' he said.

'It was long ago,' Molly said doubtfully. 'She was liked without being really popular, if you know what I mean. I remember her as a quiet sort of person. She was good to be with. Not fun, she was too quiet to be fun, but she had a sort of contentment which rubbed off on you. And she was a trusting person who always thought the best of everybody.'

'Soft?' Keith asked.

'In a way, I think she was. She was religious but she didn't force it on you. Keith, do you think that that might be the reason why she doesn't want to believe that her husband killed himself? Mortal sin?'

'It could be. On the other hand, somebody with real faith would probably reason that God would know the truth and that what people thought didn't matter.' He looked round at his wife. 'What do you think? As a practising heathen myself, I wouldn't know.'

9

'I wouldn't know either,' Molly said. 'And, Keith . . .'

'Yes?'

'That inner tranquillity isn't there any more. Help her if you can. She must be going through a bad time. Why don't you go and introduce yourself while I put the tea in? Then you can judge for yourself.'

Keith shook his head. He knew his own limitations. 'I wouldn't know how to keep up a conversation with a recent widow-by-suicide I've never met before. You go and chat to her while I get the tea. See what impressions you can get.'

Tea was already set and Keith had only to fill the teapot and push the trolley across the hall. He found the two ladies exchanging news from the intervening twenty-odd years. He left the trolley at his wife's side and waited patiently for their attention.

The widow could not have been more than a year or two older than Molly, but the years had not treated her so kindly. Molly was eternally a young woman, sometimes showing signs of middle age but as often, when happy or excited, she could have been taken for an attractive teenager. Mrs Hendrickson was inescapably middle-aged with only a soft voice, a cared-for skin and a shy smile to testify that she had ever been young. Her figure was getting out of hand, her hair was still thick but unashamedly greying and she wore a charcoal-coloured dress which he would have categorised, without being able to say why, as 'old-wifey'. But, he supposed, it was unfair to judge her dress-sense by her mourning clothes. She had a likeable face which had never had pretensions to beauty and the soft lines of her features suggested good intentions rather than a high intelligence. One of those women, he realised suddenly, who are stamped out by the million and who form the unappreciated backbone of society.

He murmured a few platitudes as they shook hands and then took the swivel-chair behind the desk.

'Molly tells me that you have a daughter,' Mrs Hendrickson said. Children were evidently her prime topic.

Keith knew better than to try to change that particular subject. 'Deborah will be taking her "O" levels soon,' he said patiently. 'She's good at art. She wants to come straight into the business and develop her own speciality as an engraver, but we think that she ought to go to college first, and then go for a training period in one of the big workshops.'

Molly looked up from dispensing tea. 'She has her own clients already,' she said with quiet pride. 'Sir Peter Hay brought her a photograph of his favourite dog chasing a rabbit and she's copying it on to one of his guns. Not a very valuable gun, though,' she added.

'It's a rubbish gun,' Keith said. 'But I've told him that the lockplates would fit his best game-gun. I'll transfer them if she makes a job of it.'

'Well, I think she's making a lovely job of it,' Molly said. 'It's in the workshop upstairs. I'll show it to you later.'

'I'd like that,' Mrs Hendrickson said. Her face clouded. 'It's nice that she knows where she wants to go. I have two, you know, a boy and a girl, and neither of them has an idea in their head beyond motorbikes and discos and . . . and things.'

Keith saw his chance to lead the conversation gently around. 'Are they here with you in Newton Lauder?' he asked.

'No, thank God.' From her lips, the words only sounded devout. 'They're staying with the family of a schoolfriend in Edinburgh. Perhaps I'd better explain.' She settled in her chair and cleared her throat nervously. 'When poor Sam had had his stroke, I was finding it difficult to cope on my own. I'm not a businesswoman, Sam always looked after the decision-making and that sort of thing.

'I still have two sisters in Newton Lauder, so I decided to move back here. My sisters and their husbands have been towers of strength, all of them. But I – we – didn't want the children to change schools just now – Beth's about to take her Highers and Michael's at university. So we arranged for them to stay in Edinburgh during the week. Luckily, they were invited to a birthday party and stayed in Edinburgh on the day Sam died. They'll be coming home for the weekend tomorrow, for the first time since that day. I didn't let them come to the funeral. I . . . I don't think funerals are good for the young, do you?' she asked.

Keith thought back to the funeral of his own mother, on a bleak hill in a blizzard. The knowledge that she had been in that box had haunted him for weeks. He pushed the thought aside

11

and hoped that it would drift away. 'No,' he said firmly. 'I don't. And your – er – Sam didn't mind moving out of Edinburgh?'

She looked at him with soft eyes – like a spaniel, Keith thought. 'I don't think so,' she said. 'It was hard to tell. His stroke left him paralysed all down the right side and his speech was badly affected. Poor Sam!' She wiped away a tear. It was a real tear – Keith had watched it welling up. 'It was hard to decide what it had done to his mind. There's a nice sort of summerhouse place in the garden, with its own heating. It was ideal for him and he had all his things out there. Sam had his own computer, one just like yours –' she looked at the microcomputer which sat on the side-table of Keith's desk, the only modern element in a deliberately old-fashioned room – 'and we brought it along. He could use it easily enough with one hand, as a sort of super-typewriter, and it saved him having to bother with putting paper in, and sometimes his old, lucid self seemed to be coming through; but, when it wasn't, you couldn't tell whether the barrier was mental or physical, or even whether he wasn't putting it on because there was something he didn't want to be bothered with.'

'It must have been awful for you both,' Molly breathed.

'I honestly don't think he was unhappy,' Mrs Hendrickson said. 'He had a friend next door, a Mr Strathling. Ben Strathling's in insurance and Sam had done business with him in Edinburgh. Ben came to visit us after Sam had his stroke, to ask after him and to say how sorry he was, and when I said that I was looking for a house in Newton Lauder he told me that the house next to his was coming on the market. It turned out to be perfect, being all on one level for the wheelchair and midway between my sisters, and a shower cubicle for Sam – I couldn't manage him in and out of a bath. It was terribly expensive, but we got far more than I'd expected for the Edinburgh house.

'After we moved, Ben Strathling visited Sam almost every day. One or two other neighbours took to dropping in to chat to him and Sam seemed to be glad. He didn't have many friends in Edinburgh.'

Or anywhere else, Keith thought. Sam Hendrickson had had the reputation of being a quarrelsome character with a savage tongue. But perhaps his illness had mellowed him. It had taken away the power of speech, and a good listener has a head start in any popularity contest. 'Did the doctors offer him any hope of recovery?' he asked.

'There's always hope,' she said earnestly, 'and we tried to keep him believing that he was going to get better. But they told me, in private, that it would take a miracle. So I prayed, of course. And it did seem that there were signs of an improvement. On his very last morning, he found that he could wiggle the toes on his right foot. Just a little bit, but he showed me and he was so pleased, we both were. That's one reason why I just can't believe that a few hours later he'd ... do what they say he did.' She choked on the last words and Keith looked away, drawing reassurance, as always, from the gracious room which was for him the symbol of his ascent from humble beginnings.

Molly gave what comfort she could and Mrs Hendrickson dabbed at her eyes and managed to resume her brave front. 'I'm sorry,' she said, several times. 'It's all been such a shock. And then that sheriff saying that he'd killed himself was just the last straw. I tried to tell him that my Sam wouldn't do a thing like that.'

'Anybody could do a thing like that, given the circumstances,' Keith said gently. 'If I ever have a stroke and get paralysed, I hope that Molly'll leave the sleeping tablets within my reach.'

Both ladies looked at him with reproach. 'You shouldn't speak like that,' Mrs Hendrickson said, 'especially not in front of Molly. It's so wrong. We mustn't throw the gift of life back in God's face.'

'But did Sam think that?' Keith asked before he could stop himself.

'Sam never could bring himself to believe in a personal God,' she said sadly. 'To him, science and evolution were perfectly satisfactory explanations for everything and he thought that all religions were just the outcome of wishful thinking. He wouldn't often discuss it, he said that he was as entitled to his disbelief as I was to my faith and that I'd no more right to interfere with his atheism than he would have had to try to talk me out of my beliefs.

'Sam just couldn't conceive of a life after death. He challenged me once to guess what an after-life would be like and then, whatever I said, he pointed out that what I was trying

13

to suggest could only be based on something physical and would be meaningless in purely spiritual terms. He wouldn't accept that there could be other dimensions which we can't even guess at.' She gave a shuddering sigh.

'Do you think that a man who couldn't believe in an after-life would be prepared to extinguish himself totally?' Keith asked.

'Sam wasn't afraid of death,' she said. 'To him, it would be just loss of individual consciousness. But he was a good man for all his disbelief. And he cared very much about his family. He'd provided for us very well, but a lot of his provision was by way of insurance policies and Sam knew all about suicide clauses.'

Silence clapped down on the room. It was out in the open. The money motive. Keith had expected it. 'Exclusion of suicide without limit of time?' he asked at last. 'Not just for one year or two?'

'Without limit,' she said. 'I'm told that the sheriff's verdict invalidates all his policies. We'll get the premiums back and nothing more. But that really isn't why I've come to you, Mr Calder,' she went on. Keith thought that the sincerity in her voice sounded genuine. 'Sam had other money put by. We can manage without his insurances. In a way, I'm almost relieved. You can have too good a start in life. It will be better for Beth and Michael to know that they'll have to work. It may give them a spur to find their places in the world.

'But I want your help to clear Sam's name. People are saying terrible things about him. That he was dishonest. That there was some trouble coming that he couldn't face. But Sam had strength, enormous strength. There was nothing he couldn't face.' She was lit now by an inner glow. She might have been speaking of a prophet or of some great hero. 'Even after his stroke, I knew that he was a stronger man than most of them are for all their health. Somebody killed him, Mr Calder, and I'm asking for your help to prove it.' She slumped suddenly and sipped at her tea. It was as if virtue had gone out of her.

Molly was looking at him, a message in her eyes.

'You'd have to speak to my partner,' Keith said weakly. 'He's the money-man. My time doesn't come cheap.'

She waved that aside. 'I'll telephone him. I'm sure we can come to some arrangement,' she said.

Keith gave a mental shrug. He seemed to be committed. 'Do

14

you have any evidence at all?' he asked. 'Any kind of a starting-point?'

'Very little beyond what I've already told you,' Mrs Hendrickson said. 'But there are just one or two things. Yesterday, after the sheriff's enquiry, the police said that it would be all right for me to clean up the room.' (Keith closed his eyes for a moment. That was all that he needed, the scene freshly cleaned and polished.) 'With the children coming home for the weekend, I didn't want the summerhouse to be as it was.'

'You surely didn't do the cleaning yourself!' Molly exclaimed.

'I thought that I owed Sam that much,' Mrs Hendrickson said, as if it were the most obvious thing in the world. 'It wasn't just his mess, you see, it was really him. He wouldn't have liked our cleaning-woman to be clearing up what he'd . . . left behind. I'd hardly started, except for wiping up the worst—' She broke off, choking.

'It's all right,' Keith said. 'We understand.'

Again, she gathered up her strength. 'In the process, I moved a couch which stood against the wall. I was going to have it taken away, because it would never clean. Underneath, there was a cigarette which had burned its whole length. The tip was left and it looked like Sam's usual brand. Mrs McShane, my daily woman, had cleaned and polished the whole place the day before and she's very thorough, so I knew that it had been dropped on the day Sam died.' She stopped and sighed again. 'Poor Sam, he'd been a compulsive smoker all his life, and after his stroke it was the one pleasure he had left, although I don't think that he could taste them any more. The doctors didn't approve, but I thought that it was more important for him to be happy. A man who could survive a cerebral haemorrhage wasn't going to be afraid of lung cancer.'

'A man who was half-paralysed could easily drop his cigarette,' Keith pointed out.

'They were always slipping through his fingers,' she admitted. 'But Sam had been afraid of fire since he was a child and doubly so since his stroke, for obvious reasons. He had an electric bell just by his hand for emergencies and whenever he dropped his cigarette he kept his finger on the bell-push until I arrived, never mind if I was in the bath or whatever. And a cigarette

15

which rolled under an upholstered couch would have made him frantic. He knew about the fumes which burning upholstery can produce.'

Keith had started making notes. Molly, who knew the signs, sat back, well-satisfied.

'It's slender,' Keith said, 'but it's there. A considerate man who was going to kill himself – which isn't really inconsistent – wouldn't throw his cigarette under the furniture. He'd smoke it right through and stub it out.'

'I was just thinking the same thing,' Molly said.

Mrs Hendrickson was looking mildly concerned. 'But why do you say that consideration and suicide aren't inconsistent?' she asked. 'Suicide always seems to me to be the most selfish and inconsiderate thing a person could do, running away from your troubles and leaving others behind to cope with them.'

'I said that,' Keith said slowly, 'because you're making me visualise things, sad things that I'd rather not think about. I usually avoid thinking about age and illness and death. I prefer to have a vague mental picture of keeping all my faculties for another fifty years and then going suddenly in my sleep. You made me imagine being paralysed and a burden to my family. I'd probably decide that I'd be doing them a favour if I left them to get on with their lives instead of having to slave for me.'

Mrs Hendrickson was shaking her head, but Molly spoke first. 'You mustn't think like that,' she said. 'It's morbid. For somebody one loved, it wouldn't be a burden.'

'I thought of it as a privilege,' Mrs Hendrickson said simply. 'Sometimes I thought that life had been too good to me. My life would have been richer if I'd had a mission, but I'd never been granted the opportunity to serve others, or only in the way that one does for a husband and children, until Sam needed my help so desperately. It was almost as if God was testing me at last. And although Sam was a dear, good man, he never seemed to worry about being a burden. That was one good thing.'

Silence fell again while Keith wondered whether anybody could be such a saint as this woman was painting herself. He wondered also whether she could really be talking about the Sam Hendrickson whose machinations over the years had scandalised even his colleagues in the trades union movement and whose inflammatory speeches had always been the first to be quoted only so that they could be condemned.

'Tell me about his shotgun,' Keith said. 'Shooting seems an out-of-key hobby for a union executive.'

'In a way I suppose it was,' Mrs Hendrickson said. 'He'd been shooting ever since he was a boy, he said, and he wasn't going to give it up. He did a lot of clay pigeon shooting. And he was a member of a syndicate in East Lothian. He kept what you'd call a low profile about that, because it wasn't the sort of image his members expected.'

'Did he have just the one gun?'

'He had three, but I couldn't for the life of me tell you any more about them. You'd better come and see for yourself.'

'I'll certainly do that,' Keith said absently. His mind was racing ahead. There would be so few lines to follow. 'What about cartridges? What brands did he use?'

Mrs Hendrickson sat up suddenly. 'That was the other thing I meant to tell you,' she said. 'Sam had his guns in the summerhouse with him. He liked to have them around even if he couldn't use them any more – I think that they were just familiar and friendly reminders of better days. But I've always been told that you should keep guns and ammunition separate, so I had his cartridges locked away safely in my wardrobe. I was going to give them away to somebody but I never got around to it.'

Keith was looking at the widow with new eyes. From being an indignant relict who, instead of facing the facts, was determined to drag the rest of the world round to her point of view, he was now seeing her as a lone campaigner for what she believed, rightly or wrongly, to be the truth. Or was there, he wondered, a difference? 'The cartridge which fired the shot,' he said. 'Was it the same brand as the others?'

'The gun and cartridge were on a table in the courtroom,' she said. 'I didn't want to look at them after the first glance, but later I thought the cartridge had been an unfamiliar colour. It was green. I thought that the others had been blue, so when I got home I went and looked and they were blue. So when I went to tell the police about the burned-out cigarette, I mentioned the cartridge as well. Mr Munro said that it was too late to re-open the case, and that if I wasn't satisfied I could think about consulting you. He said that I shouldn't expect you

17

to do more than report on the likelihood of Sam having ... done what they said, but he did say that they would certainly consider your findings very carefully.'

Keith sat up and frowned. 'Superintendent Munro suggested that you come to me?'

'Yes.'

'A long, thin Highlander with a face of gloom and a voice like a rusty hinge?'

Mrs Hendrickson nodded.

'Did he really?' Keith said. 'Well, well!'

# TWO

The former schoolfriends walked out on to the gravel together. 'The Jaguar belonged to the union. It had to go back. But it was too big for me, anyway,' Mrs Hendrickson said bravely.

Molly stood at the front door, anxiously watching her friend drive off, slowly and carefully, in a small and tired-looking car. The Jenny Kerr whom she had once known had always made her feel protective.

When the car was safely out of sight, she came back to the study. Keith was staring absently at a corner of the ceiling. While Molly waited patiently for a return of his attention, she gathered the used cups on to the trolley.

The tiny sounds broke Keith's concentration. 'I'll have some more tea,' he said suddenly. 'If there is any. Don't make fresh.'

Molly fetched a clean cup and sat down again. 'She hasn't changed,' she said as she poured. 'She always had the knack of finding the right person to solve her problems and then persuading him – it was usually a boy – to go to work for her.'

'I believe that,' Keith said. 'She's very feminine, for all she's getting on a bit.'

'She hasn't given you much to work on, though. He could have found a cartridge in a pocket. I'm always finding them in yours.'

'Maybe. Although, if he'd been paralysed for some months, all his clothes must have been through his wife's hands over and over again. A woman as conscientious as she makes herself out to be would surely have found and removed any twelve-bore cartridges. They're heavy and not exactly small.' Keith buttered another scone before going on. 'One curious thing is that nobody's mentioned a note.'

'Do suicides always leave notes?'

19

'Not the ones who do it as a sudden, desperate reaction. But, of the ones who do it as a premeditated act, I think it would be a rare suicide who didn't leave some kind of a message behind. You might want to escape from the troubles of this life, but your instincts would surely insist that you left some signs that you'd been around. Footprints in the sands of time. Mine would, anyway. Unless I was so overwhelmed by whatever I was getting away from that I couldn't think about anything else.'

'If his right hand was paralysed—'

'You'd expect him to leave a message on his word-processor, up on the screen where it would catch the eye. But, of course, that would in reality only be a tiny electronic trace. The first person along would only have to switch it off if they didn't want the message found. If, for instance, they didn't want it to be suicide. Or some people are compulsive switchers-off of electrical things. Of course, if he'd also put it on to disc or tape . . .'

'You could always go and take a look,' Molly suggested. 'You've got a good two hours before we eat.'

Keith looked at his watch. 'Not tonight,' he said. 'There's no hurry now. Mrs Hendrickson promised that she wouldn't touch anything else. I'll make a start in the morn. I'll use the rest of today to finish up my report on Mr Wilmington's gun-barrel.'

'Have you done all your tests?' Molly rather liked Mr Wilmington, a vague-mannered schoolteacher who never called at the shop without spending a few minutes gossiping about his pupils.

'At last, yes.' Keith was grateful for the change of subject. He felt uneasy in trying to imagine the mental state of a suicide, as if he himself might somehow become infected with that ultimate depression. 'He's not the first owner to come crying to me with a burst gun-barrel, blaming a faulty cartridge. It nearly always turns out to have been caused by a badly-made or carelessly-used gun. Most often it's an obstruction in the barrel. Snow or mud or cleaning materials.'

'And this time?'

'This time, it really was a faulty cartridge,' Keith said. 'He was lucky not to lose any fingers, although it's surprising how often they do get away with it. Would you like to give me a hand tomorrow? I need an extra pair of eyes and ears and somebody to take notes.'

'I was going to make a start on the laundry,' Molly said reluctantly.

The front door closed with a slam which rocked the house. 'Deborah's home from school,' Keith said. 'Bang goes peace and quiet. She might like to go along with me tomorrow. It'll be Saturday.'

'Do you think it's suitable for a young girl? She's given you a hand with things like faked or stolen guns before now, but violent death—'

'I don't think it'd do her any harm,' Keith said. 'It might even help her with growing up.'

'She's too mature for her years already,' Molly said. 'I'd keep her away from anything gruesome.'

'If you leave her behind she'll only spend the day mooning around the house, getting under my feet and asking where you've gone and when you'll be home again.' Molly thought over her duties and decided that the laundry could wait. 'All right, I'll come with you. Then, if Deborah wants to tag along, I can make sure that you don't let her get messed-up or hysterical.'

'As if I would!' Keith said.

The telephone rang soon after Keith and Molly had taken to their bed. Keith tried at first to ignore the nagging whirr of the bedside extension. He had folded Molly in a goodnight embrace and by now, with their nightwear around their respective neck and ankles, warmth and comfort were turning to delicious excitement.

The most hardened satyr could not have ignored that summons, even with Molly quivering with laughter against him. Keith bit back a rude word and leaned over Molly. Even that small action nearly undid his resolve, but he lifted the phone and made room for it between their two heads.

'Mr Calder?'

'Mm?'

'Be careful how you go in the Hendrickson affair.' The voice was unrecognisable, artificially deep and both muffled and metallic as if it were coming through cloth and an open-ended tin can. Keith felt Molly stiffen against him.

'Who's that?' Keith asked.

'Never you mind who. Poke around if you must. Charge your fee. But, if you love your family, leave the official view as it is or you'll be a sorry man.'

The connection died and the dialling tone came on.

Keith leaned across Molly again to hang up the phone. This time, the contact meant nothing. 'I'll be damned!' he said. 'The widow may have been right after all. Who'd have thought it?'

'I thought it,' Molly murmured.

'Only because you were at school with her a hundred years ago.'

Molly refused to be distracted by references to her age. 'We'll talk about it in the morning,' she said. She moved gently against him. Keith's body was quiescent, his mind away toying with this new development, but she knew how to regain his attention.

In the morning, they did talk about it. They rose earlier than was their habit on a non-shooting Saturday and held their discussion over breakfast. For once, Keith and Molly were in full agreement. They would ignore the threatening phone-call except that Keith would be accompanied on his visits by both Molly and Deborah.

Only their reasons differed. Molly's faith in Keith was as blind as Mrs Hendrickson's in God, and she wanted her old friend to have more help than the Almighty seemed willing to provide. Keith for his part always turned stubborn in the face of threats.

Deborah, when she arrived at the breakfast table, was torn between a long-standing habit of following her father every-where and impatience to get on with her engraving for Sir Peter; but the decision was made for her. Keith wanted both his ladies where he could keep an eye on them. In addition, during the inevitable delay while Molly made the house fit to be left, he loaded two small pistols. The percussion pepperbox pistol went into his own pocket and he slipped the little Derringer to Molly for her handbag. Threats, he knew, may not always be empty.

The Hendrickson home was in the most exclusive corner of the town. To reach it they drove, through a dry and calm but overcast day, into Newton Lauder. They turned in the Square, climbing a hill and crossing the canal bridge, to enter a section of private road between farmland and the canal, terminating in a group of only eight houses.

This small estate owed its existence to a local builder who, between the wars, had been inspired to aim near the top of the market, just below the purses of those who could afford to buy and run the large, old country houses. On sites of not less than half an acre he had built houses designed to capitalise on the seclusion and the views. He had been generous with space and meticulous with finishings and he had avoided any trace of the severity which the discipline of stonework imposed on traditional Scottish architecture. The result was a style of informal charm, almost of coziness. The houses had sold, even at the asking figures, and now fetched prices which made people hiss through their teeth.

The builder, realising that he had exhausted his market, had hoped to extend the road and to add houses of slightly less opulence and cost, the values of which would have been dragged upward by the exclusiveness of the neighbourhood. But by then he had the richest in the town to contend with, and those gentlemen and their ladies had no intention of being invaded by lesser souls. A trust was formed and the adjacent land was purchased and let back to the farmer. Boswell Court (named not after the biographer but for an obscure saint) remained inviolate.

The Hendrickson house was the fourth (and last) on the right-hand side. Vulgar numbers were not issued, or if issued were not used, in Boswell Court, and the house was known as Rowanbank. Landscaping had matured in the fifty years since the house was built. All the properties were well screened by hedges and specimen trees, but Rowanbank in particular turned an almost blank gable to the visitor, reserving its main outlook for the garden and the hills beyond.

Keith parked the car in the hammerhead where the road ended and turned to Molly. 'I want Deb to come and take notes while I speak to Mrs Hendrickson,' he said. 'You go and call on the neighbours. The wives may chat to you more freely than they did to the police.'

'You'll remember what you promised?' Molly gave Keith a meaning look.

'I'll remember. There'll be no screams in the night.'

23

'All right, then,' Molly said.

'I won't know which house you're in,' Keith said. 'I'll give three honks on the horn when I want you.'

Keith, with Deborah in train, followed a neatly-paved drive round the Hendrickson house until he found the front door, sheltered by a deep porch which linked the door to a substantial garage. In this sheltered corner, Keith noticed, the spring bulbs were flourishing and the shrubs were at least a fortnight ahead of his own at Briesland House.

Mrs Hendrickson answered the door herself. Live-in maids were not the tradition in Newton Lauder, the servant problem, for those who could afford it, being answered during the week by an elaborate network of 'daily women'. At weekends, the family ate out or the lady of the house was her own menial.

She looked doubtfully at Deborah, evidently assuming that her arrival on Keith's heels was coincidental. 'Mike and Beth haven't arrived home yet,' she said.

'I brought my daughter to help me,' Keith explained. 'Deborah. She's quite used to being Watson to my Holmes.'

'Or Clouseau to his Dreyfus,' Deborah murmured. Keith quelled her with a frown.

Mrs Hendrickson shook Deborah's hand and made no comment beyond raised eyebrows. 'Do come in,' she said. 'Or do you want to see the summerhouse first?'

Keith remembered Molly's admonition against exposing Deborah to a scene which, if Mrs Hendrickson had been side-tracked by her discovery of the cigarette, might still be spattered with dried blood and brains. 'Perhaps we could talk first,' he suggested.

The living room was spacious but with no suggestion that it was ever subjected to the indignity of being dined in. Chintzes and pastel colours prevailed, somehow echoing Mrs Hendrickson's own gentleness and tranquillity. Windows, double-glazed and uncharacteristically broad for Scotland, looked east along the garden. The peaked roof of the summerhouse showed above a screen of evergreens. The view to the hills had been kept open, but there was no glimpse of neighbouring houses. The illusion of being deep in the countryside was carefully preserved.

Mrs Hendrickson, true to her type, felt impelled to question

Deborah about her schooling, aspirations and acquaintances. Keith waited for the polite minimum of time before reclaiming her attention.

'Tell us about that day,' he said.

Deborah opened a school jotter on a rosewood side-table. She tried hard to listen as well as to record. Keith had given her no more than the barest outline of their task.

The mild animation which had enlivened Mrs Hendrickson while exchanging trivialities with one of the younger generation faded and died. She visibly braced herself. 'Yes, of course,' she said. 'It was the Saturday, a fortnight ago today, so I had Sam all to myself. No nurse, no daily woman. We woke quite early, about eight. To be honest, I could have slept on. I'd stayed up late to watch a play, you see.' She nodded towards a huge television set. 'But I sensed that Sam was awake and bored – boredom was his worst enemy after he became so dependent on others – so I roused myself to make a cup of tea. I brought him his breakfast in bed. He could manage very well, except that I had to cut things up for him because of his being one-handed. You're sure you want to know all this?' she asked anxiously.

'We'd rather be told everything,' Keith said. 'You can't say too much, but you could easily leave out something which could have turned out to be vital.'

'I see. Very well. Usually I have to try to stop myself from running on, but this time I'll let myself go.

'I didn't feel up to getting him into the shower, my back was still troubling me from the day before, so I gave him a sponge-down and helped him to get dressed and into the wheelchair. I got myself dressed and tidy while he used his electric shaver. There were a few letters, all bills. I slit the envelopes for him and he looked through them while I made the beds, then he gave them back to me to settle.

'I took him outside after that. He was strong enough to work the wheelchair on the flat, but there's a slight uphill to the summerhouse and anyway he had difficulty making it go straight, one-handed. It would have been a nice day for sitting in the garden, but he felt the cold terribly since his stroke. Anyway, he always preferred to be in the summerhouse with his things. It was a nuisance, having to trail up the garden, rain or shine, whenever he wanted something – especially the

25

lavatory,' Mrs Hendrickson added in a decorous aside, '– but it helped him to feel independent to have a place which was all his own. I wheeled him there and took him inside and made sure that he had everything he wanted.

'Then I came back to the house and got on with the odd jobs. Do you want to know what I did?'

'If you can remember,' Keith said.

'I can remember every moment of that ghastly day. I've been over it often enough in my mind,' Mrs Hendrickson said wearily. 'I washed up the breakfast things. I wrote cheques and envelopes for the bills, stamped them and put them on the hall table for posting. I put some dirty laundry into the washing-machine. And I started to prepare something for our lunch.'

'Can you put times to any of these things?' Keith asked.

'I'm sorry,' she said, 'but no. I wasn't watching the clock.'

'Never mind,' Keith said. 'Go on.'

'There were three phone-calls. One was from my sister Louise, to ask whether I needed anything. I didn't, but she said that she'd look in anyway during the afternoon. She was always very good about staying in the house while I went to the shops, just in case Sam wanted anything. The next – oh, but I should have explained,' Mrs Hendrickson broke in on herself. 'Sam had an extension in the summerhouse. He couldn't make himself understood, but he liked to listen and I certainly never had anything to say that he shouldn't have heard, except when the doctors phoned. The second call was for Sam. A very gruff, deep voice with a strong accent. I said that Sam couldn't speak and the voice said, "He can listen, can't he?"'

'I could always tell when Sam was on the line because it had a sort of hollow sound when his receiver was off the hook and sometimes I could hear his radio in the background. I could tell that he'd picked up the extension, so I said that Sam was listening, and without a word of thanks the voice said "This is Hughie", only he pronounced it "Shoogie", the way Glaswegians do. So I hung up and got on with my work.

'A little later, our next-door neighbours came visiting. Not Ben Strathling who's next-door proper,' Mrs Hendrickson explained carefully. 'Mr and Mrs Albany live what would be across the street except that the street stops without running in between us, if you see what I mean, so I count them as being our other next-door. They've been very good about visiting and being some company for Sam. So I made coffee and we all went out and had it with Sam. He used to like that. In the old days, he hated what he called "poodle-faking" – such a funny expression! – but after he became ill he enjoyed having guests for drinks or coffee. He couldn't join in the conversation except nodding or shaking his head, or writing it up on the screen of his computer-thing if it was important. When he tried to speak it was all garbled and it embarrassed people and he seemed to know that. And anyway he liked to use his computer for conversations because it left him with a sort of one-sided record which he could go over again later if he was bored and alone. That was the last time that I saw him alive,' she added forlornly.

'Did he seem quite as usual?' Keith asked.

Mrs Hendrickson wrinkled her brow. 'It was hard to tell,' she said. 'You see, his face didn't show expressions much, half of it being sort of frozen, and anything he wrote on the computer screen gave no hint of what tone of voice he'd have used. I thought that he seemed a bit low. Tired, perhaps.

'Mr Albany stayed on with Sam when his wife left, and I came back to the house. Ian Albany's a shooting man, as you probably know –' (Keith nodded) '– and he used to talk guns with Sam and clean them for him, things like that. I don't suppose they needed cleaning if they weren't being used, but I think that having them cleaned helped Sam to believe that some day he would be able to use them again.' She stopped and put a hand to her face. 'I didn't mean—'

'I know what you meant,' Keith said.

She nodded, gratefully. 'I sat down in here for a while, to have a little rest and read my book. I wondered whether to go out and see whether Sam and Mr Albany would like a drink, because it was getting on towards lunch-time. But Sam had a stock of drinks in the summerhouse and they were quite capable of helping themselves and anyway I soon saw Mr Albany coming down the garden and going away. He waved to me through the window. I was on the phone at the time. That was the third call, Sam's physiotherapist wanting to change his appointment.

'About half an hour later, I was just going to put the lunch on when the milkman came to the door. When I say the milkman, it's really the milkman's father-in-law. He comes round on Saturdays in a little van, to collect the money and take any special orders.'

Deborah looked up from her careful note-taking in school shorthand. 'Old Mr Rogers?'

'That's right, dear.' Mrs Hendrickson paused and braced herself. 'We had the usual argument, because he never knows anything about the days I've had too much milk left in the fridge and I've put a note out to say that I'd take one pint instead of the usual two. Or he always says he doesn't. But he always knows when we've had extra, for visitors or the family being at home.

'I'd just settled up with him, in fact we were still on the doorstep talking about something else, when I heard what I can only describe as a muffled bang from the garden side of the house. I nearly paid no attention, because it could have been somebody in the field or something, but I decided that it was time that I went and looked in on Sam anyway. So I went round the house and up the garden and ... found him. That was at about a quarter past twelve.' She kept her chin up but there was a definite quaver in her voice. 'I think that that was the worst moment of my life. You're not going to insist that I describe it all, are you? Please? I don't think I could bring myself to.'

Keith could understand the widow's reluctance to dwell on the scene. 'I'll get the details from somebody else,' he said. 'Tell me one thing. Was the video screen on his word processor switched on?'

She thought back. 'It was on,' she said. 'But there was nothing on the screen, only a sort of list of things it could do. So I switched it off, and the radio too. It was just an instinctive gesture, like closing a dead person's eyes. Oh dear! From your face, that was the wrong thing to do. Could there have been a message on the other side?'

'If his machine's like mine,' Keith said, 'it switches between that list and the text every time you hit the ESCAPE key. But never mind that for the moment. What happened next?'

'The next few seconds are just a blur.' She lowered her voice. 'Perhaps God was sparing me, just a little, by granting me a numbness. I think that I must have screamed, or at least called out Sam's name. Ben Strathling came through the hedge from

28

next door and Mr Hughes turned up and later I remember seeing Mrs Albany. It's all a bit vague. Ben took over and Mrs Albany – Theresa's her name, we call her Terry – took me back to her house.'

Mrs Hendrickson's hand was shaking and Keith could see tears in her eyes. He decided that she needed a change of subject before he pushed her any further. 'Would you write us a letter,' he said, 'saying that you've engaged me, and any of my associates, to enquire into the circumstances of your husband's death?'

'Yes,' she said. 'Of course. You want something to show to the police and other people? I've already phoned the neighbours and asked them to be helpful.' She got up and moved to a small writing-desk which stood between the windows.

'That's it. Make two copies,' Keith said. 'To whom it may concern. Deborah can take one with her now, when she goes to join her mother.'

Deborah snapped her jotter shut. 'Oh, Dad!'

'I am not taking you with me when we go out to the summerhouse,' Keith said firmly. 'Your mother would have a fit, even if you didn't. And Mrs Hendrickson will find it quite distressing enough having me along, asking silly questions. You can go and call on anybody your mother hasn't got around to.'

'But I can't go crashing in on people, just like that,' Deborah protested. 'At my age, they won't take me seriously.'

'Do you know any of the young people up here?'

'Well, yes. I've been to two parties here and I think I've met them all.'

'That's enough introduction,' Keith said. 'Have a good gossip. You may be able to find out from the youngsters something the parents hold back from your mother. See if you can find out where everybody was when the shot was heard, and what else they saw and heard at around that time. If you're half as good as your mother at getting people to talk about themselves, you'll save me an age of time. I can always follow up where it seems necessary.'

Mrs Hendrickson looked up from her writing. 'The police asked everybody those sorts of questions,' she said, 'and Mr Munro said that he'd make their statements available to you.'

'But if, as you think, they got the wrong answers, they must

29

have asked the wrong questions,' Keith said. 'We'll go over the ground again.' He glanced at the two letters which Mrs Hendrickson gave him, nodded and handed one to Deborah. 'You run along now, Toots. Give your mother some back-up. And, later, maybe you two can call on the milkman while I talk to Superintendent Munro.'

Deborah, grumbling, departed. Mrs Hendrickson, after fetching a light coat as a prophylactic against spring colds, led Keith by a side-door into the garden.

The older paths were of gravel but a new path of concrete paving had been laid in an easy gradient along the shortest route to the summerhouse, thereby introducing the only straight lines into an otherwise delightfully informal garden but greatly simplifying the to-ing and fro-ing of a wheelchair. The summerhouse emerged gradually from behind its screen of greenery as they walked – a square building, more recent than the house, with a picture-window, overlooking the view to the east, stone walls presented to the north and south and, on the west side which they were approaching, doors, mostly of glass, which could slide and be folded so that the room could be thrown open to the garden.

Mrs Hendrickson steeled herself and unlocked one of the doors. The smell of a powerful domestic cleaning agent wafted out to them. As Keith followed her inside, some recent workmanship caught his attention. 'The door's been repaired,' he remarked.

'That was some time ago, just after we moved here. There was a break-in. They didn't touch his guns, thank goodness, just took some papers.' She made it clear that papers were of little importance.

The summerhouse was a single room, almost twenty feet square, warm, dry and well-lit, painted white throughout but with bright colours to the furniture and the few pictures. The floor, which was of red quarry tiles, was bare but some rugs were rolled up against the skirting. The blank south wall was fitted with a low bookcase and cupboard, and in the angle between this and the picture-window stood a desk with a microcomputer, disc-drive, printer, television set and nearby a telephone extension. An electric bell-push had been fitted to the corner of the desk. The large ashtray held a dozen or so cigarette-ends, and beside it lay a half-empty packet of desiccated cigarettes and a gold lighter. A large cassette-player-cum-radio stood on the bookcase. It was all arranged to suit a man confined to the wheelchair which still stood by the desk.

The remainder of the room was sparse, occupied only by a low table surrounded by two armchairs and the stained couch. The arrangement was unbalanced because, Keith supposed, the couch which had stood under the picture-window had been pulled out, forcing the displacement of the other pieces. Energetic attempts at a clean-up had started but had been abandoned and these, with the disturbance left by the police and the residual stains on the paintwork, ruined the appearance of what must have been a serene room, perfect habitat for an invalid. Keith had felt an unease as he approached the building, an atavistic fear of a place made unhallowed by the events it had enclosed; but, on acquaintance and ignoring the after-the-party disorder, he found it pleasant and not unfamiliar, as if his dream of the perfect working room had been translated into reality.

'Let's sit down and talk again for a moment,' Keith said. They took the two armchairs and tried to ignore the stains which disfigured the couch. 'What papers were taken?'

'I haven't the faintest idea,' she said with complete unconcern. 'As far as I could tell, it didn't bother Sam and he wouldn't have the police called. But the police arrived a few days later, with a warrant and a solicitor representing the union. Between them, they took away the rest of his papers, except for a few purely personal files, so I'm afraid you won't find much of use.'

'Was Sam ... upset when the various branches of the law came and impounded his papers?'

'Sam was the only person who wasn't upset. He was having one of his bad days. Or pretending to, I could never tell. The phone had been busy the day before and I think that that may have decided him to stay in bed. But I'll tell you this – I was upset. I am not used to having the police around the place.' Mrs Hendrickson's tone made the forces of the law and order sound like an indecent infection and her usually affable expression gave way for a moment to a lofty scowl. 'And the others were upset because most of what they wanted had already been taken

31

in the break-in. I didn't care about the papers, but they were Sam's; and, anyway, I wasn't putting up with it.

'Sam had solicitors in Edinburgh, but I didn't know who they were even if there'd been time to call them. So I phoned the local man, Mr Enterkin, who'd done the conveyance of the house for us and made some alterations to Sam's will.' Keith looked up sharply and Mrs Hendrickson noticed the movement. 'After his stroke, Sam knew that he might . . . be at risk. His will was long out of date and so, being Sam, ill or not, he did something about it. Anyway, it was Mr Enterkin I phoned. He came rushing up here—'

'Now I know that you're exaggerating,' Keith said with a smile. 'Ralph Enterkin never rushed in his life, especially not when driving a car.'

She stopped in mid-flow and thought about it. 'I suppose I am,' she said. 'And you're quite right. I should weigh my words, shouldn't I? Well, Mr Enterkin set off straight away and crawled very slowly up here in his car. Is that better?'

'That sounds more like him,' Keith said.

'He did all that he could in Sam's interests, but in the end he said that it was all above-board and that I should let them have what they wanted. I told Sam about it when he was stronger, but I could tell that he had expected it and didn't want to hear any more.'

Keith thought that Sam Hendrickson might have been unconcerned because he thought that his health would insulate him from trouble, or because he knew that his papers had already been carefully weeded, or even because he always had the way out which he might ultimately have taken. His associates might have been less phlegmatic.

It was difficult to visualise a marriage between this gentle mother-figure and a left-wing firebrand. 'What did you think of his politics?' he asked.

'To be honest,' she said, 'I never gave them much of a thought. Beliefs are a very personal thing, don't you think? Even if somebody's making speeches, the reasons for their inner beliefs are their own, as separate from argument and logic as a faith in God. You couldn't deny much of what Sam said about class injustice and so on. He cared very deeply about the wrongs of privilege and oppression and I had to agree with him.

I think we both felt strongly about the evils of self. Our only difference was that I felt guilty that we should be so secure when other people were hungry, but Sam just said that we were entitled to the rewards of hard work and intelligence. I kept telling myself that he'd every right to come to his own conclusions even though, if I'd been politically inclined, I think I'd have come to something quite different.' She looked up at the ceiling for a moment without even seeing the terrible stain. 'I'd have decided that it was better to pull the underdog up rather than to knock the top dog down. But that wasn't for me to say while Sam was alive and active.'

Keith nodded. It was not an unusual standpoint for a wife to take. Loyalty, combined with self-interest, could obscure original thought. He could sometimes see his own views reflected in Molly.

Mrs Hendrickson, Keith judged, was ripe for the first trick question. 'What was the first thing you noticed when you came in here, after hearing the bang?'

'The smoke,' she said without hesitation. 'It caught my throat even before I looked at Sam. A sort of burning, acrid smell. And it wasn't the cigarette that he'd dropped. I thought at first that he'd set the place on fire, and then I thought that he must have been smoking something he shouldn't. Then I saw him. I suppose the smoke was left from the shot?'

Keith nodded. 'Sam smoked pot, did he?'

'After his stroke, somebody smuggled him in some cigarettes, just once or twice. They seemed to soothe him. But I couldn't approve.'

Keith could see little moral difference between cannabis resin and such drugs as the doctor might have prescribed. 'What did the police take away after Sam died?' he asked.

'As far as I know, only the gun and the cartridge. And poor Sam's body, of course.'

'And did you remove anything?'

'Only—' she began, and broke off. She lowered her head until her face was hidden.

'I understand,' Keith said quickly. He had remembered, too late, that in her cleaning-up she had, in fact, been removing material which had once formed part of her late husband. It was not a thought for her to dwell on. It was not even one which he cared to carry in his own mind. 'Don't try to say any more. It's a bad time for you. Just sit and try not to think of anything much while I look around.'

She snuffled into a small handkerchief.

He got up and looked behind the couch. Sure enough, on the otherwise spotless floor was the ash-trail of a cigarette which had burned its length. The remaining cork-tip was a distinctive colour, matching those in the open packet on the desk.

Keith looked around him, digesting the scene.

Above the bookcase, six wooden pegs were fixed to the wall, one pair above the other. The topmost pair of pegs supported a heavy, over-under, twelve-bore shotgun of Italian make. On the lowest pair, only a few inches above the bookcase, was a slim, twenty-bore, Spanish side-by-side boxlock. Both guns had been fitted with rubber butt-pads. They were well cared-for, the blueing almost unmarked and the walnut stocks showing the soft glow of a well-tended oil finish.

Despite the cleaning-up, the stains and pellet-marks told a story which was consistent with a man in the wheelchair having turned it to face the guns, loaded the gun of his choice, put the muzzles in his mouth and pulled a trigger. The plaster ceiling showed clearly an oval pattern of small punctures where the pellets had lodged, but organic material, including tiny fragments of bone, had been spread more widely.

Mrs Hendrickson had said that there had only been one cartridge shown to the court. Keith wondered why. His own instinct, in Sam Hendrickson's shoes, would have been to load both barrels rather than risk the traumatic instant if he pulled the wrong trigger on the reversed gun. Or had the missing gun been a single-barrelled repeater?

A four-drawer filing-cabinet stood beside the desk. Keith looked inside. One drawer held a few personal files of correspondence, receipts and tax-papers. Another was neatly furnished with clean glasses and a variety of bottles. Otherwise, the cabinet had been cleared out.

Keith selected a file marked 'Insurance' and looked inside. He skipped over the life insurances, noting only that the late Mr Hendrickson had either valued his life highly or had been concerned about the future of his family. Among the insurances of goods and effects, the guns were listed. The missing gun had been a double-barrel, twelve-bore, Spanish sidelock of middle price but reputable make. Keith knew the model well.

He looked through the drawers of the desk. Stationery, stamps, all the paraphernalia which a man collects, none of it significant. The middle drawer held a few basic tools and some cleaning materials for the guns. He moved a duster and found two, yellow twenty-bore cartridges.

The microcomputer was similar to his own. The guns and some other surfaces showed the marks of fingerprint powder but the computer's keyboard was clean. He decided to leave it alone for the moment. The television set would act as its display unit, but Sam Hendrickson would have had the option of watching his favourite programmes on it when he so wished.

On the bookcase beneath the guns lay a pair of snap-caps – metal dummy cartridges with sprung discs instead of primers, designed to save damage to firing-pins if triggers were pulled on an unloaded gun for practice or to relieve the springs.

Small circles which showed in the side-plates of the over-under gun were actually the ends of the axles carrying the internal tumblers or hammers, and these were marked with indicators. The engraved lines were parallel to the length of the gun, showing that the tumblers were in the fired position.

Keith examined the upper surfaces of the desk and bookcase, moving around to catch them against the light. He saw nothing. 'I'll be damned!' he said to himself.

It was his habit to carry a pair of cotton gloves, to protect his hands from grease and guns from his acid fingerprints. He pulled them on and took down the over-under gun. The police, he hoped, would already have photographed any fingerprints. He opened the gun, holding one hand over the breech, and the ejectors popped another pair of snap-caps against his palm. He replaced the gun and took down the twenty-bore. This gun, being a non-ejector, merely lifted a smaller pair of snap-caps towards him when he opened it. Under the dusting of powder, both guns looked and smelled as if they had been cleaned not long before.

The wheelchair at least had been cleaned. He was about to sit down in it but delicacy restrained him. He walked back and sat down opposite Mrs Hendrickson, who had recovered her composure and was watching him anxiously.

'Let's understand each other,' Keith said. 'For the moment, you just want me to prove that Sam didn't kill himself?'

'Yes.'

'You don't expect me to find out exactly what happened?'

'I don't think so,' she said uncertainly. 'Not just yet. If you can prove ... what you said, I think the police would re-open the case. If not—'

'If not, we can speak again,' Keith said.

'And do you think that you can? Prove it, I mean?'

'Oh, I think so,' Keith said. 'I'll want to see a few other people first, before I say any more. But I think so.'

# THREE

There was no immediate sign of Molly or Deborah. Keith gave three quick toots on the car's horn and then sat, taking in a scene redolent of comfortable conformity. He was generally contented with his lot – a good business, a fine house, few debts and a loving family – but he was conscious of a fleeting trace of envy. Then he laughed at himself. It was human nature to see others as being without the problems or self-doubts which closer acquaintance usually revealed.

The hour was approaching when civilised man takes time for a pre-prandial drink, but the scene of manicured lawns and sculptured shrubs was not devoid of people. Next door to the Hendricksons' a male figure, presumably belonging to Ben Strathling, could be glimpsed through the hedge, hosing down a late-model Jaguar. High on a ladder a window-cleaner was working. Somebody was watching him from an upper window. The window-cleaner fetched something from a small van and moved his ladder before climbing again. There was no other van to be seen, which suggested that old Mr Rogers had finished his collection of the milk-money.

Deborah appeared, hurrying along the short street with the familiar grin which was so like Molly's, and hopped in beside him. Molly came out of a different house and paused on the doorstep, still chatting to a lady. Keith pulled the car forward and Molly broke away and came to join them. Keith set off back towards the middle of the town.

'You were almost right,' Deborah said cheerfully. 'Nobody seemed to mind talking to me. One or two of the parents were a wee bit patronising about it.'

'Mostly, they said that they'd rather let sleeping dogs lie and then started to talk their heads off,' Molly put in from the back seat.

'Especially about one another,' Deborah said. 'You'd think that people like that came together in that special sort of place because they were at least prepared to try to like each other.'

'You might,' Keith said. 'I wouldn't. Except for Mrs Hendrickson, who moved there because Sam already had a friend next door, they've mostly come together because they're well-off and they'd rather mingle with others in the same bracket than expose themselves to the envy of proles like you and me.'

Deborah snorted with laughter. Even her laughter was an echo of Molly's. 'Come off it, Dad,' she said. 'You could buy and sell most of them.'

Keith looked at her out of the corner of his eye but had to return his gaze quickly to the road for the canal bridge. 'A little filial admiration's all very well,' he said, 'but don't let it go to your head. We're doing all right, but we're not in that bracket yet.'

'If you say so. But some of them aren't as well-off as they'd like one to think. Do you believe that you can smell money in a house?' she asked.

It was a serious question and Keith thought about it. 'Not money as such,' he said. 'But you can smell the results of its being spent or not. Things like the quality of soap and food. Expensive wines and tobacco. Flowers out of season. That sort of thing.'

'Polishes,' Molly said. 'They're the biggest give-away. And the freshness of the air. People who don't have to worry about the cost of heating can afford to have the windows open.'

Deborah nodded eagerly. 'Those are just the sort of things I meant. And it goes all the way from the poorest up,' she said. 'You can tell. Anyway, I got a whole scad of information, some of it quite scurrilous.'

'So did I,' Molly said. 'Do you want the highlights now?'

They were almost back at the Square. 'Not this minute,' Keith said. 'There may be a quicker way to prove that Mr Hendrickson didn't do himself in. Where's Primrose Crescent?'

'Just behind the High School. Why?'

'Because that's where Mrs Hendrickson's daily lives. I'll walk there and see her.' Keith halted the car and turned round to speak to Molly. 'You take the car and Deborah and try and catch your old milkman. He's probably back at the dairy by now. Find out what he can remember and then meet me back at the hotel.'

'For lunch?' Deborah asked keenly.

'I hope so. Ralph Enterkin always talks more freely over a good meal, especially if a client's paying for it. And I'll try to set up an appointment with Superintendent Munro for after lunch. Are you sure you know what "scurrilous" means?'

'Not really. It's what you called uncle Ronnie. Cheerio!'

It was not quite closing-time when Keith returned. The car was back, parked near his shop. This usually presented a pleasantly old-fashioned front to the Square but it was now half-hidden by a large delivery van. He unlocked the boot and carried a bagged shotgun inside. It was not in his nature to waste a journey. His partner, Wallace James, was presiding over the massed ranks of guns, fishing tackle and all the associated gear and clothing. Wallace accepted a cheque from the only customer and raised his eyebrows at Keith.

'Here's that Perazzi back,' Keith said as the door closed. 'I've got the dents out of the barrels and removed about ten years of accumulated shit from the action. Tell the silly sod to be more careful.'

'I'll t-tell him,' Wallace said, accepting the heavy gun-bag. 'But he won't. There are two more for your t-tender care. I've put a note with each of them about what's wanted.'

'Miracles, probably,' Keith said.

'I c-can't deny it.' Wallace blinked in the sudden flood of light as the delivery van moved away. 'Thank God! I was just nerving myself for another battle with old man Kechnie. Did you finish the report for Mr Wilmington?'

'Posted it last night. Duff cartridge, no doubt about it. He'll probably want me to go and argue the case with the Huddersfield Cartridge Company.'

'Let me have your time-sheet and I'll get an account out to him. He may as well square up as we go along. His m-money's as good as anybody else's,' Wallace said. 'Even Mrs Hendrickson's.'

'I suppose,' Keith said glumly. 'I'd rather hoped you were going to set a fee which would put the lady off. It's not the kind of work I like.'

'I wish you'd told me so earlier,' Wallace said. 'I don't know, though. This time of year, we have to take what we can get. Just for God's sake handle it tactfully, your efforts mustn't look like muck-raking. Have you made any progress with the suicide?'

'The alleged suicide. Yes, I think I have. But it's too early to talk about it. Wal, did we ever take in one of Sam Hendrickson's guns for overhaul?'

'Not since I've been with the firm,' Wallace said.

'And according to his insurance papers he only bought it five years ago. From the serial number, I'd guess that he bought it new. And if that's so, whatever this was I don't think it happened quite the way the sheriff said it did.'

Keith borrowed a pair of twelve-bore snap-caps out of stock, lugged the two shotguns awaiting overhaul out to lock in the car and then walked across the Square to the hotel. Deborah, sitting quietly for once, was already perched on a stool at the smaller bar beside her mother. Each had a glass of what Keith took to be sherry in front of her. There were no other customers. The hotel had been built at a time when solidity was still affordable and successive managements had ever since set their faces against the intrusion of music. There was a hush as of an empty church.

Mrs Enterkin, the plump wife of the pre-eminent local solicitor, was behind the bar. She had been a barmaid before her remarriage and her husband was content for her to continue working. He set no great store by his dignity, while her vocation helped her to remain a fountainhead of that local gossip which can prove invaluable in a legal emergency.

Keith caught her eye and, behind Deborah's back, looked at the sherry-glasses. Inconspicuously, Mrs Enterkin tapped the water jug. Keith nodded. He should have guessed. He ordered a pint of Guinness.

'Ralph phoned,' Mrs Enterkin said in her gentle, West Country voice. 'He got your message and he should be here in a few minutes.'

'That's good,' Keith said. He settled himself on to a stool

beside his daughter. 'You're very quiet in here for a Saturday.'

'There's one or two in the lounge, but most of them are in the public bar for the finals of the darts championship.' She looked up from the task of nursing the last few drops into his pint. 'They say that Mrs Hendrickson's hired you to look into her husband's death.'

'What else are they saying?'

Mrs Enterkin put the cool glass in front of him and collected his money. 'They say that, what with his stroke and all the trouble that was coming to him, the poor man had reason enough to kill himself.'

'That's true,' Keith said. 'That's very true. But people do manage to lead full lives after strokes. And, besides, if we all did everything we've got good reason to do it'd be a strangely uninhibited world.'

Mrs Enterkin laughed, sending ripples around her plump body.

The solicitor arrived a few minutes later, greeted his wife and the Calders and accepted a glass of malt whisky. He was a man of jovial appearance, as plump as his wife and, outside of confidential business, just as talkative. They considered the menu and placed their orders. Deborah was allowed to choose the most exotic and expensive dishes – a privilege, Keith decided, which would cease as soon as the learning process was over.

'If you can get away,' Keith said to Mrs Enterkin, 'please join us.'

'I can't,' she said. 'Thank you all the same. But there'll be nobody else coming in here. I can have yours served on the bar if you like.'

'Splendid!' the solicitor said. 'Just where I'd want it. My natural habitat, as you wildlife enthusiasts put it. Now, Keith, to what do I owe the pleasure of a free lunch instead of a more valuable fee?'

'Sam Hendrickson,' Keith said.

'I supposed as much.'

'I want everything you can tell me about him. I have his widow's authority,' Keith showed Mr Enterkin the letter. 'First, his will. I didn't like to question her about it. She's in an emotional state.'

41

'Small wonder, poor thing,' Mrs Enterkin said. 'Not that anyone else seems sorry at his going.'

'His will was deposited with me when they moved here,' Mr Enterkin said. He looked from his wife to Molly. 'This is not yet for general circulation, although the provisions are fairly mundane. I am, in fact, his executor. He seemed dissatisfied with his Edinburgh solicitors and he made me his executor when they moved here. The will –'

'One moment,' Keith said. 'Before you go on, and while I think of it. When they moved here, he'd already had his stroke. How did he manage to change his will?'

'Without the least difficulty. His wife relayed a message to me. I visited him. It was not easy to make out a word that he was trying to say, but he typed his instructions left-handed on that machine of his. Even then, our discourse was fraught with misunderstandings. He was not the world's foremost southpaw typist and was inclined to rattle on without bothering to correct any typographical errors. At first I thought that he was trying to consult me about his willy, which was a little outside my field.'

Mr Enterkin glanced apologetically towards Deborah, but that young lady only looked mildly amused. He coughed and went on. 'When he got his message across, I prepared fresh documents which he signed, left-handed, but in front of two witnesses. Perfectly legal, I assure you.'

'And the provisions?' Keith asked.

'Much as you would expect, except that he was including his insurance policies in the total. He left large, fixed sums to the children, but in trust until each reaches the ripe age of twenty-one. Fortunately for his widow, he was old-fashioned enough to believe – rightly, in my view – that the young cannot be trusted to deal wisely with money until that age, if then. When those dates arrive, the widow, who has to make do with the balance, may find herself in somewhat straightened circumstances unless the insurances are paid off after all or unless her offspring, in the light of the unexpected shortfall, each makes her an allowance. I have advised her to contest the will on the grounds that her husband neither expected nor intended to leave her in straightened circumstances, but she feels that his wishes were sacrosanct. And she has a touching faith in the generosity of her offspring which I hope may not prove as

42

ill-founded as I fear it might. Her only other hope is that you will prove that he did not, after all, make away with himself.'

A waitress brought three soups and a smoked salmon. Mrs Enterkin, who was also in charge of the tiny bar in the residents' lounge, was summoned away through the back-bar door.

Keith waited patiently until the waitress was gone.

'What can you tell me about the scandal that was brewing up in the union?'

Mr Enterkin looked surprised. 'Very little more than what's been in the papers, plus a modicum of scuttlebutt which has been going around in legal circles. You must know almost as much as I do.'

'I doubt it,' Keith said.

'Dad gets through the morning papers in about ten seconds,' Deborah explained.

'In that case, I shall expound,' Mr Enterkin said. 'It had been an open secret for some time that all was not well within the union. The newspapers had to be careful as to the allegations which they reiterated, but the general picture was becoming clear.

'Many of the shorter-sighted members would have supported Sam Hendrickson all the way, even had he sprouted horns and a forked tail, because their standard of living had shot up, aided by his personal brand of fertiliser and because he had an undeniable charisma in public speaking, especially for those whose upbringing inclined them towards his left-wing views. A policy of screwing the bosses always goes down well with those who have been brought up to see that as the order of natural justice. What they were unable to see was that he was enforcing his demands far beyond the point at which the survival of their jobs became endangered, and whenever a firm went to the wall they preferred to categorise it as an act of spite on the part of the management.

'But there was a sizeable lobby which wanted him out, totally and soon. His misbehaviour was only too obvious and was bringing not only his own union but the whole union movement into disrepute.

'On the other hand, his grip of the union's activities, aided by a hard core of personal supporters who had every financial incentive for his continuance in power, made it very difficult for

43

the disaffected to do anything about it. Indeed, anyone whose voice was raised too loudly in opposition was liable to find himself expelled from the union, for reasons which appeared sound enough, and thereby bereft of his right to a voice.

'Recently, however, there was an outcry about intimidation and ballot-rigging, and demands for an independent enquiry.'

Keith had hitherto been spared involvement with trades unions, and he was floundering in the solicitor's wake. 'But an enquiry into specifically what?' he asked. 'Misappropriation of funds?'

'As to misappropriation,' Mr Enterkin said, 'who could tell? Such matters, if cleverly contrived, are not easily dragged into the light of day, and unions are notoriously coy about washing their dirtier underlinen in public view. What was very evident was that he was feathering his own nest from somewhere, and the incidence of strikes just where the biggest money would want them suggested very strongly that Mr Hendrickson's services were up for sale.'

'You mean,' Keith said, 'that one firm could pay him to scupper a rival by fermenting a strike?'

'Unless the rival cared to top the offer. Don't forget that the operations of a firm can be brought to a halt by a union quite unconnected with its immediate affairs. It needs only the cutting-off of supplies, transport, mains services, fuel, maintenance or any one of a dozen other essentials. But,' said Mr Enterkin, 'such surreptitious dealings can be more subtle than that. The biggest and most recent scandal arose out of the high probability that he had accepted money from a company to foster the strike which brought that selfsame company to a standstill.'

Keith was a good enough businessman at his own level, but his experience was limited to the management of a firm which had never had more than four persons engaged directly in its affairs. 'You'll have to explain,' he said.

Mrs Enterkin had returned. Her husband gestured to her. 'Before expatiating any further,' he said, 'I require another drink. How about yourselves?'

'I'm meeting the police this afternoon,' Keith said. 'I'd better not.'

'I, on the other hand, can expect to spend the afternoon

44

listening patiently while an indignant client tells me how he has been wronged and begs me to pursue the matter as far as the highest court in the land. Being more scrupulous than some of my brethren, I shall then tell him, in about three words, that he would be throwing good money after bad, or, as the French say, beating the water with a stick. I shall endure more easily and sleep more soundly through it all with another drink inside me. And you, young lady?'

'Could I have a glass of white wine?' Deborah asked.

Keith and Mrs Enterkin exchanged a wink. The wine would be watered.

'Three steaks and a cassoulet,' said the waitress, arriving with a tray.

Keith waited again until the door closed. 'Go on,' he said.

'The most open of the open secrets to which I referred,' said Mr Enterkin, 'was that, when Netherclyde Shipbuilders found themselves without contracts, they embarked on the building of two trawlers on spec. Just as the money was running out, a most convenient strike bridged the gap until the recent announcement of an order for three bulk carriers. But for that, they would have been liable for redundancy payments on a scale which would have put them into bankruptcy. Idleness due to industrial action, on the other hand, does not constitute redundancy.'

'And Sam Hendrickson was suspected of having arranged the strike for a fee?'

'More than suspected. Some previous employees of the shipyard were prepared to swear to it.'

'That's the lousiest trick I've ever heard of,' Molly said indignantly.

'Then you've led a very sheltered life,' said the solicitor. 'But for the strong evidence of a substantial bribe, he might well have been able to defuse the situation, morally if not legally, by pointing out that a major employer had in fact survived instead of going under. This was not the first such crisis to befall him, but in the past he had always managed to slide or coerce his way around them. This time his stroke, whether or not it was provoked by the stress induced by the crisis, left his flank exposed.

'When Mrs Hendrickson telephoned me to seek my help

because hostile lawyers had come for her husband's papers, I was in two minds. But I decided that, whatever his sins, Mr Hendrickson was entitled to his rights under the law. However, I had to advise the lady that they had obtained a perfectly proper commission and diligence; and the police who, coincidentally or not, probably not, arrived separately but simultaneously, were similarly endowed. There was nothing I could do to stop them.'

'They were ganging up against him?'

'So one would suppose.'

During the lawyer's rolling periods, Keith had been thinking. 'There had been a break-in at the summerhouse shortly before that,' he said. 'Some papers had been taken.'

'That, no doubt, would have been at the instigation of his own cronies,' Mr Enterkin said. 'It explains why the arrival of the police and of the lawyers representing the hostile elements in the union caused less of a fluttering in the dovecot than I would have expected. Presumably anything exceptionally compromising had already been removed. But even that sensible if illegal move would not have helped if witnesses to the corruption were already coming forward.'

'He was in deep trouble, then?'

'None deeper. Although, of course, the state of his health might have averted actual prosecution. Or the consequences, in the event of his prosecution and conviction.' Mr Enterkin, having had his say, tackled his meal. 'This steak's cold,' he said.

'You couldn't expect it to keep hot while you talked your head off,' his wife said. 'Now, what you were saying about Mr Hendrickson. Some of his members live around here and I've heard them talk in the bars. He did no good to this part of the country. They blamed him for the collapse of Border Weavers and for long strikes at Lowland Fabricators and at the print-works, neither of which gained the workers as much as it cost them. They hadn't a good word to say for him.'

Mr Enterkin, having made some impression on his steak, was prepared to talk some more. 'Be that as it may,' he said, 'I really couldn't visualise Sam Hendrickson committing suicide. I never knew him before his stroke and God alone knows what effect that might have had on his mind, but he had risen high in the trades union movement. You don't do that unless you have the same sort of moral stamina that distinguishes politicians – the ability to take all that the world can throw at you and to let it roll off your back. Some, like yourself, Keith, have it. Others don't.'

Mrs Enterkin served them with coffee. They fell silent. A cheer was heard faintly coming from the public bar.

'The widow,' Keith said, 'speaks about him as if he was a particularly caring sort of saint. Yet, from what I've heard, he was an abrasive character who rode roughshod over everybody.'

'Sarcastic,' Mrs Enterkin confirmed. 'That's what they were saying after the news of his death, those who'd known him. From what they said, he had a tongue that could skin a fox.'

'Even the most abrasive personality,' said Mr Enterkin, 'unless he's a total misanthrope, needs a haven where he can convince himself that he is both loving and loved. Many outright villains are downright sentimental. IRA gunmen have been known to sing songs of motherhood and to shed real tears in the process. In Hendrickson's case, his haven may have been his family. Or possibly just his wife.'

'Now there's a thought,' Keith said. 'I wonder how his kids felt about him. It's not always so easy to be polite and caring towards your own children. Sometimes I wonder how I manage it.'

'Do I only get coffee?' Deborah asked. 'I was wanting to try the profiteroles.'

Keith looked at her appraisingly. 'If you go on eating like this,' he said, 'you'll be as fat as a pig before you're twenty and we'll never get you married off.'

As Molly pointed out, threats or no threats she had to do the shopping. Keith, after assuring himself that she still had the little Derringer in her handbag and did not intend to stray from the more populous part of the town, let her go off with the car while he and Deborah visited Superintendent Munro.

Behind the frontage of the Square reared the only tall, modern building in Newton Lauder, the extension to the police headquarters building. Superintendent Munro's office, however, was in the old part of the building which fronted directly on to the Square. Here he was close to the daily comings and

47

goings and to the area where the general public, it was to be hoped, came to help the police with their enquiries or to solicit their help.

Munro's office, which Keith remembered as having resembled a classroom in a Victorian orphanage, had been revamped. The tall, narrow windows had made it impossible for the architect to improve the proportions of the room, but it had otherwise been transformed and could now have been mistaken for the waiting-room attached to a television studio. The tall and loose-jointed superintendent with his long and knobbled face could well have been a character actor waiting to audition. He had managed to imprint his own ego, while destroying the decor, by hanging many personal photographs around the walls – some of them groups of unidentifiable people from Munro's past, but many being equally grim landscape shots of his native Isle of Lewis which not even the sympathetic photographer had been able to soften.

The superintendent rose from behind a desk which seemed to have strayed in by mistake and to be looking for a way out – or perhaps, Keith thought, it too was waiting to audition. He greeted Keith with unwonted affability and to Deborah was avuncular. 'I always said that this young lady should be in the police,' he said, in the careful lilt which always sounded as if he were still thinking in Gaelic and translating as he spoke. 'She has been our star witness before now and may be so again.' To the desk sergeant he added, 'Ask Inspector Gowrie to bring the evidence.'

Keith and the superintendent had, over the years, enjoyed a relationship which had swung between comprehensive loathing and occasional, uneasy alliances. Now, finding himself courteously offered a comfortable chair and the state of his health solicited, Keith felt his antennae quiver with suspicion.

Detective Inspector Gowrie arrived in plain clothes, carrying Sam Hendrickson's shotgun over one arm with the easy air of one walking between pheasant drives. The effect was spoiled by the box-file under his other arm. He was a chunky young man with a Lothians accent and a brisk and confident manner. Munro left him standing while brief introductions were made, only inviting him to sit at the last possible moment within the bounds of politeness between superior and subordinate.

The gun, Keith noted, was finished with a similar rubber butt-pad to the ones in the summerhouse. Sam Hendrickson, it was to be supposed, had been sensitive to the effects of recoil.

'You steered Mrs Hendrickson in my direction,' Keith said to Munro. 'Why was that?'

'She was dissatisfied with the sheriff's verdict,' Munro said. 'She was wanting a further investigation. You have often investigated firearms cases in the past. Who else would I suggest?'

'You could have choked her off, as you've usually tried to choke me off before now. If you'd told her that the sheriff's verdict was final and correct, she'd have accepted it from you.'

Munro pointed a bony finger at Keith. 'But do you, yourself, believe that his verdict was final and correct?'

'With all respect —' Gowrie began. Munro stopped him with a fearsome glare.

'No,' Keith said. 'I don't. But that wasn't —'

'No more do I,' said Munro. 'When the lady drew our attention to the remains of the cigarette —'

'With respect,' Gowrie said peevishly, 'the cigarette could have been thrown away by the deceased. If he was about to take his own life, he would not be greatly concerned about the possibility – the very remote possibility – of a fire. We found no other evidence pointing to anything other than suicide.'

'Wrong, wrong and wrong,' Munro snapped. 'Regrettably, I have had more than my share of experience. There are those who make apparent attempts at suicide, as a cry for help or attention. Occasionally the gesture goes wrong. The person who was to have found them in the gas-filled room or comatose with sleeping tablets fails to arrive in time. But those are the ones who allow things to continue in their usual untidy and unfinished way, because they expect to be around to tidy up. Such a one might well ignore a dropped cigarette.

'But if a man can make an appeal for help by using a loaded shotgun, which I doubt, this was not such a case.

'Your true suicide, except for a minority who act out of sudden desperation, is meticulous. He wishes to be well remembered. So he leaves all neat and tidy. He would not leave a cigarette burning under the furniture. If, as you say, no evidence was found to suggest anything other than suicide, that may have been because the investigation was inadequate.'

'With respect, the opposite is surely more likely to be true,' Gowrie persisted. 'The man who is about to blow his brains out can hardly die in a fire, whereas the one who is taking a near-overdose —'

'That is the third time that you have mentioned respect,' Munro said angrily. 'Do not use the word again while it is so clearly absent. You were confronted with a death by shotgun. If you had reported it as a mysterious shooting, a team from Edinburgh would have taken over and every detail would have been put under the microscope. You preferred to call it suicide from the very beginning, keeping the investigation in the hands of your sergeant and yourself, with the predictable result that you found nothing to indicate anything else.'

The two policemen scowled at each other. Inspector Gowrie had flushed red and his hand was shaking. Keith realised that he had been invoked as a result of a feud within the Newton Lauder police. He sat quiet and kept his eyes on a hideous and faded photograph of a younger Superintendent Munro with other members of some long-forgotten shinty team.

Detective Inspector Gowrie unlocked his eyes from those of his superior and looked coldly at Keith. He licked his dry lips. 'Might one ask why Mr Calder excludes suicide?'

'I was about to do so,' Munro said.

Keith cleared his throat. 'Somebody phoned me last night to tell me not to contradict the verdict of suicide. He made an ominous but unspecific threat against me or my family.'

'If that is your only argument—' Gowrie began.

'My wife overheard the caller,' Keith said.

A hot little silence was broken by the superintendent. 'Inspector Gowrie was not doubting your word,' he said.

The inspector seemed reluctant to contradict his superior yet again. 'Are you asking for our protection?' he enquired.

'Not at the moment,' Keith said. 'And I do have other grounds for disbelieving the verdict. I visited the Hendrickson's summerhouse this morning. Although there's a thin layer of dust by now, I noticed that the furniture seemed to have been freshly waxed.'

Gowrie raised his eyebrows. 'So?'

'So nothing for the moment. Bear it in mind for later. I also

50

noticed, in the desk drawer, a couple of twenty-bore cartridges, to fit the gun which a man in a wheelchair could most easily have reached down. Unless the police rearranged the order in which the guns hung on the wall?'

'I checked that,' Gowrie said impatiently. 'The guns were as you saw them . Even from a wheelchair, he could have reached the twelve-bore gun. He may have preferred to use the heavier weapon, just to make siccar.'

'The twenty-bore would have been just as certain,' Keith said. 'I once came back to my car from pigeon-shooting with a twenty-bore. A sheep was lying beside it, obviously at its last gasp, and under my windscreen-wiper was a note from the farmer. "Mr Calder," it said, "please shoot this sheep." So I did, and the shot drilled a neat hole clean through the sheep's skull.'

'Mr Hendrickson did not have the benefit of your wider experience,' Gowrie said.

'If he'd been shooting for some years, as his wife assured me was the case,' Keith said, 'he'd be in no doubt about the killing-power of a twenty-bore. What's more, Mrs Hendrickson had taken his cartridges away to the house for safety. Obviously, she'd missed the two twenty-bore cartridges in his desk drawer.'

'She could also have missed the fatal twelve-bore cartridge,' Gowrie said.

'Which I'm told was of a different make from all the others.'

'And is this what you're basing your conclusions on?' Gowrie asked. His twisted smile was almost a sneer.

'No,' Keith said. 'Of course not. Non-matching cartridges are part of the everyday scene. Just out of interest . . .' He put his hand into his coat pocket, where there were usually a few cartridges to be found. 'One Grand Prix,' he said, 'one Huddersfield and two Winchester. Much more to the point is the fact that the twenty-bore gun is a non-ejector.'

Gowrie grunted, frowned and then spoke. 'But the cartridge was not ejected. I do not see what that has to do with anything.'

'Then,' Keith said, in unconscious imitation of Mr Enterkin, 'I shall explain. Your chair is not unlike the wheelchair. Pretend that you're paralysed down the right side, Inspector. I'll put these two snap-caps on Mr Munro's desk, within your reach.

Don't worry, they're dummies and absolutely harmless. Let's see you pick up the gun with your left hand, open it, insert the two snap-caps, close it and pretend to shoot yourself.'

'Very well.' Showing some familiarity with firearms, Gowrie picked up the shotgun left-handed. He pressed over the top-lever and the barrels dropped through an arc of twenty degrees. He set the gun down across his knees and inserted the snap-caps into the gaping chambers. When he pressed his left hand down, the gun closed with a soft click. He lifted it again and, after a little fumbling, held the butt between his knees and touched the muzzles with his mouth. His left thumb was on the front trigger but he refrained from pressing it. 'Satisfied?'

'So far so good,' Keith said, 'although I'm in some doubt as to whether Hendrickson could have gripped with both knees. Hand me the gun, please.' He took and opened the shotgun, holding it so that the two policemen could see between the action and the barrels. 'As you can see, when the gun's opened the two extractors come up, pushing the cartridges to where you can take them out by hand. But shooting is usually a matter of a hell of a lot of walking or standing and a few moments of hectic activity now and again. So you want the fastest possible reloading time. A gun of any quality, such as this one, has selective ejectors which pop the fired cartridges right out. Like this.'

He closed the gun, slipped off the safety-catch and pulled both triggers. He opened the gun and, with the practice of years, caught the two snap-caps as they were ejected. He replaced them on the desk, closed the gun, pulled the triggers again and returned the gun to the inspector. 'Now try again.'

'Why?' Gowrie asked, tight-lipped.

Munro had been watching in silence. He was as much in the dark as was Gowrie but he was content to await Keith's revelations. 'Just do as Mr Calder says.'

'I'll explain first, if the detective inspector insists,' Keith said. 'When a gun of this design, which is one of the most common, has been fired and opened, two different springs have done their jobs, the mainsprings and the ejector springs. Two of each, if both barrels have been fired. To be ready for use again, each has to be re-cocked. With any such arrangement of cams, levers and springs, the designer can distribute the work-load in a variety of ways over the opening and closing process, but the usual arrangement, as here, is that the mainsprings are re-cocked on opening and the ejector springs on closing. But I know this particular model well, and most of the load of cocking the ejectors comes at the beginning of closure. To make matters worse, the designer wanted a good throw from the ejectors and specified springs of a strength which is frankly excessive – unless you want to knock a third bird down with the ejected cartridges. In fact, when both barrels have been fired it's stiff as hell to close at first and then suddenly goes "over the hump" and closes with a snap, often catching the skin of the unwary. As far as I know, I'm the only gunsmith who regularly does a modification on this model to make the fired gun easier to close, but this gun has never been through my hands. Now, try.'

'I still don't see the relevance,' Gowrie said.

'I see the relevance, and that is enough,' Munro said.

Gowrie flushed a dull red. With slight difficulty, he opened the gun against his leg. He laid it across his knees again while he loaded the snap-caps. And there he stuck. Struggle as he might, the gun would not close.

'You see,' Keith said, 'I noticed that the two guns still on Hendrickson's wall had the triggers pulled. Some people prefer them that way.'

Gowrie paused in his efforts. 'That doesn't mean that the third gun was the same,' he said.

Deborah, who had been listening raptly as her elders argued, stirred for the first time. 'But it was,' she said. She opened her jotter. 'I spoke to Mr Albany this morning. This is what he said. "After our wives left, I gave Sam's guns a clean for him. They didn't need it, but he liked to see it done. I put snap-caps into each of them and pulled the triggers. Sam liked to feel that the mainsprings had been relieved. I'd told him several times that that was a fallacy. But if it made him happy, what the hell?" '

Gowrie grunted again. He picked up the gun, still left-handed, and turned it so that the butt was on the desk and the muzzles rested on his shoulder. Under the greater leverage the gun at last snapped shut, pinching a neat triangle of skin on the inspector's palm. 'There!' Gowrie said, dabbing with a handkerchief.

'And now,' Keith said, 'take a look at the mark of the rubber butt-pad on the inspector's desk. That's why I mentioned that the furniture in the summerhouse was freshly polished. There's a good coating of polish and not a mark to be seen.

'You might be able to do the same trick with the butt on the floor, or by hooking the gun under the edge of the desk, but I'll tell you for nothing that the cartridges would fall out again before you could close the gun. And before you try it with the butt on your knee and the muzzles on the floor, let me point out that the floor of the summerhouse is of very hard quarry tiles and that the blacking on the muzzles of the gun is unmarked.'

'Which,' said Superintendent Munro, 'is a long-winded way of saying that there is no way in which a half-paralysed man could load and close that gun without leaving traces which you are unable to find.'

'That,' Keith said, 'is correct. And yet Mr Hendrickson would have known that the twenty-bore gun, which was closest to his hand and the lightest to lift down, would have presented no such difficulty and that there were cartridges to fit it in his drawer.'

# FOUR

That two police officers of some seniority would give immediate acceptance to Keith's view of the sheriff's verdict was not to be expected. In the ensuing discussion, strangely, it was Superintendent Munro who was determined to probe for weaknesses in Keith's argument while Detective Inspector Gowrie, once he had put behind him his initial chagrin, was eager to set off on the new line of enquiry.

Gowrie's box-file, it turned out, did not contain the relevant photographs. He left the room to fetch them.

Munro sighed and leaned back in his chair. 'I must confess,' he said, 'that I did not expect anything quite so dramatic from you. I had no more than a feeling in my water that the inspector's investigation had been superficial and that I could count on you to find something which he had missed.'

'Just to teach him a lesson.' At Mrs Hendrickson's expense, Keith added silently.

'Aye. Well, no doubt he will be the better policeman in the long run over the heads of it.'

'No doubt. So what happens now?' Keith asked. 'Do you drop the mess into Edinburgh's lap?'

'I think not. At the moment, we only have a few unexplained details to offset against an official decision which is presumed to have put an end to the matter. It may even be that some person aided and abetted Mr Hendrickson to commit suicide. Did you think of that?'

'Yes. But I didn't think much of it,' Keith said.

'As to that, we shall see. Just as long as Edinburgh is informed that we have found some unexplained discrepancies surrounding the sheriff's verdict and are continuing an enquiry, we will have paid lip-service to proper procedures. And then we

55

will see what the inspector can do with a real investigation,' Munro added smugly.

Gowrie returned with the photographs and began passing them to Keith.

'May I see?' Deborah asked.

'No way,' Keith said, his eyes on a glossy shot of the appalling wound. 'I don't want you waking me up in the night with the screaming horrors.'

'Oh Dad!' Deborah protested. 'I'm not that soft. You've taught me to gralloch a deer before now.'

'It's different when it's people. Be satisfied with reading the pathologist's report. May she see that?' he asked Munro.

'I see no reason why not. It was read out in open court.' They fell silent. The photographs were informative. They were also uniformly gruesome. Police photographers are not concerned with sparing the feelings of the viewer. Keith was glad that he had witheld them from his daughter. The general shots, which would have been taken before anybody but the doctor had been allowed to touch anything, showed the guns placed as he had seen them.

Deborah looked up suddenly from the pathologist's report. 'It says here that the contents of the brain-pan were "largely absent". But, Dad, you were telling us about a shotgun drilling a neat hole . . .'

'There's nothing in that,' Keith said. He hesitated before deciding that words alone would not turn her stomach. 'I shot that sheep from an inch or two away. If Mr Hendrickson had the muzzles in his mouth, the gas pressure would do almost as much damage as the shot. The exit wound looks surprisingly small. It was the gas pressure that did the rest. The old expression about somebody "blowing his brains out" is absolutely true.'

Deborah seemed quite undisturbed by these grisly details. She was reading on with a puzzled frown. 'Oh. It also says that the shot seemed to have passed almost vertically through the cranium.'

'The lassie's as sharp as a knife,' Munro said. 'I had wondered about that myself. It suggests that he had his head back. That was common enough in the old days, when barrels were longer. A person had to tip his head back to reach the trigger. I've known them to push the trigger with a stick.'

56

Keith took up the thought. 'With a modern gun, with twenty-seven-inch barrels, it's not natural. Not if he was of normal size.'

'Five feet eleven,' Gowrie said. 'Of course, we don't know how it would be to be paralysed down one side.'

Each of the men, in turn, tried holding the gun left-handed and bringing the muzzles to his mouth while keeping fingers near the triggers.

'We're doing it all wrong,' Keith said suddenly. 'We're trying to aim up through the top of the head by keeping the butt down. But the shot and . . . and grey matter hit a ceiling which was about six feet above his head, and hit it about – what? – eight feet behind his back, to judge from the photographs. So the gun was at an angle of about forty degrees to the horizontal. So his head must have been laid well back.'

Gowrie was making notes. 'We must ask Mrs Hendrickson whether his neck was weak after the stroke.'

'M'hm. But,' Munro said, 'I am beginning to see another picture. Somebody hits him on the head. He slumps in the chair with his head lolling back. The visitor takes down the gun, loads it with a cartridge from his pocket, puts the muzzles in the unconscious man's mouth and pulls the trigger, deliberately angling the gun so that the shot would remove the bruised part of the head.'

'What did the fingerprints say?' Keith asked.

'The usual smudged mess,' Gowrie said. He produced three more photographs, over-written in black. 'This is the gun before we lifted the prints. Several of Hendrickson's, rather more of Mr Albany's, none of them overlapping, and a lot of smudges. Heavy engraving is bad for prints, and it's easy enough to put a few prints from a dead or unconscious man on to the barrels of a gun.'

'And it's so easy to get the very thin, plastic gloves,' Deborah said.

'Where?' Munro asked.

'Almost any packet of hair tint. Suggestion,' Keith said. He put his finger on the photograph. 'You have a row of three prints here. They're marked as being Hendrickson's, but I can't even tell which way up they are. Did you keep whole-hand prints from the body?'

Gowrie nodded. 'We did.'

57

'Have them copied on to a stiff but not rigid, transparent plastic, cut them out and try moving them around to simulate that group of prints. That might tell you what angle the hand would have been at and whether those prints are in the right relationship to each other.'

Gowrie made another note. 'Worth a try,' he said.

'I suppose,' Deborah said shyly, 'that they really are left-hand prints? If not, there's something wrong.'

'It doesn't say so,' Keith said, looking at the photograph.

'They are,' Gowrie said. 'Definitely.' From his uncertain tone of voice, it was clear that he was guessing. But Munro let it pass. This time, Gowrie would check and check again.

Keith skimmed through some more of the photographs. For the moment, they had no more message for him. 'Could I see the cartridge-case?' he asked.

'Certainly,' Gowrie said. He dipped into his box-file. 'You're going to love this.' He produced a green shell and handed it over. On the brass base was stamped 'Huddersfield 12', and printed on the green plastic were the words, 'Keith Calder Guns, The Square, Newton Lauder'.

'We sell thousands upon thousands of these,' Keith said. 'They're a standard cartridge. I pay a little extra to have my name on them, but it's worth it for the advertising. Anyway, that's my belief. My partner doesn't always agree. If you can find me the wad and a few pellets, I'll check to make sure that they could have come out of it.'

Deborah turned a few pages. 'The lab says that the wad and pellets were compatible with the cartridge and that the marks of the firing-pin and extractor match the fired barrel of that gun,' she said.

'Very likely,' Keith said. 'But being compatible doesn't mean that they were ever together. Did anybody check that the marks were in register? I bet that they just opened the gun and the empty case scooted across the room.'

'I'm afraid that's exactly what happened,' Gowrie said. 'As soon as the fingerprint man had finished, I opened the gun myself to make sure that there wasn't another live round in it.'

'In that case,' said Keith, 'you can forget it. What I was thinking, rather vaguely, was that somebody could, at any time, have picked up a case which had been fired in that gun. Then, if

58

the only live cartridge which he had available was a give-away –
a reload, perhaps – he could have done the deed and changed
cartridge-cases.'

'Unlikely,' Munro said, 'But possible, surely.'

'Not possible,' Keith said. 'Not without half-dismantling the
gun. The case flew out when Inspector Gowrie opened the gun.
That would only happen if the trigger had been pulled again.
The lab would surely have noticed if the firing-pin had been
struck twice.'

'They would,' Gowrie said, 'and they didn't and it hadn't.'
He passed Keith an enlarged photograph of the head of the
cartridge-case. The single imprint of the firing-pin was clear and
sharp. 'The whole question,' Gowrie said, 'hinges on two
things. First, did Mrs Hendrickson move the wheelchair after
she found him? Second, is Mr Calder correct when he says that
there are no marks on the desk? I want to go and see and hear
for myself before doing any more.'

Superintendent Munro looked at his watch, a chromed digital
model as plain and serviceable as himself. 'We will all go,' he
said.

Keith held up the cartridge-case. 'If I can keep this for the
moment,' he said, 'I'll see what else I can find out.'

Gowrie put out his hand. 'I'll mark it for identification,' he
said. 'Now, shall we go?'

There was no sign of Molly, but Keith knew that once she had
vanished into the shops she could lose all sense of time. He left
a message for her with the desk sergeant.

As they rode back up the hill to Boswell Court in the rear of the
superintendent's car, Deborah was anxious to talk but Keith
shushed her. 'I want to get my thoughts straight,' he said.

'One of these days,' Deborah said, 'you'll find out that I'm
worth listening to.'

Munro made a sound which could have been affirmation or
amusement.

'I hope so,' Keith said. 'Until then, hold your wheesht,
there's a good girl.'

If Mrs Hendrickson was surprised at the early return of Keith
and Deborah, this time accompanied by an inspector and a
superintendent of police, she showed it by no more than one

59

enquiring glance at Keith. She took them into her living room and submitted patiently to a lengthy interrogation. The house had come alive with the muffled beat of rock music from somewhere in the further bedrooms.

Gowrie asked the questions. He returned to the same points over and over again, approaching each time from a different direction, but Mrs Hendrickson was firm and unshakeable. She had not touched the body or the wheelchair which, when she first saw them, had been exactly where they were seen and photographed by the police. And her husband had been perfectly capable of holding up his head.

The inspector seemed satisfied at last. He asked for the key of the summerhouse and Mrs Hendrickson fetched it. 'You don't need me with you?' she asked. 'Only it's my family's first day home since their father died, and I want their meal to be special. Mike's out just now, saying hello to his friends,' she added to Deborah. 'But you could stay and meet Beth.'

'I know them both,' Deborah said. 'I'll see them again. Dad, can't I come with you this time?'

'I don't suppose I'll get any peace until you do,' Keith said. The scene of Mr Hendrickson's death had not been as unsavoury as he had at first expected. The dark, dry stains had become unreal, as if on the set of some filmed thriller.

'Aye, let her come,' Munro put in. 'She's shown that she has sense.'

So Deborah, very matter-of-fact and older than her age, accompanied her father and the two officers to the summerhouse, where she confirmed Superintendent Munro's opinion of her by pointing out, without a hint of squeamishness, that a small bloodstain still detectable on the tiled floor was at least eight feet from a point beneath where the shot had marked the ceiling. She had somehow possessed herself of several of the photographs – Keith could not imagine by what means but suspected that Gowrie had fallen for her blandishments – and was quick to demonstrate that the bloodstain corresponded to a position below the corpse's head when it was found. 'And if the wheelchair was moved,' she finished, 'it would have had to be moved quickly after the shot, before blood could drip.'

The men made no comment. It was self-evidently true.

Gowrie and Munro studied the desk and the top of the

60

bookcase from every angle and finally agreed that there were no marks to suggest that either end of the gun had been rested on top of or beneath the furniture for extra leverage.

'There we are, then,' Munro said. 'We have a strong presumption of foul play but only the most circumstantial of evidence. A pity it is that we allowed Mrs Hendrickson to start cleaning the place. It may be locking the stable door, but we had better seal it.'

'Before you do that,' Keith said, 'lets take one more look. The only things which Mrs Hendrickson admits to touching before she sent for you were the radio and the computer. She says that she switched them off as an instinctive, final gesture. If he committed suicide, he would almost certainly have left a note on the computer.'

'That is true,' Munro said. 'But, of course, any murderer faking a suicide would have done the same thing. If such a note was only in the computer and on the screen, it would have been lost when she switched if off?'

'That's right,' Keith said. 'But, being important either way, it just could have been put on to disc.'

'We'd better get an expert,' Gowrie said.

'If you like,' Keith said, 'but I have almost exactly the same model. Has it been checked for prints? There's no sign of powder.'

Gowrie referred to his papers. 'Mrs Hendrickson will have cleaned it off,' he said. 'The computer was checked. No prints found. It was badly splashed with material from the corpse.'

'In that case, I can't do any damage.'

'If you're sure . . .' Gowrie said anxiously. 'It would be tragic if we wiped something off at this late date.'

Keith took the wheelchair over to the desk and settled himself in it. Habit took over. Without thinking, he reached over the computer to operate the switch at the back. A faint warmth on his wrist warned him in time. 'Christ! I'm wrong,' he said.

'What's up, Dad?' Deborah asked.

'Write down that I'm an idiot and I'll sign it. I said I couldn't do any damage, and I was on the point of moving the switch. The computer's on. It may have been on all this time and I could have wiped it clean. Mrs Hendrickson only switched off

61

the monitor, not the computer. Come to think, I should have known from what she said. Let's see what the monitor shows us.' He switched on the black-and-white television set. The screen came alive, showed fuzz and then settled. The menu of functions showed crisply.

'That's what Mrs Hendrickson thought she remembered seeing before switching off,' he said.

'Could it have been switched off and on again?' Munro asked.

Keith shook his head. 'I don't think so. Not unless somebody's altered the internal wiring. When it's newly switched on, or after a power-cut, it only shows the computer state. Here, the word-processor program's been keyed in,' He touched the ESCAPE key. The screen flicked to a jumble of apparently random letters.

Gowrie was looking over Keith's shoulder. 'It's just rubbish,' he said.

Keith nodded sadly. He put his hand out again to switch off.

'Stop!' Deborah screamed.

Keith jumped and held his hand back.

'It's not just rubbish,' said Deborah urgently. 'Leave it.' They looked at her and she blushed faintly but persisted. 'Remember, this would only be what went in last of all,' she said. 'It'd go in if the computer was switched on even if the monitor was off. I bet you anything that what you see here's the result of Mrs Hendrickson doing her cleaning-up bit and wiping over the keyboard, starting and finishing around the ESCAPE key. And,' she added, 'if you say anything about babes and sucklings I'll switch the damn thing off and you'll never know what else it says.'

'I wasn't going to say any such thing,' Keith protested.

'Well, you usually do whenever I get there first.'

'Which isn't all that often. I was only going to say that the young have an advantage when it comes to microchippery. They're brought up to think in computer jargon and binary arithmetic. But well done, Toots. Very well done.'

Keith simultaneously pressed the SHIFT and the UP keys. Instantly, the screen showed the beginning of the computer's contents. They began with a date, the date of Sam Hendrickson's death. Lines of type followed.

'It's a bittie guddled,' Munro said.

'More than a bittie,' Keith said. 'Ralph Enterkin told me that Mr Hendrickson wasn't much of a typist, especially left-handed and after his stroke. So he didn't bother with capitals and, if the person he was typing the message for understood him, he wouldn't bother with corrections. If that person got the message before he'd finished, he'd stop right there. All that, plus only seeing one side of a conversation, as in Beethoven's conversation-books, doesn't make for easy reading.'

'I've seen worse,' Gowrie said. 'My son's Christmas present list for one. Take the first line.'

The first line read: *clod shit door.*

'If there is sense there,' Munro said, 'I am not the one to see it.'

'This would be when his wife brought him out here,' Gowrie said. 'Allowing for the U and the I being adjacent on the keyboard, he was telling her that he was feeling the cold and asking her to shut the door.'

The next line was clear: *cant reach radio.* 'Still to his wife,' Keith said.

'Presumably. So far so good,' Gowrie said. 'But what about *p louis j natter cmg thispm*?' He did his best to repeat the line phonetically.

'Beats me,' Keith said.

'No it doesn't. You remember, Dad,' Deborah said. She flicked through her notebook.

'Do I?'

'Of course you do. Mrs Hendrickson told us. He liked to listen to phone-calls and the first call was from her sister. This is his note of the call. P just means phone . His sister-in-law would be Louise J. She phoned up for a natter and she was coming "this p.m.".'

'Well done,' said Inspector Gowrie. 'I won't say a word about babes and sucklings. Then we get *p* again, for another phone-call likely, and *hr*, which would be a person.'

Deborah turned a page. 'Hughie,' she said. 'That's what Mrs Hendrickson heard. She left Hughie to talk to her husband.'

'We should be able to trace a Hughie R among his acquaintances,' Gowrie said. 'Which is just as well, because just what *bd ns jc tkng plod* means, God alone knows.'

'God and yours truly, not necessarily in that order. My turn to make a guess,' Keith offered. 'Plod's slang for your outfit. I suggest that somebody with the initials J.C. is talking to the police. So *bd ns* may stand for bad news.'

'Possible,' Gowrie said. 'And that's the most you can say about it. Hughie can tell us when we find him. Who or what would *iandta* be?'

Deborah looked on through her notes. 'Ian and Terry Albany,' she said. 'Next-door neighbours. They came to visit and Mrs Hendrickson brought them up here for coffee.'

'Which explains *ok thanks*. And *ho*,' Gowrie said, 'could be the start of almost anything, probably a sociable enquiry to which he got the answer before he'd finished. *jst put 1 out* sounds as if it refers to the offer of a cigarette. Then we get *k-k-h-s-w-w-f*, followed by *ok just tired*. The last bit speaks for itself, but is the earlier part just gibberish?'

Nobody spoke.

'We seem to be agreed that it is. But what would *linseed stocks* be?'

'Exactly what it says. Mrs Albany and Mrs Hendrickson left,' Keith explained, 'but Ian Albany stayed on and gave the guns a clean for him. This is a request to give the stocks a wipe over with linseed oil. There's a bottle and a cloth in the desk drawer.'

'The barrels were greasy but I didn't notice any oiliness on the stock,' Gowrie said.

'You probably wouldn't. The trick,' Keith said, 'is to wipe nearly all of it off again. But it might be worth having his trousers examined. If there aren't traces of linseed on the knees, it would confirm that he didn't close the gun for himself. And the next words, *snp caps nd trigs*, suggest that he didn't get Albany to leave one gun with the triggers unpulled. Of course, he would have asked it and then wiped out the request so as not to involve his friend. I suppose that *fancy br* was asking him whether he'd like a beer.'

'Or a brandy,' said Munro. 'We must persuade Mrs Hendrickson to tell us about her husband's personal shorthand.'

Inspector Gowrie raised his hand and Keith saw that a spectacular blood blister was developing on his palm. 'Beer,' the inspector said. 'There were two empty tins and used glasses. Then there's another phone-call – *p ph tues*.'

'His physiotherapist phoned up to change an appointment,' Deborah said. 'Making a note of that doesn't seem like a man who meant to kill himself, does it?'

'He might have come to the decision later,' said Munro.

'In that case,' Keith said, 'it would have been too late for him to ask Mr Albany to leave the gun ready for use. Albany left while Mrs Hendrickson was taking the call.'

They had reached the bottom of the screen. While he spoke, Keith keyed to lift the text. His eyes were still down on the keyboard and he heard the others make small noises of surprise or excitement. He looked up quickly.

*'my dsrling,'* read the screen, *'you cant gonon like this tied to a cripple. ill never be mysrlf agaim. time i wasnt here. my love to mike and brth. bless yiu all.*

The remainder of the screen was occupied by the solid jumble of letters which they had already seen.

Keith looked round at Deborah. 'Run down and get Mrs Hendrickson,' he said.

Deborah looked at the two policemen. 'Won't it be an awful shock for her?'

Munro nodded. 'But only Mrs Hendrickson can tell us whether these could be her husband's words,' he said. 'You can warn her.'

Awed by the importance and delicacy of her mission, Deborah hurried out.

'We now have a new problem,' Munro said. 'Was this written by Hendrickson himself or by somebody else?'

'And when?' Keith said. 'It could have been put into the computer at any time since the death.'

'It doesn't look right to me.' Gowrie said. 'These machines make it so easy to edit out your mistakes, even with one hand. A man who was just about to kill himself would surely take the trouble to correct the very last message which he would leave on this earth. On the other hand, some other man – or woman – who was putting a false message into the machine might well try to copy Hendrickson's usual style.'

'I think,' Munro said, 'that you are making one or two rash assumptions. People under stress do not follow guidelines. Mr Hendrickson, in a desperate mood, might not have felt like lingering over his final message. He might have been in a hurry to do the deed before his courage failed or his wife arrived.'

'Irrespective of who wrote it,' Keith said, 'I'm going to print it out and also copy it on to his disc. It's been in the computer for a fortnight, but it would only take a two-second power-cut to wipe it off for ever.'

Mrs Hendrickson arrived, puffing slightly, a few seconds later. Keith had returned the computer to its list of functions. He got up and stood aside.

'Is this what the screen was showing when you found your husband?' Gowrie asked her.

Mrs Hendrickson hesitated and then nodded.

'How did you switch it off?'

'That switch there.' Mrs Hendrickson indicated the switch on the television set.

Gowrie looked at Munro.

'We have found an electronic message,' Munro said gently. 'It purports to be a suicide note from your husband. It may or may not be genuine. We want your advice. Are you ready?'

'Deborah told me.' Mrs Hendrickson braced herself and then nodded. Keith reached past her and touched the ESCAPE key. The colour drained from her face and she swayed. Keith brought the wheelchair forward and steadied her as she sank into it.

'Take your time,' said the superintendent.

'I don't think —' She broke off, swallowed and began again. 'I don't think Sam wrote that,' she said. 'He hardly ever called me "Darling", and he usually referred to Mike as "Spike".'

Mrs Hendrickson read the message through again. 'What makes me more certain is that he always detested the word "cripple" even before he had his stroke. There used to be a sign near our house in Edinburgh which said "Cripples Crossing". Sam complained to the Council until they changed it to "Disabled Persons Crossing", although I said at the time that the new wording was an awful mouthful and I couldn't see that it mattered what they were called, and I don't suppose that they minded very much either, it was the fact of being crippled that mattered. But he said that the word itself was degrading.' She shrugged and looked away out of the window, blinking. 'Why two words should be less degrading than one is among the many things I'll never understand.'

'The message is a fake?' Munro persisted.

'I'm sure of it.'

'What nonsense, Mum!' A girl of about Deborah's age was standing in the doorway. She had features resembling her mother's and yet her expression was in complete contrast, both forceful and contemptuous. 'I've heard Dad use all those expressions, often. He wrote that message.' She wheeled about and was gone.

'Don't heed my daughter,' Mrs Hendrickson said. Tears had spilled on to her cheeks but she was past caring about them. 'Beth was devoted to her father. She can't believe that anyone would hurt him. She would prefer that he had killed himself out of nobility, to spare us.'

'You, on the other hand, prefer not to believe that he killed himself,' Gowrie said. 'Should we heed you?'

Keith broke in quickly. 'If you weigh up the other evidence,' he said, 'you'll see that it supports Mrs Hendrickson rather than her daughter.'

Gowrie nodded and looked at his superior.

Superintendent Munro sighed deeply. 'We will be sealing the room,' he said, 'pending further investigations.'

Superintendent Munro and his detective inspector remained in the summerhouse, considering the scene and bickering in muted voices. Keith and Deborah returned to the house with Mrs Hendrickson. They sat in the large living room. Daylight was going and they saw the lights flash on in the summerhouse. A rabbit came out on to the lawn and crouched, alert for danger.

Mrs Hendrickson was seated at her small writing-desk. Her face was still stained with tears. She seemed uncertain what to say but her instincts as a hostess triumphed. 'You'll take a drink?' she suggested. 'Please help yourselves.'

Keith looked at his watch. The day had almost fled. 'A very quick one,' he said 'Molly has guests coming.' He poured a whisky for himself and gin for his hostess, wondering how soon he could get away without seeming rude to a client who was clearly upset. Surreptitiously, he dipped a finger in the gin and ran it round the rim of another glass before topping both glasses up with tonic water. Deborah sipped suspiciously from the weaker drink but the tang of the gin on the rim of her glass seemed to satisfy her that she was not for once being palmed off with a placebo. Keith made a mental note to warn her of the dangers before she entered other drinking company.

Mrs Hendrickson brought herself under control and listened to Keith's explanation. When he had finished, she raised her glass solemnly to the pair of them. 'I really do congratulate you both,' she said. 'I wouldn't have believed that you could persuade them so quickly.'

'Nor would I,' Keith said. 'We were lucky that there were some strong indicators. The police still have to satisfy themselves that I'm not talking through my hat, but I've no doubt that they will. I take it that that's all you want from us?'

'It's up to the police now. But they may still decide that it was suicide. Or I suppose that they might agree with you but without finding enough evidence to re-open the case with the sheriff. I can call on you again if I need your help?'

'Of course,' Keith said politely. 'But they'll be thorough this time. And Superintendent Munro's a very conscientious man. He won't make a final decision until they're sure.'

'If only he doesn't go by that silly girl of mine!' Mrs Hendrickson said. Her voice and body had been taut when they entered the room but she had gradually returned to her placid self. 'I expect he'll have more sense,' she said. 'I agreed a rate with your partner. How many hours did you spend on it?'

'Seven,' Keith said. 'Each of us. And a lunch for ourselves and Mr Enterkin.' He passed the receipt over, wondering what to do about Deborah.

'Mr James said that your daughter would almost certainly be helping you. He suggested half your hourly rate for her. I thought it was very fair.' She opened the flap of her desk and picked up a pen.

'So do I,' Keith said. Privately, he thought that 50p and a pat on the head would have been ample. 'Forget about Molly. She won't take a fee from a friend.'

'Could you make my cheque out separately, please?' Deborah asked. 'Uncle Wal phoned me. He said to get a separate cheque and he'd fix it so that I could offset it against my school books and not pay any tax.'

'But I buy your school books,' Keith said.

'That's what I told Wal. He said, "So much the better".'

Mrs Hendrickson handed over two cheques. 'I really am grateful,' she said. 'Poor Sam, luck was against him. His stroke and then . . . to die like that! He was only forty-eight, you know.

I feel that the least I can do for his memory is to see that he doesn't go to his grave as a suicide.'

The girl, Beth, appeared in the doorway. She ignored Keith, nodded to Deborah as to an acquaintance barely worthy of acknowledgement and spoke to her mother in tones of cynical amusement which somehow failed to be convincing. 'Give up, Mum,' she said. 'You're kicking against the pricks. Dad topped himself and you know it.' Her voice had the throaty tension of the highly-strung.

Mrs Hendrickson's hand clenched and then relaxed slowly. She took a deep breath. 'I know no such thing,' she said shakily. 'How can you speak to me like that? Your father would never . . . never . . .'

'He would. Like a shot, as they say.' Beth snickered at her own joke. 'Not to save you from wearing yourself out looking after him, he felt entitled to that. But he hated being ill and dependent and he'd have loathed seeing his precious reputation going down the plug-hole, which would have happened if he'd lived. So, for his own sake, not for yours, he popped himself off.'

'I won't believe it,' Mrs Hendrickson whispered.

Beth came further into the room and they saw that an older boy – presumably her brother – had been waiting behind her. 'You don't want to believe it,' Beth said, 'because of the money. It's not his reputation you care about. You don't want to be dependent on us when we come of age.'

The boy – Michael – pushed past. He caught Deborah's eye and checked for a moment, then walked quickly across the room. He looked back at his sister. 'You'd rather that Dad had killed himself, just out of spite,' he said hotly. 'But he didn't write that note. He never, ever called me Mike, and even after his stroke he still managed to blow his top if anybody referred to him as crippled.' He stooped over his mother. 'But you can count on us, you know,' he said. 'We'll look after you. I will, anyway.'

'He blew his top all right,' Beth said.

Keith forgot for the moment that he was off the case. 'How did you know what the note said?' he asked.

The boy raised his eyebrows. He seemed quite unperturbed. 'Beth told me,' he said.

'I never said a word about it,' Beth snapped and flounced out of the room.

Mike broke into a second's brittle silence. 'She did tell me, word for word.' He heaved an exaggerated sigh. 'I don't know what's got into her these days.'

'She's upset,' said his mother. 'Try to be nice to her.'

A ring at the doorbell heralded Molly's arrival. Keith and Deborah were glad to make their escape from a scene which was becoming embarrassing.

# FIVE

Keith and Molly were a sociable couple but they had no social ambitions. Rather than attend a dinner dance at the golf club they were content to spend an evening at darts in the local inn or playing snooker, not very seriously, at the club in Newton Lauder.

As Deborah approached womanhood, however, they had decided that she must have at least a nodding acquaintance with social etiquette. So on Saturday evenings, when guests could linger without dread of the alarm clock's voice soon after dawn, Molly would often give a small dinner. Her guests that evening were Wal and Janet, with Sir Peter Hay. Sir Peter, during his lady's absences abroad, was a frequent guest, not only to round up the numbers nor because he was a good friend and patron but also because, when it came to such matters as the right wine for a course or the proper fork to be used, his was a sure lead to follow. He knew such things as certainly and as unthinkingly as Keith knew the workings of a gun or Molly knew when a joint was cooked.

By custom, Keith and Wallace wore suits but Sir Peter honoured the occasion by draping the least tatty of his many kilts around his long, thin frame. Janet, Wal's blonde wife, was aglow in cream silk. In earlier days, Deborah would have waited at table; but Molly insisted that Deborah must now learn to be waited on, so Deborah was in her only good party frock while Molly kept an apron over an out-dated favourite dress, now in honourable retirement.

Good manners held curiosity in check through the preliminary drinks in the living room and soup or pâté in the heavily-panelled dining room but, when the main course had been served and their hostess was thus freed to give the

71

conversation her attention, Sir Peter voiced the question which had been hanging in the air.

'What's this we hear, Keith, about you looking into Sam Hendrickson's death. Did the scourge of the TUC not take his own life, then?'

'I can't go that far,' Keith said. 'All I've done is to show that the issue isn't as clear-cut as the sheriff was led to believe.'

'Oh, come on, Dad,' Deborah said. 'You put it a lot more strongly than that to Mr Munro.' She took a small sip of her wine. She was only allowed one glass for the evening, so she was careful to spin it out.

'Maybe I did,' Keith said. 'I had to. I was the devil's advocate. If I hadn't made as strong a case as I could, the police might well have decided that this particular hare wasn't worth coursing.' Briefly, he summarised the evidence. There was no need for detail; each of those present was familiar with guns. 'Consider, for instance, the cigarette,' he went on. 'Sam Hendrickson could have been having one last cigarette while he struggled to load the gun. If he'd dropped it at that time, he might well have decided to ignore it rather than risk being found by his wife attempting an act of which she would have profoundly disapproved. The cigarette would have been well away from any upholstery.'

'Well, you certainly had me convinced,' Deborah said.

'It won't give you nightmares, will it?' Molly asked.

Deborah considered the question seriously. 'I don't think so,' she said. 'Of course, I want to live for a million years yet, but—'

'Death itself gets less fearful as its time approaches. It's premature death that one fears. For my part,' Sir Peter said, 'I always had doubts about that verdict. The sighs of relief when his death was announced combined to blow slates off the roofs in more than one city.'

This comment was received with respect. Sir Peter was a director of a number of companies.

'But whose sighs were they?' Janet asked.

Sir Peter beamed across the table. He had been an admirer of Janet's golden looks since she had left school. 'About every alternate name in the phone-book,' he said. 'His own faction in his union, because his death will probably abort a scandal which could have ruined them all. The less fanatical among the

72

ordinary members, because they can now hope against hope for a more honest and democratic administration of their business. Several concerns who were next on his hit-list. A great number of men and women who have fetched up in the dole-queue due to his past machinations. Plus, of course, any personal enemies he may have made along the way. Myself included.'

'Golly!' Deborah said.

'You've m-met him then?' Wallace said. 'Was he as bad as they paint him?'

'As bad or worse,' Sir Peter said. 'I know all about *de mortuis nil nisi bonum,* but frankly there wasn't any *bonum* so the tag doesn't apply. I met him last when he went after a major firm with a trumped-up dispute. It seemed to be no more than a brazen attempt at blackmail, so they weren't going to give in. I was on the board and I went along to the meeting. The chair was occupied at that time by a very charming and distinguished lady and she took the trouble to speak to him as if he were a respectable colleague rather than a crook. She was wearing a dress which, in this day and age, could be considered prim rather than daring. But the charming Mr Hendrickson told her in so many words that if she thought she could get a better deal by flashing her – er – bosom at him, she could think again.'

'Crikey!' said Deborah. 'And nobody hit him?'

'Despite the temptation, no. In fact I suspect that, rather than boorishness, it was a calculated move to keep us off-balance.'

'What happened?'

'A few days later, we got the hint that a smaller but rival body was behind him. So we started talking takeover and the threat faded away. Oddly enough, I met him socially a few months later when somebody else invited me to shoot with a syndicate of which he was a member. His attitude was friendly and he seemed quite surprised when I made it clear that I would rather not know him.'

Molly got up to collect the plates and to serve a sweet. 'It sounds as if the police are going to have their work cut out,' she said.

'What's more,' said Keith, 'I don't think they can make a job of it if they keep it low-key, the way Munro intends. With so many people potentially involved, and so much money and

73

power, they're going to need the big guns.'

'I'm surprised,' Sir Peter said, 'to hear you use that particular analogy. You of all people, Keith, know that big guns are seldom needed. If you have the fieldcraft to bring the quarry within range, a smaller gun with the right load can do the job just as well or better. If Superintendent Munro cares to channel his enquiries through some of the specialist units, he may go places without asking for a full-scale murder team – which, in view of the sheriff's decision, he wouldn't get.'

'I suppose,' Deborah said, 'that Mr Hendrickson couldn't have made enemies up at Boswell Court? He only moved there after he had his stroke and I don't exactly see him using his word-processor to go on putting people's backs up.'

Sir Peter laughed shortly. 'Mrs Hendrickson would have had difficulty finding anywhere to live where nobody already owed him a grudge.' He paused and gave his host a thoughtful glance. 'You'd better watch your back, Keith. There could be powerful interests involved.'

'We've already had one threatening phone-call,' Keith said. 'But the damage is already done. I don't really expect somebody to come after me for revenge.'

'Boswell Court's where the police should be looking,' Deborah said. 'Mum thinks so, too.'

Molly seated herself and picked up her spoon. 'That's true,' she said.

'I rather thought as much myself,' Keith said. 'That phone-call came last night. Mrs Hendrickson would already have phoned her neighbours, asking them to co-operate with me. There had hardly been time for anybody else to know that I'd been called in. What are your reasons?'

'Because I went round most of the houses,' Molly said, 'and Deborah called at the others. Not everybody was in, but we talked to at least one person in each household. Apart from a window-cleaner and the milkman, there was nobody there at all that morning except the residents. And we don't see how a stranger could have got in without being noticed.'

Deborah looked at her father. 'That's what I was trying to tell you in the car.' She went to work on her banana split, seeming unaware of the silence in the room.

'You can't be sure, Toots,' Keith said gently. 'You didn't have very long.'

'Long enough. You were ages with Mrs Hendrickson. And Mum got the same story.'

'All the same . . .'

'Let me finish my sweet,' Deborah said, 'and we'll explain. I'll need to make a sort of map.'

Sir Peter moved the decanter out of her way. Deborah bolted her sweet and for once Molly did not reprove her. The mood was one of mildly alcoholic contentment. There had been gin, whisky or sherry before the meal and with it a wine – from a supermarket, but highly recommended by Sir Peter – and now they were to be given entertainment enriched by reality and spiced with a touch of the macabre.

'Now,' Deborah said. She seemed not to be displeased at being the centre of attention. 'The road into Boswell Court comes along the canal bank and then jiggles sideways to make room for houses. Right? Then you've got four houses on the left of the road, with gardens backing on to the canal.' She laid out four mints in their dark envelopes. 'They don't have numbers up there, just names and nobody uses the names much except the postie, but we'll call them One to Four.'

'Four being Mr and Mrs Albany?' Keith said.

'That's right. And, opposite, another four houses which we'll number Five to Eight coming back, so that the Hendricksons are Number Five and Mr Strathling is Six.' She laid out another row of mints. 'And, just to be sure that we're looking at it the same way round, this is the wood beyond the houses.' She placed a table mat. 'It borders on Numbers Four and Five and it's all ringed with barbed wire. There are small clumps of trees as you arrive at Boswell Court, but we won't count those. And here's the canal.' She placed two forks and then looked at her mother. 'You tell the next bit.'

Molly nodded. 'It was the first fine weekend of spring,' she said, 'so there were a lot of things going on out of doors. I'll take them in numerical order. At Number One, Mr Kechnie was washing the cars in front of his garage.'

Wallace jumped as if he had been stuck with a pin. 'Kechnie? Is that the K-kechnie who has the grocer's shop two doors along from us?'

'And several others in the region. One and the same,' Sir Peter said.

'He's a miserable, vicious old bastard,' Wallace said. The

75

complete disappearance of his slight stammer was enough to show that his anger was genuine. 'Frame him for it, Keith, if you can.'

'He may not need framing,' Sir Peter said. 'He's one man who had a genuine grudge against Sam Hendrickson.'

'How's that?' Keith asked.

'I don't suppose that I know the whole story, but several years ago Hendrickson's union was in dispute with one of Kechnie's suppliers. Hendrickson approached Kechnie, trying to persuade him not to patronise a supplier whom the union had blacked. Kechnie told him to go and boil his head, but not so politely. The dispute with the supplier was soon settled, but Hendrickson had his knife into Kechnie by then. Ever since, the grocer's been plagued by stoppages, and by deliveries which arrive late or damaged or even contaminated.'

'Surely that would have stopped when Mr Hendrickson fell ill,' Janet said.

'That I wouldn't know,' said Sir Peter. 'But habits die hard. And don't quote me but, from what I hear, Kechnie was hit hard enough that he's still carrying a bank loan which is making his life difficult. Remember, now, you didn't hear that from me.'

The table fell silent while the implications sank in. 'Go on, Deborah,' Keith said at last.

'Golly!' Deborah said. 'Some people play rough games. Who's next? At Two, Mr Pollock was mowing the grass at the front. At Three, Mrs Orton and her daughter, Pat, were at the back of the house, clearing beds ready for planting-out while, upstairs, Mr Orton's mother was sitting at her window looking across the road in the general direction of Number Six. Mr and Mrs Albany we know went next door to visit the Hendricksons, but they were indoors after they got home.'

'I know Ian Albany,' Sir Peter said. 'Met him shooting. Good enough chap, but I wouldn't breed from him.'

'It's a pity you didn't tell him that sooner.' Deborah said. 'His daughter's a blot. Mr Strathling, at Six, isn't much help. He was indoors until he heard the shot, watching the racing on the gogglebox – he seems to be a fan, he was doing the same thing when I called on him. His wife was out shopping both times, she works in the bank so that Saturday's her best day for shopping.'

76

'I saw somebody I supposed was him washing a car this morning,' Keith said. 'It must have been between races.'

'I know Ben Strathling,' Wallace said. 'But I'd forgotten that he lived up there among the nobs. He gave us a good quote for our insurance.'

'He covers me as well,' Sir Peter said. 'And I've met him socially. Bumped into him once or twice at the races or in gaming clubs. His company's one of the biggest and best although they've been getting sticky about paying out on claims recently.'

'If you've quite finished chatting,' Deborah said severely, 'I'll take up the story. At Seven, Mr Beecher was away fishing but his wife was digging the back garden. The McLaings, at eight, were away on holiday.'

'Beecher's a customer at the shop,' Wal said. 'Not fishing tackle, though. Cartridges. He shoots sixteen-bore. You altered the cast of his pump-gun last year, Keith.'

'I remember the gun. I don't know that I ever set eyes on him.'

'On top of all that,' Deborah said firmly, 'the window-cleaner was working. He comes round some of the houses weekly and some fortnightly, so he was there again today and I spoke to him. Despite the sound of Mr Orton's mower – it's electric, so it isn't too noisy – he heard the shot and he'd got as far as Number Six, the Strathling house. Of course, he was facing the windows; but he says that he sees most of what goes on.

'The milkman, old Mr Rogers, was going round collecting the money for the week.

'All those people,' Deborah said, 'or at least most of them – the Kechnies went out before we got there this morning – were positive that no strangers were around the place. There was some to-ing and fro-ing among the residents, but no strangers.

'And to top it all, Kenny Stuart, the farmer, was working the field which runs behind Numbers Five to Eight and round the corner of the wood. He was drilling barley. Mrs Beecher swears that the tractor never stopped for a minute. And you know what Kenny is about intruders.'

'No,' Molly said. 'I don't.'

'Kenny's brother runs a family shoot on the land,' Keith explained. 'They get poached now and again by ... well, I won't name any names, but they come from the council houses further along the canal. So Kenny only has to see a strange figure on his land and he'll uncouple the tractor and go after them. He doesn't have the rights to that wood, but a lot of his pheasants pick nesting territories there. The residents are always complaining, Kenny says, because they have more than enough trouble with the rabbits without pheasants getting into the gardens and making dust-baths in the flower-beds.'

Sir Peter knew all about pheasants in the garden. 'It's not so much the flower-beds,' he said, 'but when they get into the potato-patch they uncover the young tatties, which go green and toxic in the sunlight. Still, I don't suppose anybody grows anything as plebeian as potatoes up there.'

Molly preferred to stick to the original subject. 'Kenny couldn't do anything about somebody walking along the towpath,' she said.

'The towpath's the other side of the canal,' said Deborah. 'The fields and gardens come right to the canal bank. There is a footbridge over the canal, from a footpath between the gardens of Three and Four, but Mrs Orton's sure that nobody used it except Mrs Pollock, who was coming back from a quick visit to her cousin and stopped for a chat just before they heard the shot. There was an angler on the towpath, but Mrs Orton says that he never moved, not even to catch a fish.'

'He wouldn't c-catch a fish,' Wallace said. 'Not there. Not more than a couple of inches long.' He passed his cup for more coffee.

'The point is,' Deborah said, 'that those people saw each other moving around, and they didn't miss much. Well, of course, nobody's in the same place all the time. People do go for a pee or a cup of coffee or to fetch tools. But not one out of all those people saw a stranger. So unless somebody got into the wood during the night and waited for Mrs Hendrickson to wheel her husband up the garden, or Mr Rogers smuggled somebody up in his van, I don't see how any outsider could have got there at all.'

The conversation checked again.

Wallace broke the silence. 'A pheasant can m-make the devil of a noise when it's disturbed,' he said. 'Nobody heard a cock squawking, or saw any of them rocket up?'

'Not to mention,' Deborah said. She looked at her father. 'I could go back and ask.'

'Definitely not,' Keith said. 'We've done our job and been paid off. We're in good odour with the police for once, but that won't last long if we start interfering.' He hesitated and then decided to dangle a bait. 'And we have a satisfied client for the moment,' he said. 'If we go on, we may find that we're throwing suspicion in the direction of that son of hers. He seemed to know a little too much and you're so sure that no outsider could have come in.'

'He was in Edinburgh,' Deborah protested.

'Maybe. And maybe he was such a familiar sight that nobody noticed him. You go ahead and type up a report of all that you and your mother can remember between you, give the police a copy and one to Mrs Hendrickson, we owe her that much. And then we're finished.'

'You'll be having it quiet for the next couple of weeks, then?' Janet asked.

Keith looked at her sharply. He knew the warning signs. 'I was going to update the price list of vintage guns for sending out,' he said.

'I could do that for you,' Molly offered. Keith gave her a look of reproach.

'The thing is,' Wallace said, 'Janet and I wanted a break up Speyside. We thought we'd have to p-put it off. But if you've finished with the Hendrickson case . . .'

Keith sighed. Minding the shop while keeping up with the gunsmithing and other work meant long hours. On the other hand, he could not get away from the fact that he was, in reality, a shopkeeper, or that Wallace was overdue for a holiday. 'All right,' he said.

They moved to other subjects. Deborah went to fetch the lockplates from Sir Peter's gun. She had rubbed them with black grease and then wiped off the surfaces so that the engraving stood out sharp and black.

Sir Peter was pleased. 'You've brought the two animals closer together, which is an improvement,' he said. 'And you've caught Bael's expression better than the photograph did. That

79

look of "I'll be walloped for this but it's worth it". The wicked old beggar!' he added affectionately. 'If he was a person, he could sue you for libel.'

Deborah accepted the praise modestly. Her manner for the rest of the evening was subdued.

When their guests were gone and Deborah had been sent upstairs, Keith, in a mood of mildly alcoholic benevolence, offered to help with the washing-up. His offer was declined. Molly set great store by her best glass and china and Keith, when he had a drink in him, could get careless.

'You go on to bed,' Molly said. 'I'll finish up.'

Keith was not sleepy. 'I need a winding-down period after all that talk,' he said. 'Otherwise I'll just lie and do some pondering that nobody's going to pay for. I think I'll go and potter. I never cleared up after testing Mr Wilmington's cartridges. Set the burglar alarm after me and I'll knock when I want back in.'

'All right. But put your coat on; it's cold outside. And leave me the pepperbox pistol, if you've got it on you. Just for my peace of mind.' Molly was not thinking of the threatening phone-call but of Keith, slightly fuddled, deciding to check or unload the distinctly tricky antique.

In the former coach-house, Keith cleaned and oiled his pressure-barrel and gathered up the spent cartridges. Thrifty as ever, he dropped the used crushers into his pocket. The small cylinders of lead could be added to his melting-pot, the next time that he was pouring bullets or balls for use in his muzzle-loaders.

When all was tidy, he switched off the single overhead bulb and stood for a moment in the doorway, waiting for his eyes to adjust.

It was a black night. The lamp over the back door washed a little light over the courtyard but it was soon swallowed by the greedy darkness. Keith was about to set off towards the glow when he thought that he saw a moving shadow.

'Who's there?' he called. His voice had risen, along with the hairs on the nape of his neck.

There was no answer. He thought that imagination had tricked him but a foot scraped on gravel and suddenly the vague

80

shadow was the silhouette of a man, very close, and two hands grabbed his lapels. He expected a butt and lashed out, low and hard, but his fist bounced off a wall of solid muscle. The hands against his chest pushed him with a weight and strength sufficient to send him reeling back from the door until he fetched up against his bench.

A large shadow came through the doorway, black against the lesser darkness outside, and the door was pulled to.

Keith thought, frantically. He was in no doubt that the man was larger than himself and stronger, probably younger and he might very well be armed. Mixing it at close quarters would not be a good idea. Rather, this was a man to hit with something hard and heavy while remaining well outside his grasp. He heard, faintly, a slithering sound which, after a moment of panic, he identified as hands sliding on the wall, seeking the light-switch.

The dark was to his advantage – Keith knew the layout as surely as he knew Molly's soft contours. The single light-bulb was above his reach. He took one of the crushers from his pocket and tossed it to one side, to cover his own sounds while he fumbled on the bench. It would take all night to unbolt the pressure-barrel from its bench but surely there must be something . . .

With an upsurge of relief, he felt Mr Wilmington's gun-barrels under his hand – two conjoined, lightweight tubes, jaggedly burst at the heavier end. He swung them overhead.

The first three swings found nothing. The fourth hit the light-bulb. It must have coincided with the man finding the switch, because there was an instant of light, too brief for vision, and then darkness again and the sound of thin glass falling on the cobbled floor.

Keith stood and strained his eyes. If any starlight was filtering through the skylight above, he could not see it. But the other man had been waiting in darkness. If his night vision were good . . .

'Where are you, ye bugger?' said a voice. 'I can wait as long as you.' It was deep and gruff, accented with the Glasgow-Irish growl of the Scottish industrial belt. Where had Keith heard such a voice recently? No, not heard. Mrs Hendrickson had described it.

Wrong, he could do no harm. But if he were right, he could unsettle the other man.

Keith took three soft paces to his left. His prayers were answered and his soles did not crunch on glass. 'Hello, Hughie,' he said. He flicked another crusher against the wall and slipped back towards his bench. Somebody seemed to have removed it.

His shot in the dark seemed to have struck home. The man started to speak and bit his words off. When he began again, he was speaking carefully. 'You didna' heed the warning you was given on the phone.' he said. 'I'm here to give you another that you'll no' forget so quick.' He seemed to be waiting near the door, as Keith would have expected.

The words 'shot in the dark' came back to Keith. He had found the corner of his bench by cracking his knee against it. He put down Mr Wilmington's barrels where he could find them again and waited for the agony to abate. There was no sound of movement. Perhaps he had not, after all, groaned aloud. He felt in his coat pocket. He usually carried a few cartridges there in case of sudden need and habit had not let him down. He found the three cartridges which he had shown Inspector Gowrie, only that morning.

He covered the noise by lobbing a small handful of crushers into the corner while he stuffed a cartridge into the breech of the pressure-barrel. He wondered whether to use another crusher to hold the piston down over the pressure-vent, but decided that an extra flash would be all to the good. He heard the sound of a footfall. The man was moving. Well, if he had wandered in front of the barrel that was his problem.

Keith turned his eyes towards the door and hit the trigger.

The blast of the gun and the slam of the shot on iron almost drowned a squawk of surprise. In the bright flare, Keith saw the man to his right, almost in the path of the shot but looking away from him. In the newly intensified darkness and silence, Keith took two paces and swung Mr Wilmington's gun-barrels, in a downward chop in case his man had ducked.

The blow landed solidly and he heard the man say 'Shit!' with deep feeling. Two seconds later, as he was beginning another swing, came the sound of a falling body.

Keith stopped his swing and walked to the door. He met bare wall, fumbled the wrong way, came back again and put his hand on the doorknob. An instant later, he was outside in the cold, clean air.

When he came back a few minutes later with a torch and a shotgun, there was no sign of the man and only the smell of gunsmoke, the broken bulb and a few drops of blood to confirm that he had ever been there. The man's skull, Keith decided, must have been built on Clydeside. The remains of Mr Wilmington's barrels had bent into a hoop.

A pair of tired-eyed, uniformed constables had dealt with Keith's Saturday night call, but Detective Inspector Gowrie arrived in time for coffee on the Sunday morning. Keith received him in the study.

'Your visitor last night –' Gowrie began.

'I'm surprised you don't say "alleged visitor",' Keith broke in.

The inspector raised his eyebrows. 'Your past dealings with the superintendent seem to have left you a bit on the touchy side. He has that effect on folk at times. But you needn't be scratchy with me. I've forgiven you for making me look daft and we're quite prepared to believe you this time around. Last night –' Gowrie produced and opened a typed report – 'you told our officers that your visitor's voice bore some resemblance to the voice of "Hughie" as described by Mrs Hendrickson but not to the caller who threatened you on the phone.'

'My caller disguised his voice,' Keith said. 'But he'd been reared in an altogether classier neighbourhood than Hughie.'

'He couldn't have been putting it on? Talking "pan loaf" as they say?'

'If he was, he was bloody good at it.'

The inspector shook his head. 'The weekend isn't the best time to get information from a union about its members and officials, but we have word of a Hughie Reynolds who was a hanger-on of Sam Hendrickson and his crowd. He doesn't sound the type who'd be a good enough actor to fool you. Odd-job man, keeping recalcitrant members in line, that sort of thing. Our informant described him as "the size and shape of a brick shithouse and with a voice like a randy mastiff".'

Keith thought back. It was some years since he had listened to a randy mastiff. 'That sounds like last night's caller.' he said.

'There's no sign of him around his usual haunts,' said Gowrie. 'Probably keeping his head down until the lump on it goes away. There's nothing much else to incriminate him. There was nobody lurking by the time our men got here. I'll ask you again, do you want protection?'

'Unarmed?'

'Of course.'

'Don't bother. I've no immediate intention of using firearms,' Keith said carefully, 'but there are a number of guns in this house. Because of their value, I have the latest in electronic alarms; and, just in case the wires get cut, my nearest neighbours have instructions to phone your boys if the alarm goes off. I'll call you if I have any doubts about coping but, for the moment, thanks but no thanks.'

Gowrie put his coffee mug carefully down on a table mat. 'The least amount of force compatible with self defence,' he said. 'I'd hate to have to prosecute you or one of your family for manslaughter or culpable homicide.'

'I'll remember,' Keith said. 'Have you made any other progress?'

'Miracles take a little longer,' said Gowrie. Away from Superintendent Munro, he was given to enigmatic statements. 'You only dropped your bombshells yesterday afternoon. And I'd been looking forward to a free weekend for once, Ho-hum! Have you had any more thoughts?'

'Some,' Keith said. 'I've done my bit and been paid off, but I'd have to be a vegetable not to go on thinking about it. And you?'

'Thoughts, yes. Progress, no. I tried to recover Mr Hendrickson's trousers from his widow but she'd already sent them to Oxfam; although, as the super pointed out, any traces of linseed oil could have been there for months for all the lab would've been able to tell, so there's no harm done. Before I invest a lot more police time, I'd like to pick your brains.'

Keith made modest noises. 'Go ahead,' he said.

Inspector Gowrie's face was usually unlined but now his brow furrowed with thought. 'Difficult to express clearly,' he said. 'We know that a noise, as of a shot, was heard. We know the approximate time of that. Unfortunately, because it was so obviously a case of suicide, the police surgeon was even less precise than usual in his estimate of the time of death. But how crucial is that time? In other words, did Sam Hendrickson necessarily die at the moment when that bang was heard?'

'It's a vague question,' Keith protested.

'I'm thinking vaguely. To be more precise, do I disregard everybody who can be accounted for at that time? Or would it have been possible for somebody to have shot him earlier and to have left some device to make the bang while he was safely in other company, returning later to remove the banger?'

To gain time, Keith poured himself another coffee which he could well have done without. 'There are two parts to that question.' he said at last. 'Could somebody have shot Sam Hendrickson without attracting attention? And could he then have arranged for a delayed-action noise to simulate the shot?'

'True,' Gowrie said. 'But you can concentrate on the first part. The second is my baby.'

'I'll comment on the second anyway. Like my wife, I always pass remarks about other peoples' babies. You're thinking of some kind of a firework?'

Gowrie nodded. 'Or possibly a tape-recording.'

'I think you can discount the idea of a recording. There was only Hendrickson's own cassette-radio around and its speaker wouldn't have a tenth of the necessary volume. I really can't see somebody lugging a hi-fi system into the Hendrickson's garden on the end of a long lead and getting it out of sight before Mrs H arrived. As for the firework idea, a squib doesn't sound anything like a shotgun.'

'I was thinking of something like an army thunderflash.'

'Ah.' Keith thought again. 'Mrs Hendrickson describes "a muffled bang". A thunderflash might be suitable. But it's pretty powerful as fireworks go. It would be difficult to use without leaving traces.'

'Down the nearest drain?' Gowrie suggested.

'When I was young and wicked – which was a long time ago,' Keith pointed out quickly, '– I once dropped a thunderflash down a drain. It was after a party and I was showing off. Every brander in the street erupted like a fountain. You think nobody in Boswell Court would have noticed something like that?'

'Leave it for now,' Gowrie said. 'We may find a scorched patch in the wood. What about the sound of the real shot?'

'Difficult. There's no doubt that he really was shot, or that the muzzle was inside his mouth at the time. Right?'

'Right,' Gowrie said.

'You can't fit a silencer to a double-barrel gun. There are silencers, of a sort, to fit a single barrel. One of the neighbours, Beeching, has a sixteen-bore pump-gun which would suit. But such silencers as I've seen fitted to shotguns weren't very effective, and they were too big to go into anybody's mouth. Why are you so keen to upset the time element?'

The detective inspector looked at Keith in mild surprise. 'I'm not busting a gut to upset the time,' he said, 'but how can I not question it? Those who were nearest to Sam Hendrickson are too well alibied for my peace of mind. One, for instance, was seen waiting near your road-end at about the critical time.'

Gowrie got up to look out of the window. It was drizzling steadily. He turned and sat on the window-sill. 'Stop me if I'm wrong,' he said, 'but I think that what's loosely called a silencer is only a sort of expansion-chamber to modulate a single, violent pulse of gas pressure and let it emerge gently and over a longer period.'

'Near enough,' Keith said.

'You pointed out that gas pressure literally blew Sam Hendrickson's brains out. Wouldn't that, inside a solid and double-glazed building, be enough to modulate the sound of the shot?'

'I doubt it,' Keith said. He thought about it. 'The human skull acting as a silencer? I doubt it very much. You could prove it experimentally, one way or the other. Your nearest police lab could surely knock up something which would perform like a human head. Or perhaps you could call for a volunteer?'

Gowrie straightened up. 'Any man who volunteered would have a skull too thick for shot to penetrate,' he said. 'Tell me something else. My sergeant suggested that, if Sam Hendrickson was shot with a different gun, one with a silencer, the empty case in Sam's gun and the dirty barrel could be explained by the murderer having fired through it a cartridge which had been previously fired and then fitted with a new primer only. He said that would be very much quieter than a shot. Possible?

'Not possible,' Keith said. 'You fire a primer up a barrel and you don't get burned powder, you get a sticky, grey guck which doesn't look the same at all.'

Gowrie sighed deeply. 'Thank you for your time. And the coffee.'

'I've something else to contribute,' Keith said. 'Come back and sit down. It hurts my eyes, looking at you against the light.'

In silence, Gowrie walked back and resumed his seat.

From his desk drawer, Keith produced the three main components of a conventional shotgun. 'I've just poured cold water on part of your thinking,' he said. 'Yet I've been doing a little more thinking of my own. I made a mistake yesterday. Put it down to trying to think of too many things at the same time.' He hooked the pair of barrels to the action-body and closed the gun before clicking the fore-end under the breech-end of the barrels. 'Assume that you've solved the other problems and that Sam Hendrickson was shot either by another gun or by his own gun using a cartridge which would be a giveaway – even a sixteen-bore cartridge, which could, with some difficulty, be fired in a twelve-bore gun. The murderer has a spent cartridge which was once fired in Sam's gun. Watch.'

Keith slipped the safety-catch and pulled one trigger. The firing-pins clicked. He removed the fore-end, pressed the top-lever and allowed the gun to swing open. It moved freely. 'The cocking-action and the tripping of the ejectors are transmitted by the fore-end,' he explained. He took a fired cartridge from the drawer and inserted it, closed the gun and replaced the fore-end. 'There you are. If you open it now, the case will eject just as it did when you opened Sam Hendrickson's gun. And just as if it had only now been fired in this gun.'

'Now that,' Gowrie said. 'is very interesting. It opens up a whole spectrum of possibilities. I'm much obliged to you.'

'Not at all,' Keith said. 'Glad to have been of help. Of course, you'd still have to explain the dirty barrel in Sam's gun and how the murderer knew in which barrel the spent cartridge had originally been fired. The lab report was quite clear. It said that the marks of the firing-pin and extractor matched the dirty barrel.'

Inspector Gowrie sat in thought for a full minute. 'So Sam Hendrickson was shot with his own gun?' he said at last.

'That's how I see it.'

'Which could not have been fitted with a silencer?'

'No way that I can think of.'

'And any alibis for the time the shot was heard will stand up?'

'Yes.' Keith watched with amusement as emotions chased each other across the inspector's countenance. 'You can swear if you want to,' he added helpfully.

# SIX

Responding to the demands of the alarm clock on a damp Monday morning and trailing into Newton Lauder to open the shop came close to being Keith's idea of hell. Years of leaving the retail side to Wallace James while concentrating on the gunsmithing, antique arms and general wheeling and dealing had accustomed Keith to a freer way of life. He might rise earlier or later as the mood took him, but he preferred to do so when he awoke of his own accord and not at the command of an impersonal machine.

Wallace had promised him a quiet fortnight. Keith found it busy if not very profitable. The complicated logistics of ensuring that Deborah never travelled alone and that Molly was either in company or armed and safe behind the alarm system at Briesland House saved him from any risk of boredom.

The game-shooting season was over and fishermen seemed already to have equipped themselves for the summer. But the clay pigeon season was beginning and there was a steady outflow of cartridges and clays. Heavyweight over-unders came in for a quick check or overhaul and lighter game-guns were left to be readied for the autumn. The workshop in the back premises had long since been absorbed by the retail side of the business, so any guns requiring more than minimal servicing had to be taken home for attention during the evenings.

Keith would have forgotten Sam Hendrickson, as most of the late union leader's acquaintances were trying to do, but for a succession of visitors, each with something to say about the case.

On the Monday afternoon Keith finished answering, on the telephone, a series of penetrating questions about the history and condition of a flintlock fowling-piece which had figured in his last catalogue of antique arms, to find a customer waiting patiently for his attention.

He recognised Ian Albany immediately. The chairman of the local shooting club was a distinctive figure, stocky and so squat and lantern-jawed that Keith had had to alter several guns to allow for his unusual proportions.

'We're shooting for our various trophies on Saturday,' Albany said without preamble or greeting. He placed an order for clays and cartridges. 'And can we hire an extra trap from you as usual?'

'No problem,' Keith said. 'Do you want Deborah to come and work a trap for you again? I can ask her.'

Ian Albany smiled. He had a friendly smile but his teeth were not quite straight, the canines protruding so that his smile sometimes looked like a snarl. 'I asked her myself,' he said, 'when she came to see me about Sam Hendrickson's death. She thought she'd probably be available. I think I'll use my Perazzi on Saturday. Do you have any sixteen-bore skeet cartridges?'

Keith climbed the step-ladder. As he searched, he spoke over his shoulder. 'One of your neighbours shoots sixteen-bore, doesn't he?'

'Jim Beecher,' Albany said. 'And that's all he shoots. If you can call it shooting. He won't come to the clay pigeons and sharpen up, although I try to tempt him. From what I hear, if he hits a sitting rabbit he buys drinks all round.'

Keith found him two boxes. Wallace had tucked them away behind some bags of hardened shot. 'According to Deborah,' Keith said as he descended, 'you cleaned Sam Hendrickson's guns for him on that last morning and left all three of them with the tumblers down on snap-caps.'

The smile changed subtly, became more snarl-like. 'Are you still stirring up the mud? Haven't you done enough damage?'

'All I did,' Keith said, 'was to point out to the police that the sheriff's verdict didn't account for everything. My part's finished. Now I'm no more curious than the next man. I'd be grateful if you'd pass that word around.'

'That's all very well,' Albany grumbled. 'But the police are making our lives a misery and they've got us looking at each other and wondering what happened and which of us was responsible. It's the widow I'm sorriest for.'

'What I did was at her request,' Keith pointed out. 'She had to twist my arm.'

'I wish somebody would twist my arm, using money as the lever. She's a fine woman, Calder. Don't take advantage of her. And leave the business alone now. You've done enough damage. God alone knows what skeletons may come tumbling out of closets if the police go on prying.' Albany paused and seemed to realise that he had worded himself carelessly. 'Not out of Mrs Hendrickson's closet, I don't mean that.'

'Blame the police, not me,' Keith said patiently. 'I'm taking no more part in it. I only asked because I was interested. You can't expect me not to take an interest. And not many people worry about relieving their springs these days.'

Albany shrugged and his smile was a smile again. 'I told him over and over again that it was unnecessary.'

'Well, that's right,' Keith said. 'I've got a hammerless Lancaster in stock which I don't suppose has had its springs relieved in the last hundred years and it's still as good as new.'

'But you can't tell them that.' Mr Albany lit a cigarette from a gold lighter. 'If somebody's got that particular bee in their bonnet . . . I'll take an aerosol of gun-oil.'

Keith bagged the purchases. 'Just to satisfy my curiosity, how long after you left Hendrickson did you hear the shot?'

Albany looked at him sharply but decided to reply. 'I wasn't looking at my watch,' he said, 'but it must have been at least an hour. Ben Strathling came across about half an hour after I got home. Some question about the serial numbers of my guns. I have them insured through him. His business took about another half-hour. It wouldn't have taken ten minutes, but my wife came in to get some change for the milkman and when she caught sight of Ben she wanted to chat about Sam's condition, she thought that he'd looked even worse than usual. Ben was visibly losing patience, but he had to put on a show. I don't suppose the old milkman was any too pleased at being kept waiting on the doorstep.' Albany chuckled. 'I got Ben out as soon as I reasonably could. The shot came within the next five minutes. That's my nearest guess.'

'You often buy my brand of cartridges, don't you?' Keith asked.

'Usually.' Albany accepted his package and his change but seemed to be in no hurry to depart. 'I wish you kept them in sixteen-bore. I'm getting a bit past carrying the heavier gun when I'm not expecting a shot. In twelve-bore, I like your cartridges better than the standard ones. I seem to get fewer runners.'

Keith suppressed a smile of his own. As he had told Detective Inspector Gowrie, his brand of cartridges was absolutely standard; but the most important factor of any load is the user's confidence in it. 'You must have handled that gun quite often,' he said. 'If you left it with the tumblers down, didn't you wonder how on earth he'd managed to re-cock it with only one arm working?'

Albany drew himself up to his full, modest height. It brought the top of his head level with Keith's chin but, armed with all the arrogance of money and status, he managed to seem taller 'Now you listen to me,' he said. 'I never knew which gun he'd used until that cocky young inspector came badgering me yesterday. It took me some time to wake up to the trend of his questions. He was having the bloody impertinence to suggest that I'd left the twelve-bore side-by-side ready for Sam Hendrickson to use on himself – maybe even loaded it for him.

'I sent the young pup off with a flea in his ear. I wasn't going to aid and abet a crime, I told him, in my position, when Sam could perfectly well have used the twenty-bore. If anybody had good reason to help Sam to end it, I pointed out, it was that wife of his, poor soul. I'm sure that she didn't, but she had the motive. She'd no life of her own, waiting on him hand and foot, but she never complained. Never. Just slaved away, trying to make life tolerable for him. You had to admire her, and to help when you could.'

Keith nodded sympathetically. 'Mrs Hendrickson thinks that somebody helped make life tolerable for him by smuggling joints to him from time to time.'

'Joints?' Albany looked genuinely puzzled.

'Joints,' Keith said. 'Pot. What used to be called reefers. Cannabis cigarettes'.

'I've never even seen one of those,' Albany said. His voice rose. 'If you're suggesting—'

'I'm not,' Keith said.

'—that I brought illegal drugs to Sam Hendrickson, I'll have you in court for slander before you can turn round. You'd better ask somebody like Ben Strathling about that sort of thing.

'And I'll tell you something else.' Ian Albany had taken time to work himself up into a temper, but his voice was beginning to shake. 'The club's been a good friend to you and your shop, but if you go around making insinuations there'll soon be an end to that. I'm in Edinburgh almost every day and I could strike just as good a deal for clays and cartridges with one of the gunshops, yes, and take members' guns in and out for overhaul. You'd soon feel the pinch, don't you kid yourself.'

Albany gathered up his purchases, turned and stalked out. He tried to slam the shop door but the spring closer spoiled his gesture.

Another familiar face came into the shop on Tuesday morning, although Keith could not have put a name to it. It was an elderly face, lined and hollowed by the passage of time, and its owner was a small man in clothes which had seen better days. He bought some very small fish-hooks and a large pike-lure.

The unusual combination triggered an idea.

'You fish the canal quite often, don't you ?' Keith said.

The other nodded gloomily. 'It gets me out of the house in my time off,' he said. 'If I hang about, the wife has me at the decorating. If there's one thing I can't thole,' he added peevishly, 'it's painting things. I haven't the patience for it.'

'You're still working, then?'

'Gateman at the tweed mill.'

'You'll need plenty of patience, to fish beside the footbridge,' Keith suggested.

'That's different. That's sport.'

'But Wallace says that there can't be anything there.'

The old man looked slightly less glum. 'Och, your Mr James is a nice lad but he doesn't know it all. I just bide there until I've caught a few wee perch or bream to use as live bait. Then I'm away a mile along the canal, to Wilkie's Pool, to try will I get a pike. There's pike in there the size of your leg. I've hooked one afore now. Never landed one yet, though.' He relapsed again into his habitual gloom.

'You were by the footbridge on the Saturday Sam Hendrickson shot himself, weren't you?'

'Aye. That I was.' The old man paused and scratched his chin. He gave Keith a sharp look. 'It's you that put the police up to speiring into it a' o'er again. And I'll save you asking the same damned questions. Not a soul came past me, except two wifies that crossed the footbridge. Nobody along the towpath. Nobody on the far bank. Not a boat going by nor a frogman coming out of the water or a hang-glider out of the sky. I'd have seen them.'

'You'd have been watching your float,' Keith said.

'Not me. I don't watch a float. I feel –' he drew the word out while slowly raising his fingers in an unintentionally obscene gesture '– for the fish. If there'd been anybody, I'd have seen them. All morning I was there, and not even a wee fish to show for it. And so I told the police.'

'They've been on to you already, have they?'

'Aye, surely. That Inspector Gowrie,' the old man added in tones of great dislike. 'Trying to make out that I'm keeping something back, just because I was with Border Weavers before they went bust. But I'd rather be a gateman than a weaver, and so I told him. The money's less and the wife thinks I've gone down in the world, but the hours suit me better for the fishing. And now, if you'll kindly take my siller I'll be getting along.'

'I won't charge you, this time,' Keith said. 'Good luck! And if you catch a pike the size of my leg I'll get it stuffed for you.'

'If I get a pike,' the old man said, 'I'll eat it.' He left Keith wondering whether to accept the statement literally or as a measure of improbability. The thought was driven out of Keith's head by the realisation of something the old man had said. He went out into the Square, but the stooped figure had vanished.

A belt of rain swept over during the Wednesday night and Keith spent the Thursday, when the shop was closed for the day, working on guns which had been left for overhaul. The Friday morning dawned brighter and once again spring-like. If Keith had not been tied to the shop he would have made some excuse to drop out of sight and take to the countryside with a gun, in search of rabbit or pigeon among the young crops.

94

He was standing in the shop doorway, wondering whether Wallace would ever hear about it if he closed up for a few hours, when a business-like estate-car pulled up in the Square and a gentleman, very dapper in a black jacket and striped trousers, got out and looked around the signboards. The shop was again half-obscured by a parked van but enough was on show to catch his attention and he walked across. Keith backed inside to clear the door and retire behind the counter.

The newcomer glanced around the shop's interior. He seemed unimpressed. He had a tiny moustache and a loose mouth which he used skilfully to express disdain. A shop which aims to serve a wide catchment area with a full range of shooting and fishing gear has to stock a huge volume of goods and a certain clutter becomes inevitable. Keith had always preferred to have the stock and the clutter rather than a tidy shop which failed to satisfy the customer's needs. When he had first opened the shop he had envisaged an air of dignified calm, where gentlemanly pastimes could be discussed as between gentlemen; but the clutter, seen in daylight darkened by the presence of a van delivering to Kechnie's shop, created the opposite impresson.

'Can I help you?' he asked.

'Mr Calder? Or Mr James?'

'Calder,' Keith said.

'Salmont. Huddersfield Cartridge Company. I had a letter from you last week.'

'About Mr Wilmington's gun,' Keith agreed. 'You've come to settle?'

'I think that's very unlikely,' Mr Salmont said 'We get many such ill-advised claims. This seems to me to have been the usual case of obstructed barrels.' His voice, which was North of England, sounded patronising. Keith rarely took kindly to patronage, especially from Sassenachs.

'Then either you haven't read my report,' Keith said, 'or you've read it but couldn't understand it. Either way, there seems to be little point in wasting our time discussing it. We'll see you in court.'

Mr Salmont never blinked, 'You will, if you're determined to have your client throw good money after bad. But—'

They were interrupted by a customer in search of a

camouflage net and some pigeon decoys. Keith spun the transaction out. Mr Salmont took the shop's only chair and looked at the ceiling. Before the first customer was out another entered, wanting fishing-line. When they were alone again, Keith turned back to Mr Salmont and raised his eyebrows.

'Perhaps you'd tell me why you're so sure you can put the blame on to our cartridges,' Salmont said.

'Very well. It was all in my report but perhaps I'd better spell it out for you. First, I never saw a burst caused by an obstruction which didn't show a clear ring-bulge around what was left of the barrel.' For ten minutes, interrupted only by a customer in search of an impossible bargain, Keith led Mr Salmont through the pointers which indicated excessive cartridge pressure. 'Finally,' he said, 'you recalled a batch of cartridges about a year ago.'

'That was just precautionary,' Mr Salmont protested. 'We never had any complaints of burst barrels.'

'Then you were bloody lucky. You've got one now. And if Mr Wilmington had had the burst in his left barrel instead of the right, you'd have had a claim for two or three fingers at a few thousand apiece. At the time of your withdrawal notice, I was interested enough to retain some of the batch you'd recalled and to examine them. Some were normal, but some were grossly overloaded. I checked the weights, and it seemed that two-and-a-half-inch cartridges had been going through one of your machines which was fitting a magnum primer and cramming in a three-inch magnum load.

'Mr Wilmington had kept the rest of his cartridges and I found several among them which corresponded exactly with the overloaded ones in the batch you withdrew. I tested them with lead crushers in a pressure-barrel and I was finding pressure up to ten times the normal.'

Keith allowed a patronising note to creep into his own voice and Mr Salmont recognised it. His lips tightened further. 'And you think that that sort of evidence would stand up in court?'

'Friend,' Keith said sadly, 'it always has done, so far. Two years ago, in Glasgow, I spent three hours under cross-examination by the Dean of the Faculty of Advocates, after giving just this sort of evidence about the damage done by one of Salisbury's Hyperclay cartridges. I find it hard to believe that you didn't read about the case, it was widely reported in the technical press. He couldn't shake me and we won hands down. What's more, we got more in damages than we'd have been prepared to settle for, and they collected a whole lot of very bad publicity and all the costs on top.'

Having dropped his hint with a shade of emphasis in his voice, Keith waited for a calculated interval. 'It's all in my report, for those who care to read and digest it,' he finished. 'Show it to your lawyer. Perhaps he could explain it to you.'

They were silent. Keith could hear voices in the Square and the hum of a distant car.

At last, Mr Salmont stirred and sighed. 'Suppose I were prepared to give you an immediate cheque, what would you settle for it?' he asked.

Keith relaxed. The other had only been probing to see how he would be likely to show up in court. 'The gun's a total write-off,' he said. 'A new one the same would cost over a thousand pounds. But Mr Wilmington's taken a fancy to a used gun I have in stock, a faster handler with regulated chokes. I could put it in at six-fifty plus VAT. You buy it for him and pay my fee and we'll settle. He wanted to go after you for the loss of his shooting but I think I've talked him out of it.'

Mr Salmont had brought with him a blank cheque already signed by Huddersfield's financial director. Ten minutes later, Keith dropped it into the till. 'Now,' he said, 'you owe me a favour.'

Mr Salmont's eyebrows rose. 'I strongly suspect that you've ripped me off, and I owe you a favour?' But his mouth had relaxed at last.

'That's right. Over the years I've headed off three other clients who wanted to go after you for the cost of burst barrels. Each time, it turned out to be an evident obstruction burst – one mud, one snow and one twenty-bore cartridge up the spout in front of twelve-bore one – and I choked them off without even referring to you. I think that counts as a favour. Three favours, really, but who's counting?'

'I'll decide whether I'm counting when I know what the favour is.'

'Nothing large.' Keith patted his pockets. He was almost sure.... Yes. The cartridge which had come out of Sam

Hendrickson's gun was still in his pocket, protected by a small polythene bag. 'Can you tell me anything about this?'

Mr Salmont accepted the case gingerly. 'This wouldn't be another complaint?'

'I shouldn't think so. It fulfilled its function perfectly. What can you tell me?'

'Nothing whatever. It's a standard case, we've made millions of them. By the printing, it was supplied to you. Number six shot.'

'What else?'

'Nothing. How can I possibly . . .? It's been fired once, never reloaded.' Mr Salmont studied the extractor-marks on the brass head. Obligingly, the van outside pulled away, releasing a flood of light into the shop. 'It was fired in a conventional gun, a double gun, not an auto or a pump-gun.'

'Go on.'

'What d'you mean, go on?' Mr Salmont retorted irritably. 'There's nothing to go on about.' He turned the case and looked at the flat of the head. 'Nice, central firing-pin impression.' He looked closer. 'By gum!' he said. 'You're in luck. After we had to recall those cartridges, we overhauled our machines and brought in new safety procedures, and we changed the style of lettering so that we could be sure we could tell the new cartridges from the old. But it took some time to make new dies, and we were rushing to get out replacement orders to such as yourself, so in the meantime we knocked the dot off the I in Huddersfield, just as a stop-gap. This came out during that time.'

'And how long were you putting these out for?' Keith asked.

'Not more than ten days. You'd have got one batch like this and your next order would have had the new lettering.'

'What else can you tell me?'

'That is absolutely the lot.' Mr Salmont's manner suddenly changed. He became ingratiating and even managed a smile. 'While I'm here, perhaps I can take an order and save you the cost of a phone-call?'

After Mr Salmont had departed, Keith had peace for an hour. He used the time to look back through the firm's records. Wallace was meticulous in his record-keeping,

Janet only slightly less so, and Keith had little difficulty in building up at least part of the picture.

The Huddersfield Cartridge Company had issued its recall notice early in April of the previous year. This had left the firm short of twelve-bore cartridges for its customers just when the season of clay pigeon competitions was getting under way, and Keith noted that Wallace had bridged the gap by placing small orders with two continental manufacturers. The next delivery from Huddersfield had been on 19th April and the invoice showed that the cartridges had carried the shop's own brand-name. A larger delivery had followed after another fortnight.

Keith scratched his head and muttered something rude. There was no way of knowing whether any of the first replacement batch had been left when the next batch arrived. Any remaining boxes might have been pushed to the back of the shelves and only have emerged for sale during the last few weeks. Nevertheless, he dug out the sales slips for the month following 19th April.

Most cartridges are sold a few boxes at a time, at values insufficient to make it worth noting the name of the purchaser. There were a dozen sales to 'Cash', and several corresponded to a multiple of the price of a box. Keith embarked on an attempt to identify purchases which could have comprised cartridges plus some other specific item but several prices had changed during the period and he gave up when he realised that the permutations were almost infinite.

The small purchaser would usually buy cartridges as he ran short, and could be expected to have used up those cartridges long ago; but Keith knew that some men always take cartridges from the end of the cartridge-belt which comes easiest to hand, refilling the empty pockets before the next sortie. With such a man, cartridges from a particular batch could linger at the unhandy end of the belt for years. Not long before, he had noticed a brown, wartime Utility cartridge in another man's belt.

The only purchasers of twelve-bore cartridges whose names were noted were Ian Albany (because his four boxes had been added on to an order for waxed cotton, waterproof shooting clothes), one local man who had since emigrated, and James Beecher – the last because Molly, who had served him, was excessively meticulous.

The total of cartridge sales during the period seemed to add up to much less than the delivery of 19th April, unless a remarkable number were buried among the sales slips, in Wallace's neat script or Janet's scrawl, which mentioned only 'Cash' or 'Goods'.

Which, Keith decided, went a long way towards proving nothing at all. He wrote a note to that effect for Inspector Gowrie. He then re-opened the envelope to add that a purchase of twelve-bore cartridges by a man who shot only sixteen-bore could be explained a dozen ways although, if the purchase had been made for himself, it left unanswered the question as to whether any had remained in his possession a year later. He left the note at the Police Station on his way home.

# SEVEN

Keith Calder had often grumbled against the law which, in Scotland as well as in parts of England and Wales, forbade the shooting of most live quarries on a Sunday – a law which, as he never failed to point out, was hard on the shopkeeper of a sporting bent, preventing him from shooting with those companions who worked a more conventional week.

On the other hand, since the addition of Wallace to the firm it had not usually been necessary for Keith to work shop hours; and while he would have preferred to get out with a gun and a dog on the day of leisure which others counted as the Lord's Day, he would have had to admit that any such change in the law would have been to the detriment of the Briesland House garden which rarely felt his shadow on other days.

On the Sunday morning just a week after the visit by Inspector Gowrie, he was weeding a bed of flowering heathers when Deborah joined him and stood silently watching. 'Do you want some help?' she asked abruptly.

Keith beamed at her. 'There's nothing I want more,' he said. 'Help me get the couch grass out. These ericas have never really got away. This clay doesn't suit them. I think I'll interplant them with periwinkle, the big variety.'

'You'll end up with a bed of periwinkle,' Deborah said. She went down on her knees.

'If I do, it'll be a damned sight easier kept.'

They worked on. The labour kept them warm despite a cool breeze which found its way between the azaleas.

'Dad,' Deborah said suddenly in a very small voice, 'Dad, you didn't mean what you said, did you, about Mike Hendrickson having something to do with his father's death?'

'I don't think I suggested that he had anything to do with it,'

101

Keith said carefully. 'Just that he might have questions to answer if his sister stays determined to drop him in the clag.'

'She's a bitch,' Deborah said.

'Perhaps. That would have nothing to do with whether she was telling the truth or even whether she'll blurt out something stupid in the wrong quarter. The inspector,' Keith said, keeping his eyes firmly on what he was doing, 'hinted that young Mike had been seen near here at about the time his father died. Anyway, if he was safely in Edinburgh it can't arise.'

Another few plants were lifted and the trailing roots of the couch grass removed.

'He wasn't,' Deborah said miserably. 'He came through on his motorbike to meet me.'

'Motorbike?' Keith said. He looked up in spite of himself. Deborah was faintly pink. 'Gowrie didn't say anything about one of those.'

'I don't suppose he knew. Mike only bought it a few days before that, so I don't think it'd be on the records at the computer-place yet. He's been keeping it secret because his mum's terrified of motorbikes. His people weren't expecting him, so he didn't go home. He went back in time for the birthday party. There!'

'I see,' Keith said. He went on working without looking up.

'You guessed?'

'I knew there was something, from the way you looked at each other. And you changed the subject in a hurry when I brought Mike into the conversation, the day we lunched with Mr Enterkin. You could have told us you were meeting him, you know. We try never to ask where you're going at the weekends, but you could have told us.'

'I expect so.' Deborah sat back on her heels and looked at the sky. 'It's just not the kind of thing you want to tell parents. Not because of anything wrong, I don't mean that, but because if it was talked about it wouldn't be quite so special any more. You know how Mum would go on. And he's a bit shy about getting his leg pulled, because I'm still at school.'

'Hoy!' Keith said. 'Don't stop working. It's all right, Toots. I know exactly what you mean. So you can give your boyfriend an alibi.' His own concern, he was surprised to find, was less over the possibility of a romantic entanglement than the picture of that fragile body on the pillion of a motorcycle. He was at one with Mrs Hendrickson on that subject.

'I hoped I wouldn't have to say anything,' Deborah said in a choked voice. 'Mike didn't get on with his father, but he didn't have anything to do with killing him. I know that for a fact, and anyway he wouldn't. He's the gentlest person I know. But the police know that he was near here and ... and Beth will say something awful, and if I have to back him up I didn't want it to come at you out of the blue. And, if you don't mind, I'd really rather you didn't tell Mum unless and until it's absolutely necessary,' Deborah finished quickly. She fell to work energetically, to the ruination of several plants.

Keith considered his next words carefully. It would be so easy to say the wrong thing. 'You do realise,' he said gently, 'that if you have to help him to account for his movements, you'll have to go into rather more detail than that.'

'I suppose that means that you want to know what we were doing?'

'Don't get on your high horse,' Keith said. He tried to keep the amusement out of his voice. 'I don't want to know anything you don't want to tell me. And that isn't because I don't care, it's because I do. We try to remember that you're not a child any more. But you're not an adult woman yet either. We hope for the best for you, but we've never tried to overload you with predigested ideas about morality. There are some things you have to make up your own mind about, when your time comes.'

'I suppose so.'

'I'm going to empty the trug.' He got up stiffly. While he made the journey to the compost heap, he did some more worrying. He had always known that some day he would have to face the fact that he had a daughter who would be a temptation to any man. He knew that form of temptation only too well although as the years had passed his lapses from grace had become fewer and fewer. Molly, who had been his mistress long before she was his wife, would be of little help. Her first priority would be that her daughter should arrive virginal at the altar. Keith would prefer the same, although inwardly he questioned their right to impose rules which they themselves had not obeyed. He knew, moreover, that an unreasoned embargo might only add the gloss of the forbidden. But surely,

103

he told himself, the time for worry was not yet.

When he returned Deborah was still on her knees, picking away at the weeds. Even in jeans and a duffle coat, and even to her own father, she was visibly on the way to becoming an unwitting man-trap.

'You made sure that I knew all the facts,' she said, head still down. 'And about diseases and babies and things.' She looked up suddenly. 'Uncle Ronnie says that you were a devil of a lad in your day.'

'This is my day, Toots,' Keith said. 'Yours hasn't come yet. And your Uncle Ronnie talks too much.'

'He does,' Deborah admitted. 'But I suppose it's true, what he said. Mum hinted at the same thing.'

'They exaggerate.' It was the only time he lied to his daughter. 'I wish I'd known then what I know now.'

Deborah dropped the hand-fork and looked at her father. 'But that's the point,' she said. 'You usually talk to me about the important things. What do you know now?'

Keith met her eye and suddenly he knew what he wanted to say. 'Nowadays, the doctors have taken away the fear of disease. At least, they had until this new one came along. And because the State will provide, there isn't the stigma that there used to be about one-parent families. So people are more promiscuous. But, despite all that, we'll always come back to one-for-one relationships, because they're the best.'

'But tell me why,' Deborah insisted. 'Dad, people keep making me learn rubbish at school which can't really matter very much, but these are the important things and nobody will talk about them. I can spend my whole life finding out by making mistakes, or you can tell me now and I can go on from there. Are you talking about love?'

'Perhaps I am, although it's not a word I'm much given to using. Isn't it a bit early in your life to be filling your head with these things?'

'I don't think so,' she said. 'Some day, if I'm lucky, I'll be alone with a real charmer. He'll be saying sweet things and coaxing me along. What do you think I'm going to say? "Keep the mood going while I phone my dad and find out what he was on about"?'

Keith shrugged. Her questions were sensible; indeed, there could have been a lifetime of wisdom in her words instead of a few short years. 'Keep your voice down,' he said. He paused and looked around. He would not have liked to find Molly behind him when he came to his peroration. 'Whatever you set out to do, Toots, try to be very, very good at it. If, which God forbid, you decide to become a whore, try to be a brilliant one. Nature gave us certain lusts, so that the species would continue. Sex. And sex can be a wonderful event or an embarrassing mess which leaves bad blood behind it. A one-night stand may gratify the urge for the moment but it's messy and confusing and it doesn't mean anything in the long run, because sex is at its best when it's entered into not to take pleasure but to give it. Then, believe me, Toots, it is marvellous beyond belief. But that demands a lasting relationship, each studying how they can please the other. That, I suppose, is what we mean by love. Try always to think of sex as the nicest possible way of saying, "I'll always love you" and you won't go too far wrong. You may even come to understand a little of what I mean.'

'I think I do understand,' Deborah said softly. 'Thank you. When my day comes, I'll remember. You may care to know that it hasn't come yet. Really not.' She paused and met her father's eye squarely. 'Mike's kissed my cheek once or twice in a big-brotherly way. That's all and it's enough for now. I like him a lot. If we're still in touch in a few years . . .'

'I'm glad. Any time you have any more questions, don't hesitate, ask your mother. And don't practise your wiles on Mike,' Keith said. 'You could get him into serious trouble.'

'That much I do know. It's getting him out of trouble that bothers me at the moment,' Deborah said. She got to her feet.

'Hold on a moment,' Keith said. 'You'll have to help me up. I'm getting too old and stiff for squatting on damp ground.' She pulled him up and he kept his grip on her hand. He put aside the thought that perhaps she had understood him too easily. He had a feeling that she wanted to say more. 'You'd better tell me what you were doing, if you weren't having a cuddle in the bushes. Just so that I'll know what not to say.'

He waited anxiously. If she refused, their old intimacy was over.

'I suppose you're right,' she said at last. She pulled him to the seat which stood under the sycamore. 'Rest your weary old bones,' she said lightly.

'Thank you.' He took a seat. She perched on the further arm.

105

'Before you begin,' he said, 'tell me one thing. Mrs Hendrickson suspected that somebody was fetching funny cigarettes to her husband. Do you know anything about that?'

'It wasn't me and it certainly wasn't Mike,' she said quickly. 'Listen. You remember, last October, you let me go beating on the Dawburn Castle estate?'

'I remember. You wanted to make some extra pin-money. You didn't stick it very long.'

'You said I wouldn't like it and you were right. I only went twice. The money was useful but the keeper's a pig. Mike went too. I introduced him. Mr Beecher's a member of the syndicate and he used to give us a lift there and back. Mike wanted to make some money towards the bike – his father ... kept him pretty short,' Deborah said after a brief struggle with herself. 'You're not to think too much of that.'

'I won't.'

'Mike stuck it longer than I did, because of wanting his bike. It's not easy to get in with better shoots, where beaters and pickers-up tend to stay all their lives.

'Anyway, the other beaters were talking about Mr Gregor, the keeper. They're plagued with foxes over there, so he has to keep a line of snares going right through the season. But the beaters were saying that as soon as Mr Gregor gets paid on the Friday he's away to the pub. Maybe that's why he was always so bad-tempered on shoot days,' Deborah added, as if making a discovery.

'Very likely.'

'They were saying that he never visits his snares on Fridays or Saturdays and not often on a Sunday. That's bad, isn't it?'

'Very bad. Also illegal.'

'And they said that he didn't usually bother with the foxes he caught, just threw them into the midden, because the pelts weren't the keeper's perk. If he sold them, the estate claimed the money.'

Keith caught on suddenly. 'You mean that you've been taking that poor boy poaching fox-pelts on non-shooting Saturdays?'

Deborah nodded. She looked happier, now that her guilty secret was out in the open. 'I had to show him how to skin them. He turned green the first time but after a bit he got very good at it. That Saturday was the last time. The foxes were beginning to lose their winter coats. Up to then, Mike had been getting us good prices in Edinburgh. Dad, if I have to alibi Mike, are we in trouble?'

Keith kept his face straight. His daughter was a chip off the old block. 'The police couldn't prosecute,' he said. 'The estate would have to do it, and they certainly wouldn't want to go into court and testify that their keeper had been leaving his snares unvisited.'

'That's good,' Deborah said. 'Otherwise I might have had to say that we were having what you so charmingly called "a cuddle in the bushes",' she finished in disdainful tones.

Having put her father firmly in the wrong she wandered off. But she was back in a few minutes. 'Dad . . .'

Keith looked up from the weeding which he had resumed. 'Yes?'

'If I saved up a whole lot of the best pelts, would you have them made up into a coat for me, like Mum's?'

'No I ruddy well wouldn't,' Keith said sternly. 'You pay for it by selling the lesser skins, just as I did.'

# EIGHT

A new week began – the second week of Wallace's absence, the second Monday morning of early rising to face imprisonment in the shop.

Keith was already slightly late and angry, mostly with himself, when he pulled the jeep up in the Square. Two vans had stopped on the yellow lines and were delivering to Kechnie's grocery, but they had managed to hide the gun shop and to obstruct its entrance while leaving most of the grocery's frontage clear.

Matters were only worsened by the arrival, after a few minutes, of a van from Huddersfield, carrying among other goods the cartridges which Keith had ordered from Mr Salmont. The driver, understandably anxious to get on with his journey, was not prepared to wait for the space to clear. One glance was enough to establish that the other vans could not pull far enough forward to let the new van in without closing off the entrance to the yard which housed the local taxis and a firm of undertakers.

Keith managed to divide his time between serving a few early customers and helping the Huddersfield driver to carry the heavy cartons across the road while keeping an eye on the shop's door as best he could. His ire was further aggravated by an impression that the deliveries of groceries seemed to include nothing heavier than potato crisps. To complete his chagrin, the grocery vans departed within minutes of his own delivery being finished.

The heavy labour of stowing away the new stock kept him busy for a while. Then, dusty and sweating, he had time to make a telephone call. Mr Kechnie, he was told, was not in the shop. Keith left a strongly-worded message, inviting the grocer or his shop-manager to call round for a discussion.

The invitation bore no fruit until the afternoon of the following day. Then Mr Kechnie walked into the shop and waited, tapping with his foot, while Keith dealt hurriedly with the only customer in the place.

'You wanted to see me. Well?' Kechnie snapped. He was an older man than Keith, small and lean with a full head of white hair and a bristling, white moustache. His manner was impatient, and Keith knew that his staff lived in terror of his temper.

Keith kept his own temper and thanked the other politely for coming in. 'I've wanted a word with you for a week,' he said, 'and especially since yesterday morning when you had two simultaneous vans blocking my shop off and making lightweight deliveries to you while I was left to hump boxes of heavy cartridges across the street.'

Mr Kechnie's moustache twitched above a cold smile. 'They could only block you off one at a time,' he said.

Keith bit back a reference to the picking of nits. 'They were simultaneously outside here at the kerb,' he said, 'and one of them was hiding my shop and blocking the door. Is that clearer?'

'And what do you want me to do about it?'

'You could try staggering your deliveries,' Keith suggested, 'and, if you left orders that the first van was to pull forward until it was almost at the archway, customers could get into my shop and visitors might be able to see where it is.'

'That's true,' Kechnie said.

'You'll do it?'

'No. I'll tell you what I've told your partner a dozen times. As long as the drivers observe the law and obey the police, I'm not going to interfere with them and get charged extra for it. I don't owe you any favours.'

'Can you look me in the eye and say that you haven't told them to park in front of my shop instead of yours?'

'I could, but why the hell should I? If you're fool enough to get your deliveries while I'm stocking up for the new week ...'

Keith held on to the ragged edges of his temper. 'We try to get our deliveries on Fridays,' he said, 'when you're usually running down stocks for the weekend. But we can't always dictate to our suppliers.'

'I see,' Kechnie said. 'So you can't dictate to your suppliers but I'm to dictate to mine?'

'That's not what I'm saying and you know it.' Keith could hear the rawness in his own voice. 'I'm only asking you to try to keep my frontage as clear as you can.'

To judge by the glint in his eye, the signs that Keith was nearing flashpoint only seemed to delight the grocer. 'You've a funny way of looking for favours,' he said. 'You haven't cared what muck you've stirred up and now you act surprised when we don't all go out of our ways to make life easy for you.'

That did it. Keith sneered back. 'What were you trying to hide?' he asked.

Kechnie made no effort to hide his triumphant smirk. 'You'll never know,' he said.

'That I will.' Keith pointed with a furious finger. 'It was you. You phoned up and threatened me and you sent a thug to warn me off.'

'Did I indeed. And why would I bother to do that?'

'You hated Sam Hendrickson,' Keith said. 'You, more than anybody, wanted him dead. Well, your threats didn't work. I've set the police working again. Whatever skeletons you're hiding in your cupboard, you'd better get them out and bury them deep.'

' I may bury you deeper. You watch your back, laddie, I'm not through yet. And I'll tell you something else, for nothing. I didn't want Sam Hendrickson dead. I loved having him alive. Whenever I met him being wheeled along by that wife of his, I tipped my hat to him just so that he'd remember that I was having the last laugh.' As he turned about and left the shop, Kechnie was having the last laugh again. His cackle drifted back on the still air.

Keith looked around for something inexpensive to kick. He had set out to sue for a favour but he had let himself be provoked into saying too much too soon and he had made a fool of himself.


On Thursdays, when the shop was closed, Wallace James, obsessively conscientious, often spent much of the day sorting stock and doing the books but Keith, who worked to live rather than lived to work, put another much needed hour into the garden and then, after muttering some inaudible excuse to Molly, whistled up the young dog and escaped in the Japanese jeep which was their second car.

On setting out, he had no more firm intention than to combine a little shooting with a lot of training of the young spaniel. Herbert, a liver-and-white springer, had a much longer name on his pedigree; but he was nicknamed, by way of Herbert Hoover, after the famous vacuum-cleaner because of his talent for hoovering up any crumbs which the family let fall. A happy and willing little dog, he had performed well throughout a lengthy basic training while awaiting the retirement or death of the Calders' old Labrador. A rapidly deteriorating heart had put an end to the old dog's career and life, and Herbert was now in an early stage of his introduction to real game.

Any piece of farmland which carried a few rabbits or was being visited by woodpigeon would have done. Keith was always welcomed by any of a dozen farmers who were happy enough to be relieved of pests and knew that their hospitality would be repaid in time by his help in need or by the gift of cartridges abstracted behind Wallace's back.

But Keith called to see whether his brother-in-law was free to go with him and, getting no answer at Ronnie's door, continued out over the canal bridge. That way took him past Kenny Stuart's road-end and, on another impulse, Keith turned in, nursing the hard-sprung jeep between the pot-holes in the gravel road. He parked near the farmhouse and found Kenny waiting beside his Land-Rover. Kenny Stuart was a fit, middle-aged man with a jovial expression, rough hands and, when the occasion demanded, a rougher tongue. He looked out of place in his going-to-town suit.

Custom and courtesy demanded an enquiry after the state of the farm.

'The spring sowing's finished at last, thank the Lord,' Kenny said. 'It's late, but look at the winter we had! Much of the land's only just come dry enough to take the machines.'

'You're in time,' Keith said. 'Any growth you got earlier would only have been feeding the pests.'

'That's true enough.' Kenny sighed. A farmer confronted with a silver lining will usually prefer to look for the cloud.

'Would you mind if I had a go at the pigeon?' Keith asked. 'I see they're dropping into the oilseed rape along that burn at your north end.'

'Help yourself. But I'd rather you worked along the boundary of Boswell Court. Nobody'll mind a shot or two. They've been complaining of rabbits at their young plants, carnations especially.'

Keith thought about the lie of the land. 'There's not much I can do at this time of day,' he said. 'The rabbits'll mostly be in that wood, which is too thick to ferret and far too thick to shoot even if it didn't have pheasants in it. I'd be giving the pup a workout and that's about all.'

'Just so the residents see somebody's trying,' Kenny said, 'There'll be few enough pheasants in the wood after the way the police went through it.'

'I could maybe come back after dark some day with Ronnie and his long net. There's no other way to tackle a place like that, except snares.'

'That'd be fine. Just as long as it's only you and Ronnie, and maybe that lassie of yours if she feels like it,' Kenny said. 'I don't want every bugger feeling free to come around the place. The residents want me to give Mr Albany the run of the land nearby. What d'you think?'

Keith shook his head. Ian Albany was not in his good books at the moment, and shooting permissions are not lightly shared. 'He's chairman of the shooting club. He'd soon be pressuring you to let them all on.'

'That's what I was thinking myself.'

The two men nodded at each other. Kenny seemed to be in no hurry. For lack of anything else to say, Keith asked, 'You remember the day Sam Hendrickson died?'

Kenny nodded solemnly. 'Aye. Yon policeman Gowrie's been at me about it. I was drilling barley just behind Boswell Court. Not that I kenned ocht about it at the time. I'd not hear a shot over the noise of the tractor.'

'You began that morning?'

'That I did.' The farmer looked steadily at Keith for a few seconds before going on. 'I'll save you asking the same damn questions Gowrie asked me. By the time the shot was fired, the verge along the road, the back gardens and the canal was all

112

freshly drilled and chain-harrowed. Any footprints on that bit were made since then – likely by Gowrie hisself. And I'd've seen anybody coming over the fields or along the canal, but apart from a car or two on the road there was nobody. I could see folk moving in the gardens, here and there, and old Mrs Orton at her window. She gied me a wave as she aye does, and I waved back. You've more need to speak with her.'

'I'm not investigating,' Keith said. 'I did my bit ten days ago. All the same, I wonder what time she got to her window.'

'That I can't tell you. If it's any help, the laddie Beecher went off along the road in yon red sports car of his about the time we waved. He must've been doing ninety before he braked for the road-end. He'll kill himself or somebody else before he's through, yon lad will.'

Keith heard the sound of a door being locked and Mrs Stuart arrived. Like her husband, she was town-smart in an inexpensive fur. She nodded and smiled to Keith and climbed into the Land-Rover.

'Time I wasn't here,' Kenny said. 'You do what you like. The sooner this business is sorted the better.'

'It's not my business now,' Keith said. 'I was just chatting.'

He watched the Land-Rover drive away and then fetched his gun, boots and cartridge-belt from the jeep. He let Herbert out and the spaniel sailed over the fence into the neighbouring pasture, raced in a few circles around the handful of curious bullocks and leaped back, panting and obviously pleased with himself. Having blown off his steam, he was ready and even anxious to come under control.

The weather had recovered. It was a beautiful day of springtime promise. Keith knew that the promise was probably as meaningful as a tart's smile, that even the snow could come back again before summer, but for the moment all was comfort and hope. The deciduous trees were still bare, reaching hopeful fingers towards the sky, but at ground level the countryside was bursting with the sights and sounds and smells of a new season. Over a distant wood, pigeon were soaring in their courtship flight, while on the further hills the shadows of small clouds lay still. It was a day for doing something special, buying a car or acquiring a new mistress – but no, he reminded himself, those days were behind him. He had meant what he had told his

113

daughter. He kept his mind on the business in hand.

They followed the line of a long hedgerow and Keith worked the spaniel through its base. A rabbit bolted on to the bare ground and he bowled it over. Herbert had dropped as the rabbit departed, and he stayed fast at the shot. Keith was pleased. This was a crucial stage of training when the young dog must learn that his mission was to respond to his master's directions without any idea being implanted that he was free to act on his own initiative. Giving the pup a word of praise, Keith left him sitting – the dog must never think that retrieving is his task alone – and fetched the rabbit himself, paunched and legged it and hung it on the hedge for collection on the return journey.

From half a field away, Boswell Court was mostly roofs, spaced well apart above a barrier of trees and hedges. Splashes of blossom painted the smaller, specimen trees.

Their route brought them down to the corner where the access road entered Boswell Court. Here, as Deborah had said, the road took a swing away from the canal bank and a small spinney had been planted in the triangle so made. This was balanced by a slightly larger spinney on the other side, a decorative grove of smaller garden varieties, mostly cherries and rowans and some laburnum. The ground beneath was deep with last year's uncut grass. Keith placed himself where the easiest escape was cut off and sent Herbert in.

The tips of the grasses betrayed the movement of a rabbit. Keith felt a familiar surge of excitement. No matter how humble the quarry the hunter's instinct, that exclusively male urge to gather meat, would always take over. He directed Herbert with hand and whistle. The rabbit broke across the road. Keith missed behind and caught it with his second barrel. The sound of his shots echoed flatly back to him.

A round, female face topped with iron-grey hair appeared at the corner of the first garden as Keith was picking up his rabbit. 'Did I frighten you?' he asked. This would be Mrs McLaing. She and her husband had been abroad when Sam Hendrickson died.

The face broke into a broad smile. 'Not really,' she said. 'And if you had, it would have been worth it. You wouldn't believe what those little beasts are doing to the gardens.'

114

'Believe me,' Keith said, 'I would. I get them myself. Kenny Stuart asked me to see what I could do.'

'We had to give up trying to grow brassicas,' Mrs McLaing said sadly. 'I'll phone round and warn the others. It might help if I knew your name.'

'Calder,' Keith said. He hung the rabbit, like his earlier victim, on a branch to await his return. Rabbit fleas soon desert a dead host and he had no wish to carry them home.

He put Herbert through the smaller spinney but without result. Blackthorn hedging overhung the canal and there was no way past on that side. He was close to Kechnie's boundary and half expected the older man to burst out at him with some complaint about noise or danger; but the grocer seemed to be away, probably, thought Keith, spreading gloom and despondency among the staff of his other shops which took a different closing day.

Mrs McLaing reappeared as he crossed the road again. 'That'll be all right,' she said. She paused and then hurried on in some embarrassment. 'I phoned Mrs Hendrickson specially to warn her, because I thought that the sound of shots might upset her, so soon after her husband . . . You know what I mean?'

'I know,' Keith said.

'She said to ask you to call in on her before you leave.'

'I'll do that. You were away when it happened, weren't you?'

Mrs McLaing nodded happily. 'What a stramash to come back to! We had a week in Tunisia. We like to get away when the Scottish winter's gone on long enough. It's nice to see the spring happen somewhere warmer and then come back to see it happen again here. But it quite spoiled it, arriving home to hear that a neighbour was dead. And everybody quite sure what had happened but no two of them agreeing with each other.'

'Your house was all right when you got back? No break-in?'

'Nothing like that. I worried about it while I was away, but I needn't have bothered.'

'It's always a worry, isn't it?' Keith said sympathetically. 'Do you leave a key with anybody?'

'No, never.' Mrs McLaing glanced anxiously over her shoulder and lowered her voice. 'I did once, with Mrs Strathling. But when I got home I could see that she'd been through all my things. Just nosiness, but it's not very nice, is it?'

115

A car was approaching. Keith was unsure whether the road had ever been adopted by the local authority but had no desire to find himself in an argument with a policeman over the definition of the word 'recklessly' or as to whether the road near which he had been shooting constituted a public thoroughfare. He gave Mrs McLaing a nod and a wave and made his way back into the field.

He took Herbert along the margin of the field at heel. Only one set of footprints preceded him along the soft soil and he guessed that they would be those of Detective Inspector Gowrie.

It was his intention to work the hedges back from the thicker wood at the far end; the rabbits would have an easy escape into the gardens but at least he would be pushing them away from their safest haven. He could trace the garden boundaries by the hedge materials – holly for the McLaings, berberis for the Beechers, cypress at the Strathlings and beech at the Hendricksons. He walked on around the wood, studying the fencing. He was on his way back and had just come abreast of the beech hedging when another female head appeared, disembodied above the hedge like that of the Cheshire Cat, but not grinning.

This, he guessed, was Mrs Strathling. She was older than he had expected, perhaps in her fifties, with a patrician face and a recent, disciplined home-perm. Her complexion was slightly too perfect to be true and her hair was tinted. He had seen her at the bank without knowing who she was.

'Psst,' said the head. 'Come through. Quietly.'

There was a thin place in the hedge, almost a gap, and Keith squeezed awkwardly through. The remainder of Mrs Strathling was in keeping – thin, thanks in part to an excellent corsetière, neatly tweeded and with a brisk sparkle of costume jewellery at her throat.

She soon dispelled any idea Keith might have had that she expected him to emulate D.H. Lawrence's gamekeeper. 'Three or four rabbits come out of the shrubbery every dusk,' she whispered. 'Come with me.' The shrubbery, a thickly-planted display of almost every shrub known to horticulture, bulged out from the hedge on the Hendricksons' side of a large lawn. Above it, Keith could see the peaked roof of the summerhouse. Mrs Strathling placed him outside her French windows and retired to the hedge.

'This is the only gap,' she whispered. 'The rest of the hedge grew around a chicken-wire fence. If you sent your little dog in now, they should bolt across the lawn.'

'It may damage the turf,' Keith warned.

'Once. But those damn rabbits damage the garden every day. Get on with it.'

Keith loaded his gun and took two spare cartridges between the fingers of his left hand before sending Herbert in. One rabbit bolted almost immediately and he dropped it in the open. He took advantage of a pause in the action to slap his barrels down. One spent cartridge went over his shoulder. He slipped another in and closed the gun, dropping his left hand to his belt for a replacement. There was a sudden flurry of activity among the shrubs and two rabbits bolted, followed a second later by a third. Keith dropped one, and hit another, which rolled over but scrambled back to shelter. He reloaded in one quick movement, missed the third rabbit as it vanished through the cypress hedge, but took a fourth which made a late exit just ahead of the spaniel.

Herbert looked at his master enquiringly. Keith reloaded and sent him back in. Half a minute passed. 'That seems to be the lot,' Keith said.

'You missed two,' Mrs Strathling said accusingly. She seemed quite unperturbed by the noise of the shots.

'Only one.' As he said it. Herbert came out of the bushes, carrying a dead rabbit and very concerned as to whether he had sinned. Keith could see the marks of shot on the fur, so all was well. He reassured the dog and picked up the other three rabbits.

Mrs Strathling looked past the house and waved. 'That damned old woman!' she said. 'She gets very hurt if you don't wave to her, and tells everybody that you think yourself too good for the likes of her. How's business at the shop?'

She was talking down to him as a shopkeeper. Keith met her eye. With a faint emphasis on his first word, he said, 'My shop's doing very well, thank you. How are things in the bank?'

Her mouth tightened. 'All right,' she said. 'Well, don't hang about. That's all for the moment.'

Now that the favour which she had sought had been granted, she was very much the *grande dame* dealing with a serf. Keith was tempted to give her an ironic tug of the forelock but

117

decided that she might take the gesture at face value. Her accent, while good, was not quite perfect enough to fool him.

She had moved on to the lawn and was smoothing a scar in the fine turf with the sole of her shoe. 'What do you do with your rabbits?' she asked.

Keith usually ate them or gave them away, but if Mrs Strathling wanted to treat him as a tradesman then a tradesman he would be. 'I sell them,' he said. 'Would you like a pair?'

'Are you sure they're quite clean?'

'Not a trace of myxomatosis,' Keith said.

'How much? I used to love a rabbit pie,' Mrs Strathling said, thawing slightly, 'but you don't see them in the shops since that disease started.'

Keith quoted a price, pitched carefully at a level high enough to annoy her but which he was sure she would pay rather than let him think that she could not afford it. The lady surprised him. 'Ridiculous!' she said. 'That's rank profiteering.'

Keith had conceived a dislike of Mrs Strathling, and he was not given to concealing his dislikes except when the person concerned was a good customer. He was hesitating between three different retorts, each of quite devastating sarcasm, when there came the sound of footsteps and Michael Hendrickson arrived at the gap in the hedge between the gardens. Incongruously, he was dressed in pyjamas, dressing-gown and slippers.

'Mr Calder, come quickly please'.

Keith dropped his rabbits on the grass and went.

They hurried, half-running, down the side of the Hendricksons' garden. At the garden door, Michael paused. 'Two men came to the house,' he said breathlessly. 'They looked rough. I heard angry voices. Mum sounded frightened and, although you mightn't think it, she doesn't scare easily.'

'Shouldn't you call the police?' Keith suggested.

'They'd take half an hour to get here. And it might turn out to have been just the wrong thing to do.' Michael wrung his hands in nervous uncertainty. Keith thought that he was looking very strange. 'I'd heard your shots and knew where you were. I thought maybe you could ... do something not too drastic. I don't know what.'

118

'I know exactly what,' Keith said grimly. 'And I'll do it. Back up whatever I say. But what are you doing at home, mid-week?'

'We've got German measles, both Beth and I. Mum fetched us.'

'You'd better get back to bed and leave this to me.' Keith told Herbert to stay where he was. Then he closed his empty gun and walked firmly into the living room.

An altercation, which reminded Keith for all the world of two dogs going after a cat, was cut off. Silence and stillness fell heavily, like snow off a roof.

One man was built like a wrestler and roughly dressed in blue jeans, a black leather jacket and safety boots. He was leaning over the seated Mrs Hendrickson with a heavy stick between his two hands pressing against her upper chest, just below the throat. He turned his face as Keith entered and Keith noted narrow eyes, a blob of a broken nose and blubbery lips. The other man, older, smoother in appearance and more conservatively dressed, had Beth in a corner and was holding her there with a hand between her small breasts. Beth, like her brother, was dressing-gowned and, now that he knew, Keith could recognise the rash and the feverishness of rubella.

At a first tasting of the atmosphere Keith thought that real violence was not intended; but it would take little to trigger an outburst and he decided to quell it before it could begin.

Keith levelled his shotgun. His mouth was dry. 'If either of you wants to live,' he said, 'come out into the middle of the floor and stand still.' The men obeyed, taking their time about it, testing him. Beth collapsed into a chair.

'Do you want the police?' Keith asked Mrs Hendrickson.

'Here,' said the smaller man. 'There's no need for that.' Keith noticed that his face, which he had at first thought unremarkable but for the thinness of the features, was etched with a cunning smirk.

'Did they threaten you?' Keith asked.

Mrs Hendrickson moistened her lips and hesitated. 'Not really,' she said.

'Oh Mum!' Beth said tearfully. 'You know they did.' Behind him, Keith heard Michael breathe in sharply.

'Not in so many words,' Mrs Hendrickson said. She sounded calm but her hand was shaking.

Keith thought that she was deliberately avoiding provocation. 'Is that true?' he asked. 'Or are you saying it under duress?'

'We're making too much of this,' the smaller man said pacifically. 'Look, we're going to sit down on the settee, where we won't seem so threatening, and we can talk it out.' He sat down quickly.

The other stood, undecided.

It was obvious that the large man was the dangerous one, probably with a reputation to lose, and Keith sensed that he was bracing himself to try something rather than sit down passively and lose all initiative. A bruised lump showed through his thinning hair.

'Sit down like a good boy, Hughie, when you're told,' Keith said. 'I've already bent one set of gun-barrels over your head. You want the same again?' He was guessing, but the odds were heavily in his favour.

The big man blinked twice. He started to make a hushing gesture and then decided that the moment had passed. He lowered himself carefully beside his partner. 'It wasn't all that sair,' he said plaintively. 'But loosing off that cannon in my ear could ha' gi'en me a heart attack. Did you think o' that?'

'I thought of it, but no such luck. Right.' Keith said. 'Getting up before I tell you to will be treated as an act of war.'

The smaller visitor was stiff with suspicion. 'What the hell was that about?' he demanded of his henchman.

'Hughie paid me a visit.' Keith told him. 'He offered me a beating because I'd ignored a threatening phone-call telling me to leave Mr Hendrickson's death alone. Was that your idea? Did you make the phone-call?

'Bloody hell no!' The smaller man rounded on his large companion.'What the devil did you think you were doing?'

Hughie wriggled uncomfortably, for all the world like a small boy caught with his hand in the biscuit-barrel. 'It was just something,' he said. 'Nothing to do with the union. Somebody paid me to scare him off.'

'And a fine hash you made of it. Who were you working for?'

Hughie clenched his fists and his face. 'I'm not telling,' he said. 'You can't expect it.'

Keith wanted to know, but this was not the time to force the issue. He glanced at Mrs Hendrickson. 'What did they want?'

Mrs Hendrickson touched her face as if to wipe away fear. 'They never got around to making that clear,' she said. 'They just seemed to be furious because Sam's death had been going to be passed over as a suicide and then I got you to persuade the police to re-open their investigations. This is Mr Calder,' she added.

'I gathered that,' said the smaller man.

'The bogger,' said Hughie. 'I'll remember you, Chiel.'

Keith restrained himself from giving the big man a rap over the lump on his head with his barrels. It was too good a gun to abuse. 'You may have good cause,' he said. 'Or again, you may never remember anything any more. Depends whether you're a good boy. You came here for something. Tell us. Start with just who you are. Hughie what?'

The big man flared up immediately. 'See you, it's nane o' your bluidy business!'

'Reynolds,' Keith said patiently. 'You see? It wouldn't have hurt to tell me.'

'I know the other man,' Mrs Hendrickson said suddenly. 'Sam introduced us at some reception but I forgot his name. The big one sounds like the Hughie who phoned.'

'He is,' Keith said.

The smaller man nodded. 'I'm Jim Talbot,' he said, 'and, as you say, this gowk is Hughie Reynolds. There's no point being secretive about it, nor about our reason for coming. We came to say something and we'd have got around to saying it without any more nastiness if you hadn't come in waving that thing around. We may as well spit it out.

'We were associates of the late Mr Hendrickson. Close associates, with all that that means. We had a good thing going. Up to last year, we had the union like that.' He showed a clenched fist. 'And the employers as well. Then came trouble. All kinds of trouble. No need to upset Mrs Hendrickson by going into details. But the fact is that Sam could have gone to jail, and he'd have taken us with him.'

'I don't believe you,' Mrs Hendrickson said firmly.

Talbot gave the shrug of a man who knows what he knows. 'You believe what you want to believe, Mrs H. I'm telling it as we see it. Things looked bad. Then Sam fell ill. That was

121

unlucky for you, and in one way it was unlucky for him and we were all very sorry, but there's no denying that it was a blessing in disguise. Sam was safe enough, there'd be no point the law going after a man who was half-paralysed and couldn't speak. He'd never see inside a jail, he was his own prison already. And, not to put too fine a point on it, any earlier irregularities could easily be laid at his door. The others in the union let up on us, because there'd be fresh elections when Sam ran out of sick-leave and they'd have their chance to take control.'

'In that case,' Keith broke in, 'why did Hughie have to phone Sam Hendrickson to say that somebody – J.C. – was talking to the police.'

'The filth don't give up so easy.' Hughie said in his deep rumble.

'Sam died,' Jim Talbot resumed. 'The sheriff brought it in as suicide. We reckoned that Hughie's phone-call must've pushed him too far. Jim Christie – well, there's no point going into details, let's just say that he was the one man who could really do damage. Sam would know damn fine that he'd be left to hold the baby. Damn it, that's what he'd expect. Once he was known to have topped himself, it seemed to be all over.

'But then, according to what we hear, you, Mrs Hendrickson, called in Mr Calder here and he showed the police that the sheriff got it wrong. We didn't know about it at the time and we didn't authorise any phone-calls or other action. And you fairly put the cat among the pigeons.'

'Didn't he just?' said Hughie gloomily.

'You weren't to know that that was just about the worst thing you could do,' Jim Talbot told Mrs Hendrickson generously. 'We don't blame you. From your point of view, it was only right. But, as for you ...' He glared at Hughie. 'When you knew that Calder had been called in, you should have reported back.'

Hughie scowled at the floor.

Talbot returned his attention to Mrs Hendrickson. 'But the fuzz think it's down to one of us and—'

The chime of the doorbell stopped him in mid-sentence.

'I'll see who it is,' Michael said. He left the room and his sister followed him out. Keith heard faint voices at the door and then the sound of footsteps.

The youngsters did not come back. There entered a woman of middle age. She wore a coat of a fur which Keith could not identify but which he was in no doubt was expensive. Her face was round and bland and cared for and her manner was businesslike. She could have been the kingpin of a fashion firm, or a wealthy man's wife.

'I might have known it,' Jim Talbot said disgustedly. 'Mrs Harriet Bloody Griegson.'

Mrs Hendrickson sat up straight and lifted her chin. 'You're not welcome here,' she said. 'I've heard Sam talk about you.'

'And nothing complimentary, I'm sure,' Mrs Griegson said cheerfully. 'But then, in union politics I could have been called the leader of the opposition. So whatever I did or said had to be wrong.'

'Sam was sure that you were behind the break-in when his papers were taken.'

Mrs Griegson seemed genuinely surprised. 'Why would we do a bloody silly thing like that?' she asked. 'Sam was pulling the wool. We got his papers legally, what was left of them, and because of that we can use them. Papers get stolen for information or to suppress them. And I'll give you three guesses who wanted them suppressed.' She looked at Keith. 'Would the gentleman with the gun be Mr Calder?'

Keith had forgotten that he was still holding his shotgun although the danger of active aggression seemed to be long past. He laid it carefully on a table. 'I would,' he said.

'You'd better hang on to it,' Mrs Griegson said with a chuckle. 'Either of these buggers would snatch your ears off, just to amuse the bairns.' She seated herself, uninvited, and carefully checked the hem of her skirt before looking at Mrs Hendrickson again. Keith noticed that she had pretty legs. 'What have they been trying to con you out of?'

Mrs Hendrickson looked uncertainly at Keith.

'Nothing, yet,' Keith said. 'They'd only got as far as telling us how satisfactory Sam Hendrickson's suicide had been and complaining that I'd rocked the boat by suggesting to the police that he might not have killed himself after all.'

Mrs Griegson nodded. 'That figures,' she said. 'A renewal of police activity wouldn't suit their book at all.'

'See here, you —' Hughie Reynolds began to rise but when

Keith picked up his gun he subsided again.

Jim Talbot jumped in quickly. 'If you're hinting that one of us killed him, you're wrong. He'd become a danger, but I've been round every sod mad enough or frightened enough to do it, and none of them did. I know them and I know where they were, and it's a fact. Not good enough for the police, though.'

'And while they're digging, they're not going to turn a blind eye to any other irregularities they happen on,' Mrs Griegson suggested.

'You think that's just great,' Hughie Reynolds ground out.

'You're miles out,' Mrs Griegson said. 'I think it's the biggest fuck-up since the Crucifixion. Anything they bring out from Sam Hendrickson's day reflects on all of us. But what's worse is the way they're going about it. Instead of setting up a full-scale murder enquiry and getting the business over one way or the other, they're using all the back doors. Fraud squad, tax inspectors, even the Health and Safety Executive. Every one of them digging through the files, backed by the appropriate legal steps, and carting away whatever takes his fancy.'

'I didn't know that,' Talbot said. 'I've kept out of the office this past few days.'

'You couldn't've changed anything. In fact, they aren't caring what they find. I can't prove it, but it's general harassment. It's brought all union business to a standstill. And that man Gowrie took me aside today and hinted that it'd stop as soon as we became helpful in the matter of murder. One good nominee's all he wants. Devious bastard!'

Keith sensed a fine Hebridean hand in the background. From his experience, Superintendent Munro and not Detective Inspector Gowrie was the devious bastard. He would have recognised the description anywhere.

'We can't nominate anyone,' Talbot said. 'I'll tell you again, nobody we know was involved.'

'Since when were you so concerned with truth?' Mrs Griegson enquired. 'There's at least one we could well do without.'

'Hey?' said Hughie.

'No, not you. Not this time.'

Talbot seemed to be in no doubt as to whom she meant. 'We thought about him,' he said. 'But he was in a snooker club with a dozen friends.'

'That's it, then,' said Mrs Griegson. 'I came here this afternoon to tell Mrs Hendrickson to get her boy working again.'

'Get him to implicate one of us, you mean,' Hughie Reynolds grunted.

Mrs Griegson sighed heavily. 'Can't you get it through your thick head that we're on the same side for the moment?' she asked. 'The one thing we all need is for the heat to come off so that we can get back to union business.'

'Back to the power struggle?' Talbot suggested.

'Struggle? We can talk about that – very seriously – once the police are off our backs.' (Talbot nodded slowly.) 'How about it, Mrs H?'

Mrs Hendrickson looked at Keith. 'I'd already asked for Mr Calder to come and see me. I want him – and his . . . assistants – to help me again. Inspector Gowrie,' she said in tones of distaste, 'has paid me three visits. His questions seem to assume that I, or a member of my family, killed my husband rather than have me spend years of my life nursing a cripple. He hinted to me – he's good at hinting is Detective Inspector Gowrie – that if I pleaded guilty but made a case of euthanasia out of it I'd get off with a nominal sentence.' Her voice, which had been rising higher and higher with indignation, ended in a squeak.

'So he's exploring two blind alleys.' Mrs Griegson looked at the other two. 'That one could be the best solution. But not yet.' She switched her eyes to Mrs Hendrickson. 'You knew, of course, that you were due for a substantial payment from the union's insurance if Sam died in harness?'

'But not if he died by his own hand,' Mrs Hendrickson said. 'It's the same as with his insurance policies.'

Mrs Griegson nodded approvingly. 'Exactly. And so, you have a financial incentive to have Mr Calder solve the case. But we'll make it easier for you. Between us,' she said, 'we carry enough clout to be able to promise that the union will pay half of Mr Calder's fee and expenses if he'll go back to work and clear the matter up.'

'I'll back you,' Talbot said.

'If Mr Calder goes back on the case,' Mrs Hendrickson said, 'I think I'd prefer that he was working just for me.'

'Just a holy minute,' Keith said. 'Don't I have any say in this?' He caught Mrs Hendrickson's eye. 'If I take it on, I go

125

after the truth. Unless that's agreed I won't touch it. So don't turn down an offer to share the cost. Just get it in writing.'

'The laddie's talking sense,' Talbot said. (Keith was at least five years his senior). 'You'll get on to it straight away, Mr Calder?'

'I'm committed to looking after the shop tomorrow,' Keith said. 'If my partner gets back in time or if my wife will help out on Saturday, I'll start then. Mrs Hendrickson had better warn her neighbours again. Can I count on full co-operation from the union?'

'You want somebody to look after your shop?' said Talbot.

'I want your assurance that your members will talk openly, frankly and truthfully to me,' Keith said.

'If you wish it. But you'll be wasting all our times.' Talbot turned his attention back to Mrs Hendrickson. 'You agree with his condition?'

'Without hesitation,' Mrs Hendrickson said.

Mrs Griegson looked at her for several seconds. 'I believe you,' she said suddenly. 'And yet, you make me wonder. By reputation, you and Sam were very close. Yet you were as different as chalk and cheese. What on earth did you have in common?'

'Not that it's any of your business,' Mrs Hendrickson said, 'but we had something for each other that was very special.'

Mrs Griegson frowned. 'Without a single view in common?'

'Do you really think that a man and a woman have to agree about politics before they marry?' Mrs Hendrickson retorted. 'I know that Sam had several affairs. They never lasted. You see, I was all that he needed.' She seemed unaware of her audience. Her mind was turned inward, looking back over the years. 'In all the years we were married, not once ... not once ...' She stopped abruptly, suddenly aware that she had been stung into revealing too much, and hid her face in her hands.

'No need to go on,' Mrs Griegson said. 'I think I understand. That's more than most happy couples could claim.' She got to her feet. 'If his heart had killed him I'd have known what brought it on. Come, you two, it's time we left.'

'I'll see you out,' Keith said. He escorted the three to the door. As a precaution he took his gun with him. Mrs Griegson made no bones about her right to walk first.

When the other two were outside, Jim Talbot hung back. His

manner was quiet, businesslike and utterly convincing. 'Just in case you don't understand what Mrs Griegson and myself were saying,' he told Keith, 'I'll spell it out for you. You go back to work and you find out the truth or something near enough to be accepted for it. We don't care who the villain is, not even if he's one of us – anyone who matters a damn is bomb-proof.'

'Find out who Hughie's client was,' Keith said. 'That'll tell us.'

'Not necessarily,' Talbot said. 'Anyone with something to hide could have hired him. But I'll try. Now listen. We want somebody nailed, and fast. Otherwise you may find Hughie coming up behind you some time you don't have that gun in your fist. After which, we'd put pressure on the widow Hendrickson to do what the inspector said, plead guilty to euthanasia. Have you got all that?'

Keith had never taken kindly to threats, but he decided that the moment for confrontation had not arrived. He said that he had got it. He slammed the door and went back to calm the very disturbed widow.

Before he left Boswell Court he collected Herbert. He looked into the Strathlings' garden, but his rabbits had vanished. He gave an amused grunt. With a bit of luck, Mrs Strathling might find herself with more than she had bargained for. Rabbit fleas do not normally attack any other host, but when starvation set in there would be no guessing what tasty mouthful they might be prepared to settle for.

As a bonus, he saw from a distance that a pair of carrion crows had found his first rabbit where he had left it. With Herbert firmly at heel, he crept up the far side of the hedge and got both with a right-and-left. He hummed as he walked back to the car, wondering how many other birds' fledglings would now be spared from being taken to feed a new generation of crows. Kenny Stuart would be pleased.

The phone rang that evening while Keith was preparing for bed. Keith sat down on the coverlet and took the call.

Jim Talbot was on the line. 'Hughie won't talk,' he said. 'I've put all the pressure on him. He's as thick as pigshit but he has his own code.'

'Thanks for telling me.'

'Don't hang up,' Talbot said urgently. 'That's not why I called. Hughie had another call from his former client.'

'With the same instructions?' Keith asked. He spoke absently. Molly was undressing and he always gave his attention to the important things of life.

'Virtually the same,' Talbot said. 'In view of the new circumstances, he turned it down. But the client may go elsewhere. I thought you ought to know.'

'Thank you,' Keith said.

'No thanks necessary. If somebody duffs you up, you can't work for us. Not if he does it properly.'

Molly had left for the bathroom. Keith concentrated again. 'Can Hughie be trusted?' he asked.

'All the way. He's either for you or against you. He's for whoever's paying him at the time.'

'Could he be trusted to bodyguard my wife tomorrow?'

'Certainly.' There was a whispered discussion at the other end of the line. Talbot came back on the line and quoted a fee.

'Tell him to report to me, at home, eight-thirty a.m.,' Keith said.

# NINE

The first Friday of each month was Molly's day for visiting an aged aunt some ten miles off and, since the old lady was not on the phone and was inclined to relish a pleasurable panic if her niece failed to arrive, it was easier to treat the engagement as the one fixed point in the month than to attempt to vary it.

Before he set off for the shop. Molly gave Keith a purse containing some notes and a few coins.

'Let me guess,' Keith said. 'You're buying me lunch?'

'Don't be silly,' Molly said austerely. 'If you want your lunch from me you'll get sandwiches. There's some cold mutton left over. Old Mr Rogers calls into the shop for the milk-money on Fridays. I usually give it to Janet.'

'I thought it was on Saturdays that he made his collection.'

'He does the middle of the town on Fridays and the outskirts on Saturdays.' She checked her shopping-bag for cleaning materials. 'Try to be good.'

'I always do,' Keith said.

'But you don't always manage.' She kissed her husband. 'Hughie should be here in a minute. I hope he's quick. Deborah's waiting in the car. Are you sure this is a good idea?'

'It's the only one I've got. I'm told that he's absolutely loyal to whoever's paying him at the time, and today that's us. Remember, see if you can charm or bluff him into saying who his previous client was. Try him with Mr Kechnie's name if you like. And don't forget to set the alarms.'

Keith drove the jeep into Newton Lauder. At the road-end, he passed Hughie in a late-model but already battered van. The big man gave him a cheerful wave and, grinning, rubbed the top of his head. Bygones seemed to be bygones.

The spring weather had relapsed into chill and drizzle. As

usual, a few customers looked in on their way to work and then all became quiet. Keith decided to look over the stock of modern guns, to make sure that all were in good order and properly lubricated. But he had only got as far as to put the kettle on when the bell jangled and Mr Rogers walked in.

The old man was carefully dressed for the job in a blue overall and peaked cap. He counted the money, accepted Molly's total as correct and stored the takings away in a leather satchel.

The kettle decided to come to the boil. 'You'll take a cup of tea?' Keith asked. 'Or coffee?'

'Tea would go down fine,' the old man said. He lowered himself stiffly into the customers' chair. 'I was up at five to help load the floats and I'm getting past that sort of caper. Mrs James aye gives me a cup. That's a fine woman.'

'I just hope I can still rise at five when I'm your age,' Keith said, 'and have an eye for a fine woman.'

'An eye's all I've got left these days.' Mr Rogers had a jolly face and there was usually a twinkle in his eye but now he was looking serious. 'They tell me you're back at looking into Mr Hendrickson's death.'

'That's true,' Keith said, wondering how on earth news managed to travel so quickly. He tested the tea. It seemed to have reached a respectable strength. He filled the two mugs.

Mr Rogers accepted his mug gratefully. 'I'll be damned glad if you can sort the thing,' he said. 'My life's been a misery this past week.'

'How's that, then?' Keith asked.

'That dratted man Gowrie. He's made up his mind that no outsider could have shot Mr Hendrickson unless I'd brought him in in my van. But that's my own fault, I told him myself that there were no strangers about the place. I told that daughter of yours too. There's a grand lass, now! She'll be a beauty in a year or two.'

'You're getting to be a dirty old man,' Keith told him.

Mr Rogers looked pleased. 'Chance would be a fine thing,' he said modestly. 'It's not just that Gowrie's been back and back at me, but he's been asking folk about my movements and who'd looked in the back of my van and the like. It's got so that my customers are talking.'

130

'Why does he think you'd do a thing like that?'

'Money. I bought a new van. But I can account for every penny I've spent, and so I told him. See, I was a member of the union up to five years ago, but that's nothing to do wi't. The union did me nothing but good, fought my redundancy for me and all like that. Gowrie makes out that I'd be known to the union, if so be as they wanted somebody to fetch one o' them in wi'out being seen.' The old man fell silent and took a long drink of tea.

'But who, in the union, knew that one of their ex-members toured round Boswell Court every Saturday?'

Mr Rodgers considered. 'Only Mr Hendrickson,' he said at last.

'Right. And I don't see him putting your name forward to the union, to help his own murderer. If your van was parked in the road,' Keith said, 'your man'd have had a hard job getting into cover unseen, what with gardeners and car-washers and the window-cleaner, not to mention old Mrs Orton at her window. You didn't pull off into somebody's driveway?'

Mr Rogers shook his head violently.

'Put it out of your mind, then. He's clutching at straws. Tell me this instead. Do you know the noise a pheasant makes when it's disturbed?'

The old man brightened up. 'I do that. Worked as beater most of my life until I could no longer swing my leg over a fence, let alone a woman.' Mr Rogers chuckled happily and winked. 'Great days, out in grand country, getting paid for it and aye a bird to take home! I mind seeing you on some of the shoots.' Mr Rogers looked at Keith sharply. 'Are there pheasants in the wee wood? You're thinking that somebody might've lain up there from one night to the next? I'd like fine to agree, but that's not the way it could've been. The whirr of a pheasant rising or the chortling a cock makes, those are still sounds that'll make my heart skip a beat. No, take my word, there were no strangers there except the laddie that cleans the windows, unless they were countrymen as could move through a wood without putting the birds up. And that's not easy just after the season, when they've been shot at a few times. You'll need to look closer to home.'

'The neighbours?' Keith asked. 'You were talking to the

131

widow at the time of the shot.'

'I was, and nothing yon mannie Gowrie says can make me change my story. As if I couldn't tell the odds between a shot and a squib after my years as a beater. And, as I said to him, if it was a squib I heard, what happened to the sound of the real shot?'

'Was Mr Kechnie still polishing his cars when you reached Mrs Hendrickson's house?'

'He'd finished by then. But Mr Strathling was visiting wi' Mr Albany and I watched him go back over the road.' The old man finished his mug of tea and pulled himself to his feet. 'Instead of going in by his door, he went round the corner of the house on the Hendricksons' side. What would he do that for? Where was he going? You ask him.'

'I will,' Keith said. 'Probably.'

Keith dealt with a phone-call, sold a pair of rubber boots and cleaned one gun. Then Detective Inspector Gowrie walked into the shop.

Keith paused in the act of passing a cleaning rod through one barrel of the second gun. 'Are you buying or talking?' he enquired.

'Talking.'

'Then it won't bother you if I go on with what I'm doing?'

'If it does, I'll tell you,' Gowrie said placidly. He stood watching, easy on his feet like most policemen. 'Thanks for your note. Not that it takes us very far. All we know is that Mr Albany could have had some matching cartridges. But so could anybody else.'

'True,' Keith said. 'Especially Mr Beecher.'

'We followed that up. He was thinking of buying a twelve-bore from Albany so he borrowed the gun and bought the cartridges for a trial. He didn't like the gun and he gave Albany what was left in the box. Albany confirms.'

'But you've no way of knowing whether Beecher kept back one or two cartridges or found them in his pocket afterwards.'

'Forget about Beecher,' Gowrie said. 'Take my word for it, he's clear.'

Keith thought that the inspector was nursing a secret smile, but he decided to move on. 'By the way,' he said, 'why are you

132

bugging the widow? She was with the milkman when the shot was heard. If, as you seem to have suggested, that bang was some sort of a firework, you should be going after Mr Albany. Did you test the place for noise?'

'I've just come from there,' Gowrie said. 'We had a technician firing shots into a drum of water. We carved some turnips to represent a human mouth. Not very precise but near enough. According to Mrs Hendrickson, a shotgun fired in the summerhouse with the door closed was exactly what she heard. We're trying to intercept the old milkman to repeat the experiment.'

'You just missed him. Did you find any signs of a squib?'

Gowrie shook his head and protruded his lower lip. 'But there'd been plenty of time for some such device to be removed.'

'Well, if it was, the widow didn't plant it,' Keith said. He applied a greasy cloth to the metalwork. 'Why would she fake a suicide and then hire me to prove the reverse? You think she hates money that much?'

'If she only heard about the suicide clauses after she'd done the deed. . . .'

'Look at it this way,' Keith said. 'Somebody would have had to do the deed with a silenced shotgun. So he would have had a single-barrel gun and a cartridge made with the same components as the other. Was the wad recovered?'

'I tracked it down. The pathologist had kept it. Twelve-bore.'

'So the murderer would have had to have had a single-barrel, twelve-bore gun and a silencer to fit it. And one of the barrels had been fouled in Sam's gun, so the gun would have been taken away, one barrel fired, the gun been replaced and that barrel missed out when the guns were cleaned by Mr Albany that morning. Who do you suppose that puts in the firing-line?'

Gowrie nodded sadly. 'Albany,' he said. 'But as far as I've been able to discover, he had no motive.'

'Nor had the widow, for a faked suicide.' Keith gave the gun's stock a wipe with another cloth and put it back in the rack.

'Assuming the suicide clause in her husband's insurances was known to the family as she says. In which case,' Gowrie said, 'the money motive belongs to the children.'

Keith felt a definite unease in his lower bowel. 'You're

133

stretching it a bit, aren't you?' he said.

'Well, maybe I am. They both say that they were together all day. But there's more to it than that. I've seen the sister looking at the brother. I just don't know,' Gowrie said. 'The only useful fact I've got from the union so far is that they had Sam's life covered. So any of the family could have had a motive for having him die before his sick-leave ran out.'

'But not as a suicide,' Keith said, polishing energetically at a gunstock. 'The widow told me that the summerhouse was full of the stink of burned powder when she got there. The place has its own combined heating and ventilating system which would have cleared most of the fumes away before too long.' Keith pulled out another gun and admired the engraving for a moment before taking it apart. 'Also,' he said, 'I took a look around the wood yesterday. I could see where your men had been plowtering around—'

'They found some faint tracks,' Gowrie said.

'Rabbits,' Keith said. 'And I saw where you tried to get over the barbed wire and couldn't make it. More to the point, pheasants are using that wood and they make a hell of a noise when they're disturbed. They're almost as noisy as guinea-fowl. And nobody heard them that morning.'

'Pheasants can sit pretty tight if the intruder moves softly,' Gowrie said. 'And it doesn't take them long to realise that they're out of season. I'm a country loon myself.'

'How many did your men put up?'

'Dozens. But they weren't trying to sneak through unnoticed.' Gowrie sighed deeply and shrugged his shoulders. 'I'm finding it harder and harder to believe that anybody killed Hendrickson,' he said glumly. 'We tried your test on the fingerprints, by the way, and all it told us was that there was nothing to be learned that way. The local residents and the milkman and window-cleaner are all swearing blind that there was no stranger around.

'But, just in case every one of them was mistaken, let's imagine that somebody was lurking in the wood. He chose his time when the milkman was keeping Mrs Hendrickson talking. He killed Hendrickson. Then what? Either he hurled himself back over the fence before they could get there, and without breaking a twig or scaring a pheasant, or else he squatted down behind the summerhouse just when there were bound to be people milling around the scene for the rest of the day. It just doesn't add up. Perhaps it was suicide after all.'

'Definitely not,' Keith said. He slapped the third gun back together. 'There's another point which has only just occurred to me. Let's suppose that Sam Hendrickson had a cartridge in his drawer. He took down the twelve-bore although the twenty was handier and much easier to load. He solved the problem of closing it, although that part of the action, which was also re-cocking the ejectors, is very stiff.'

'That's for sure,' Gowrie said. He showed Keith his palm. The blood blister had hardened to a lump like a raisin.

'But when he opened the gun,' Keith said, 'there's no way that a man who was paralysed down one side could prevent the snap-caps being scooted all over the room. You need one hand to open the gun and at least one other to prevent ejection. Sam's gun has particularly ferocious ejectors. Sit down and try it.'

Keith put snap-caps from a drawer into the gun which he happened to be holding and pulled the triggers. Detective Inspector Gowrie sat down in the customers' chair and tried for himself to open the gun one-handed while catching the expelled snap-caps. He was attempting the feat, as a last resort, with the butt of the gun on the floor and the muzzles against his shoulder while with his left hand he tried both to open the gun and to prevent the ejection of the snap-caps, when the door opened and a customer walked in, catching him in an undignified contortion with his right arm dangling as if useless and his tongue protruding in concentration. The fact that the newcomer was an attractive young lady did nothing for his composure.

When she had bought her salmon-flies and, grinning over her shoulder at him, had departed, Gowrie stood up. 'Sam Hendrickson could have picked up the snap-caps before finishing off his suicide,' he said.

'He could,' Keith agreed, taking back the gun. 'He could have wheeled himself around the room, although he found it difficult to direct himself one-handed. He might even have been able to retrieve them from under the furniture, which is where they'd inevitably have fetched up, Sod's Law being what it is. But if you were half-paralysed, desperate enough to knock

135

yourself off and half-expecting a visit from your wife who would strongly disapprove of self-slaughter, would you go to all that bother?'

Inspector Gowrie almost slumped back into the chair. 'I don't know,' he said. 'I'd have to be that desperate before I could make a guess. I'll ask one of our consultant psychologists. It's time they did something useful.'

'The way it looks at the moment, you'll be lucky to make a case for anything worse than aiding and abetting a suicide. I can see Sam Hendrickson asking somebody – Mr Albany, likely – to leave the gun loaded and then wiping that request off his word-processor,' Keith said. 'But it's not a lifelike picture. The more I learn about Sam Hendrickson, the more I see him as having the kind of indomitable stubbornness which would never give in to anything. Mrs Hendrickson has asked me to do some more work on the case. Do you mind?'

'I can't object, as long as you stay within the law and tell me what you find,' Gowrie said.

'You ask Munro,' Keith said. 'He'll tell you that, provided I'm not buggered about, I'll play fair. Give me most of tomorrow to ask questions and you can meet me at Boswell Court late in the afternoon and I'll tell you what I've got. Munro told Mrs Hendrickson that I could have copies of the statements you took from the residents. Bring them up to me and I can look for discrepancies from what they've told me.'

Gowrie was looking unhappy. 'I can't make late afternoon,' he said. 'I'll come up around noon and see how you've got on. You may even learn something useful. But I think you're wasting your time and Mrs Hendrickson's money. We've passed the stage where a skilled amateur has a chance of putting his finger on the crucial fact.'

'It isn't only Mrs Hendrickson's money,' Keith said. 'The union has agreed to pay half, and if I need to speak to their members they'll talk freely. I met Hughie, yesterday. And you were right, his name's Reynolds. He's bodyguarding for me today. Leave him alone while Molly tries to coax the name of his former client out of him.'

'Twenty-four hours,' Gowrie said slowly. 'After that, I want to talk to him. You know, you may not be wasting your time

136

after all. I'll give you a list of things you could try to find out for me about the union.'

'Get knotted,' Keith said.

The real rush of business came just before closing-time as those with sporting engagements over the weekend called after work to stock up with cartridges or fishing tackle.

There were three customers in the shop when, out of the corner of his eye, Keith saw a man of late middle-age enter. The newcomer took up a waiting position by the gun-rack, and even when a last-minute customer dashed in for a packet of swivels he did not assert his right to be served but waited patiently until he could get Keith's undivided attention. Then he stepped forward and offered his business card.

The card was of a major insurance company, and bore the name of B.Strathling.

'I'm pleased to meet you at last, Mr Strathling,' Keith said. 'I've seen you in the distance. Are you here as a customer?'

'I called primarily about your insurance.'

'Then I'll shut up shop before we talk.' Keith locked up and put the CLOSED sign in the door. Ben Strathling, he noticed, was a tall man, balding, neatly but inexpensively dressed. He had cold eyes and his mouth was too wide for his narrow head, giving him a fish-like look. Keith decided not to hold that against him. Some of his best friends reminded him of fish or fowl, or of dogs.

'I was going through my papers,' Strathling said as Keith turned back to him, 'and I noticed that your insured value hadn't been increased for two years. With inflation running the way it is, I thought I'd ask whether you weren't under-insured. It can work to your disadvantage in the event of a claim.'

'You'll have to speak to my partner about that,' Keith said. 'He's the money-man. But we took stock only a month ago. If you haven't heard from him, either our insurance is adequate or Wal hasn't got around to it yet. He doesn't forget such things. I'll have him write to you. He'll be back on Monday.'

'No need for that,' Strathling said cheerfully. His wide mouth could produce a warm smile although his eyes remained cold. 'I'll call in on Monday.'

137

'Do you go round all your clients personally?' Keith asked curiously.

'Only the bigger local ones. It's often easier to deal face-to-face. I was manager of the Newton Lauder office until we closed it several years ago,' Strathling explained, 'and now the locals tend to feel cut off from personal attention. I became manager for south-east Scotland, and I'm responsible for Kelso as well as Edinburgh and several other offices, so it was handy enough to go on living here and be able to give some continuity of service.'

'I understand,' Keith said. 'Well, Wallace James is your man.'

'I'd another reason for calling in,' Strathling said. 'Mrs Hendrickson has been asking her neighbours to co-operate with you. She says that you're trying to clear up any remaining mystery about Sam Hendrickson's death.' He frowned at something above Keith's head. 'Just what further clarification is needed, I must admit, evades me. I'd have thought that more than enough unpleasantness had been generated already. A suicide doesn't do a neighbourhood any good.'

'I don't suppose it'll affect property values,' Keith said.

Strathling pretended not to hear. 'But she's the widow, poor lady, and if she's not satisfied I suppose we'd all better help you to set her mind at rest. The thing is, I understand that you may be doing the rounds tomorrow. I'm expecting a phone-message which might call me away. So, in case I missed you, I came in to see you now. Mostly, I'm afraid, to tell you that I can't tell you anything. I was doing some homework while watching the racing on television – I like my little flutter on the gee-gees, it helps to keep me sane.' Strathling gave a little giggle. 'And my wife was out shopping.'

'Did she walk over the canal footbridge?' Keith asked.

'She took my car. She likes to do the whole week's shopping in one go.' Strathling paused. Keith's interruption had broken his train of thought. 'I . . . I wasn't looking out and, what with the noise of the telly, I didn't even hear the shot. Sorry.'

'So what was the first you knew about it?'

'I heard Jenny Hendrickson let out a yelp when she found him. Not surprising, really, when you remember the state he was in. At first I thought it was on the television, or kids

138

playing. But I decided to pop round – I was always anxious about poor old Sam. Jenny and the milkman were already there.'

Keith was still leaning against the door. Strathling, satisfied that he had had his say, moved towards it but Keith frustrated him simply by remaining where he was. 'It was good of you to come in,' Keith said, forcing a little extra warmth into his voice. 'Let's not waste the journey. You weren't stuck in front of the goggle-box the whole morning.'

Strathling nodded. 'No more I was,' he said. 'My apologies! I went over to see Ian Albany about something when the racing gave way to gymnastics – I'm not enough of a voyeur to sit and watch young girls doing the splits. Ian and his wife were both at home. But that must have been some time before the shot.'

'Not by the time you returned home,' Keith said. 'The milkman called at the Albanys' for his money while you were there. He moved straight on to Mrs Hendrickson and was talking to her when the shot was heard.'

'Is that so?' Strathling produced a twisted smile. 'But then, he's the worst gossip in the town and she's almost as big a chatterbox. If they got on to the subject of some local scandal, they could have been talking for any given period.'

'Perhaps,' Keith said. 'Who else did you see?'

'Not a soul, to remember. I think the window-cleaner was at Ian's house when I arrived. He was doing the front of mine when I went home.'

'You crossed straight over and back?'

Keith had asked his question as casually as he could but Strathling looked at him sharply. 'More or less.' He hesitated. 'I'd quite forgotten. I meant to look in on poor Sam Hendrickson. See if he was all right and try to cheer him up a bit. So, when there was a break in the racing, instead of going out by the front door I went out of the French windows. I paused at the gap in the hedge. But I could hear a man's voice – you can hear quite well if there's a window open – so I decided that he wouldn't want to be bothered.'

'Was that coming or going?' Keith asked.

Strathling hesitated again. 'I don't know,' he said at last. 'I just don't remember. I was thinking about other matters. I'd no cause to make a mental note about it at the time. I just have a

139

recollection of sticking my head through the gap in the hedge and hearing a voice.'

'A man's voice?'

'Yes. Of course, it might have been his radio, or the television. I didn't hear any words.'

'Did it sound like a conversation? Or a talk? Or did it sound excited, like a sports commentator?'

'I didn't hang around long enough to hear more than a word or two.'

'You said, "If there's a window open". Was there an open window when you arrived on the scene?' An open window would have cleared the smell of smoke more quickly. But Hendrickson had felt the cold after his stroke. Keith was sure that the police photographs had shown the windows to be closed.

Strathling frowned. 'I don't remember. Anyway, the door could have been open.'

'If . . .' Keith began, 'if I told you that the voice belonged to one of your neighbours, who would you think it was?'

'In that event, I'd say that it belonged to that grocer chap, Kechnie. I wondered at the time. I didn't want to see him – can't stand the man – so I turned back.' Strathling glanced at Keith with a hint of malice. 'You could ask him why he crossed the road that morning, before the shot.'

'You saw him cross? Or did somebody tell you?'

'Neither. Something else I'd forgotten. That scene in the summerhouse drove it out of my mind. When I heard Jenny Hendrickson squeal and I came out of my French windows, I glanced around because I wasn't sure where the noise had come from. I glimpsed his head over a low point of the hedge. He was in my neighbours' garden. The Beechers.'

'Have you let the police know about this?'

'I told you,' Strathling said irritably. 'I'd quite forgotten about it. I'll go and tell them now.'

'Don't bother,' Keith said. 'I'll pass the word along.'

Strathling chose to take offence. 'Now, you look here,' he said. 'You've no official status in this and I think you're taking too much on yourself. I can carry my own messages to the police. Are you suggesting that I'm not to be trusted to go and make a statement? Well?'

'Do by all means go and tell them yourself,' Keith said. 'They may be better able to jog your memory.' He stood aside.

Strathling walked out without another word and headed across the Square, but half-way across he curved aside from the direction of the police headquarters and got into his Jaguar. Keith shrugged. Strathling might well have decided to phone from home. He was the sort of man who would stand on his dignity and expect the police to come to him.

# TEN

As they shared the family meal that evening Keith, who had arrived home barely in time to wash his hands and sit down, asked Molly, 'So who was the client?'

'What makes you so sure that he'd talk to me?'

'You could trick a Trappist into spilling the secrets of the confessional,' Keith said. 'You bring out the chatterbox in people.'

'Oh. Well, I did find out. Hughie's rather a sweet person.'

The right man had certainly turned up. Keith remembered meeting Hughie at the road-end. 'Hughie is?'

'Yes. He's big and tough and not very bright, so he gets used for the rough stuff, but inside he's just a softie.'

'So who —?'

'He sat very quietly in the car until we were most of the way there and then he explained, very shyly, that he'd taken on the job of warning you off but that he wouldn't have laid a finger on Debbie or me.'

'That's a comfort to know,' Deborah said.

'Did you know that he has a little girl of his own?' Molly asked.

'No,' Keith said. 'I didn't. Who did he —?'

'Well, he has,' Molly said firmly. 'But when I asked him who'd hired him, he'd only say, "A mannie who was feared the polis would fin' o'er muckle".' Molly's accent was a perfect imitation of Hughie's although she could not manage the deeper voice.

'Who —?'

'Anyway, it was just as well he was with me because when we arrived Aunt was having one of her turns. And you know what a weight she is. I couldn't have managed her on my own, but

142

Hughie picked her up very gently and carried her up the stairs as if she was no more than a pillow. He wanted to go out of the room while I got her to bed, but she was still woozy and I couldn't lift her on my own, so he stayed and helped me but with his eyes tight shut, and by the time the doctor and the district nurse got there she was quite respectable and rather pleased with herself. She'd been forgetting to take her tablets, silly old thing. But she still refuses to go into hospital.

'I made us some lunch and Hughie helped me to clean the place through. He's good about the house,' Molly said. 'Much better than you are. And that seemed to break the ice a bit, because on the way back he was very apologetic. He'd been engaged to do a job, and part of the service was confidentiality. And I said that he was being paid to keep me safe but we didn't know who to look out for when he wasn't around.'

'That got him talking?'

'Not just then, but when we got back and I'd paid him what you said, he was just getting into his van when he paused and said something about the client who paid being worth more than the one who didn't. Then he looked at me very seriously and warned me, sounding just like a fortune-teller with a crystal ball, that I should never trust a bald-headed man with green eyes and a ginger moustache.'

'Mr Beecher!' Deborah said.

'Is that so?' Keith said. 'I don't think I've ever laid eyes on the man. First thing in the morning, I'd better try to find out where he goes on these so-called fishing-trips. Wal says that he never buys any tackle from the shop.'

'He could buy it somewhere else,' Molly said.

'Do you want my help tomorrow, Dad?' Deborah asked.

'Depends. Your mother said she'd mind the shop if Wal and Janet aren't back in time. I could use some help and I don't want you running around where somebody could get at you, but I'd hate to have you think I couldn't manage without you. Aren't you supposed to be trapping for the gun club?'

Deborah smiled broadly. 'At that rate of pay,' she said, 'which would you expect me to prefer? I'll phone and cancel. Their whip-round for the trapper's hardly worth having. About two quid and a toffee-apple.'

'She's her daddy's girl all right,' Molly said. 'Mercenary. You shouldn't let people down like that.'

'I won't be leaving them stuck,' Deborah said. 'There'll be other volunteers. Anyway, I think Mr Albany may be rather relieved. He never wins anything when I'm trapping. I see to that. And I'll go on seeing to it until he treats me like a grown-up person. If I'm old enough to have my bottom pinched I'm too old for a sort of adolescent version of baby-talk.'

'Does he do that?' Molly asked in ominous tones.

'It was only once and I think he'd been drinking that lunch-time.'

Keith knew that Deborah could look after herself – if only she wanted to. He was more interested in an earlier remark. He was usually either shooting or coaching and had never given much thought to the trapper's part in competitive shooting. 'How could you make sure that he didn't win anything?'

'That's easy,' Deborah said. 'You get to recognise most of their voices when they call for their first bird. Then there's all sorts of ways of making it fly off at an angle, or making pairs fly apart. And with most traps you can speed them up slightly, or slow them down. If it's somebody I like, I can almost make the clay hang over his head.'

'I've had some damned difficult birds when you've been trapping!'

'You'd probably annoyed me,' Deborah said blandly.

Molly decided that a change of subject was overdue. 'What are you going to spend all that lovely money on?' she asked her daughter.

'Clothes.'

'But we buy all your clothes,' Keith said.

Deborah humphed. 'These aren't clothes,' she said. 'They're coverings for my nakedness. I don't want to be a schoolgirl all my life.'

'We wouldn't expect it,' Molly said.

'Maybe not, but I can't see you buying me the sort of clothes I could show off in a disco or at a pop concert. One of these days, I'll want to do a tour of the boutiques.'

'Being a swinging chick comes expensive,' Keith said after a pause.

'That's why I'm trying to build up a kitty of my own.'

'I think she does have a sort of a point,' Molly said. 'Not a lot, but some.'

Keith pushed away an image of Deborah in punk gear with a Mohican hair-style in fluorescent colours. 'Come through to the study,' he said, 'and we'll put what we know into the word-processor.'

'Help me with the washing-up first,' Molly said. 'I want to sit in with you. Jenny Hendrickson's still my friend, even if I've hardly seen her for umpty years.'

'How many years?' Deborah asked.

'Never you mind. Keith, do you have enough information to put together yet? I thought you'd be going off on one of your tours, seeing hundreds of Sam Hendrickson's old contacts all over the place.'

'I thought so too,' Keith said. 'But when I came to think a little more, I decided that Detective Inspector Gowrie was only making life difficult for himself, worrying about how some outsider arrived in Boswell Court. The signs, all but one, are that you and Deb were right all along and that there was no outsider. And chasing around for motives never pays dividends, because the motive often turns out to be the last thing you'd have thought of or else it's too trivial to have been believed. So we concentrate on the time around the shot and we tabulate who saw or heard whom or what where and when and we go on asking questions until discrepancies show up. And then we go on asking more questions until we've explained them.'

'And if that doesn't work?' Deborah asked. 'Are we up the creek without the proverbial paddle?'

'Not necessarily. Either we've satisfied ourselves that it was a local job or we haven't. Come on, let's get the washing-up over.' He began to stack dirty dishes.

'What's the sign which doesn't point that way?' Molly asked, getting up to help.

'The fisherman said that two women came over the foot-bridge. But Mrs Orton only mentioned Mrs Pollock. There's a faint possibility that some disgruntled ex-mistress killed him, although his wife is pretty positive that infidelity wasn't among his more regular failings. Or would you say that she was as capable of closing her mind to adultery as she is to his other defects?'

They had reached the kitchen. Molly dumped dishes into hot water. 'If you have faith in one thing,' she said, 'you can have faith in another.'

Keith thought about it. Molly's meaning began to poke through. 'You mean,' he said, 'that if you can believe in a personal God you can believe anything?'

'Yes. No,' Molly said indignantly. 'Don't put words into my mouth. But, Keith, what about that lady from the union?'

'I'm curious about her myself.' Keith began to dry, passing dishes to Deborah to put away. 'When they were talking at Mrs Hendrickson's yesterday, there were a lot of things being said which weren't said aloud, and it was as if I didn't know the language.' Deborah left the kitchen with a tray of cutlery and Keith took advantage of her absence. 'Mrs Hendrickson seemed to be saying, woman-to-woman, that whatever differences she and Sam might have had between them they were terrific in bed.'

'I expect you're right,' Molly said. 'She hinted as much to me. And she isn't the sort of person to say that sort of thing if it wasn't true.'

Deborah returned. They dropped the subject quickly. 'And Mrs Griegson seemed to be saying, to Sam's former henchmen, that she was ready to take her place in a fresh carve-up,' Keith said. 'If Sam's continued existence was standing in her way, she could have had a motive. She could have walked up to see him, perhaps to demand that he put in his formal resignation. He refused and she dunted him on the head, expunged any record of their discussion from the word-processor and replaced it with the suicide message and then finished the job the way Munro suggested.'

'Where would she get a cartridge?' Deborah asked.

'Spotted it in the open drawer, perhaps. But after that she'd only have had a matter of seconds in which to do a vanishing act, perhaps a minute at the most, during part of which Mrs Hendrickson was approaching to see what the noise had been.'

Deborah paused in the act of drying pans. 'Plenty of time,' she said, 'for somebody to get round the back of the summerhouse and to sit down under the picture window. Do we know that anybody looked there?'

'No. It'd be a hell of a risk, though,' Keith said.

'Well, what about diving through the hedge into the Strathlings' shrubbery?'

'It's a beech hedge reinforced with chicken-wire,' Keith said.

'You'd have to be ectoplasm to get through it without leaving tracks. But there's a gap where Ben Strathling used to go through when he visited Sam Hendrickson.' Keith became motionless, still holding a plate and towel.

'Hoy!' Molly said. 'You can talk and dry at the same time.'

Keith wound himself up again. 'There'd be a strong risk of being seen. But let's suppose that a killing had been done on the spur of the moment, in unthinking temper. What Deb's suggesting might be the least dangerous of the various risks available. You can take that one on tomorrow, Toots.'

'Me?' Deborah said.

'You thought of it, you look into it. Speak to the fisherman, if he's there, and to Mrs Orton. We want to know who the other woman was and roughly when she came over the footbridge. The ground in the Strathlings' shrubbery looked rock-hard and no doubt Detective Inspector Gowrie's been through there, but you can take a look. I'll want to see Granny Orton anyway, so I'll find out what she saw.'

Molly took the dish-towel out of his hands and dropped it into the washing-machine. 'That's the lot,' she said. 'And nothing broken for once. Bless you my children.'

They settled down in the study in front of the microcomputer. Keith keyed in the word-processor program.

'Now,' he said. 'Read me the notes of what Mrs Hendrickson told us.'

'All right. But we don't have any times to put against things,' Deborah said.

'No. Folk don't walk around looking at their watches and memorising times. But we should have a sequence. I'll be satisfied if we get a framework to hang any new snippets on.'

They settled down to work, from Deborah's notes and their memories. When they had finished Mrs Hendrickson's account Keith said, 'Now we'll thread in what we think was meant by what we found in the computer, where we think it makes sense.'

'Won't we be guessing?'

'The great thing is to make a guess. If it turns out to be wrong, we've learned something.' A few minutes later, he said, 'Now we'll put in what I was told by Kenny Stuart and by Mr Albany.'

The list now read:

*Mrs H takes Mr H to summerhouse.*

*On computer – cold, shut door, can't reach radio.*

*Mrs H back to house, takes phone-call from sister Louise. Noted on computer.*

*Phone-call from Hughie R.*

*On computer – bad news, jc talking to the plod (police).*

*Mr & Mrs Albany visit. Coffee in summerhouse.*

*On computer – ok thanks, no, ho —*

*Mrs H to house again, Mrs A leaves.*

*Mr A cleans guns.*

*On computer – just put one out. kkhswwf ok just tired. linseed stocks, snap-caps and triggers, fancy a beer?*

*Physiotherapist phones.*

*Mr A leaves.*

*Mr Strathling visits Mr Albany at No. 4. Milkman (Rogers) arrives at A's door for money. Mr S returns home, going round the side of the house.*

*Old Mrs Orton waves to Kenny Stuart.*

*Milkman arrives at Mrs H.*

*Sound of shot.*

*Mrs H finds husband. Computer was on menu. Switches off monitor but suicide note remains in computer.*

*Strathling and Hughes arrive, followed by Albany.*

Molly had been writing a letter on her knee. Keith had wondered whether she had pretended an interest in order to get help with the washing-up, but she looked up suddenly and peered at the screen. 'It asks as many questions as it answers,' she said. 'But I suppose that's half the objective. "Ho —" could be the start of "how are you?"'

'Or "How can you do this to me?",' Keith said.

'What about Mr Strathling hearing a man's voice?'

'He was too damn vague to be any use,' Keith said. 'If he heard it at all and wasn't just trying to divert my attention away from himself. He thought it might have been the radio, or possibly Mr Kechnie's voice, and he said he couldn't remember whether he heard it on his way round to the Albanys' or on the way back, which makes about a half-hour's difference.'

'We could find out whether there was a talk on and at what time,' Deborah said.

'It could have been somebody introducing a piece of music,' Keith said. 'We'll take a look tomorrow and see what wavelength the radio's set to. I'd rather know exactly when, in this time-scale, people started and stopped what they said they were doing. It doesn't take all morning to mow a lawn or wash a car.'

'It does if you have to trim the edges or polish the bodywork,' said Deborah, who was pressed into service rather oftener than she felt was fair.

'And I want to know how the movements of the milkman and the window-cleaner fit in.'

Silence fell. All three stared at the list on the screen, willing it to yield some meaningful message.

'Assume that we're right,' Molly said suddenly. 'Assume that nobody came in from outside. Also assume that it was one of the residents. Who would it be?'

'That's really tomorrow's question,' Keith said. 'But you went round most of them, between you. What do you think so far? And give us a brief description of each household as you go along. It's time I saw them as individuals instead of animated chess-pieces.'

Deborah took a deep breath. 'All right,' she said. 'I'll start. But that's a lot of assumes. What do we assume about people covering up for each other?'

Keith thought about it. He imagined a similar crisis within his own immediate circle. Such had not been unknown. 'For starters, assume that people will cover up for their own family,' he said. 'Not for anybody else. But tell us if any two families seem to be exceptionally pally.'

'Seems reasonable. Would you and Mum cover up for me if I killed somebody?'

'That would depend on whether you'd tidied your bedroom,' Molly said. 'Get on with it.'

'Really,' Deborah said. 'You are the end! We'll work outwards from the Hendricksons. You both know Mrs H. I'd like her very much if she wasn't quite so top-heavy with virtue. She and Mr Rogers give each other perfect alibis. Unless, of course, they were having an affair and one of them killed Mr Hendrickson so that they'd be free to run away together.' She glanced at her parents to see whether she had managed to shock them.

149

Molly considered it seriously. 'I think he's too old to be having an affair with anybody,' she said.

'How old —?' ˙

'We'll tell you if it ever happens,' Keith said. 'Molly, would you say that your old friend had a passionate nature? You didn't react when Deb suggested an affair.'

'I was wondering. She used to be very much a romantic,' Molly said, 'and her sex-life seems to have been Grade A. I think she's too conventional to . . . to . . .'

'Throw her knickers over the windmill?' Deborah suggested.

'Deborah!' Molly said. 'Where do you get these expressions?'

'I heard Dad say it once. I thought it was very . . .'

'Rude?'

'Expressive,' Deborah said. 'That's the word I wanted.'

'Clype,' Keith said.

With a single glance, Molly made it clear that he was in disgrace. 'I don't think that she'd have a physical affair,' she said. 'Jenny takes the Bible literally. But she might have a romance. I can see her getting a kick out of nobly renouncing her love for the sake of her crippled husband.'

'Maybe allowing some neighbour to believe that if she wasn't lumbered with Sam she might go off with him?'

'I suppose it's possible,' Molly agreed doubtfully.

'Did she seem to have a fancy for anybody in particular?' Keith asked.

'Not that she told me,' Molly said. 'I got the impression that she only put up with Ben Strathling for Sam's sake. But when she mentioned Mr Albany, her voice seemed to soften.'

'And he seemed very concerned about her,' Keith said. 'But could anybody fancy that hairy ape?'

'He could be very attractive,' Molly said.

'Oh Mum! He must be a hundred years old!'

Keith decided not to point out that Ian Albany was about his own age. 'I suppose his wife must once have fancied him or he wouldn't have one. Do they still get along?'

'They bicker,' Deborah said.

'Much?'

'About the same as you and Mum.'

'A case for the divorce lawyers,' Molly said, hiding a smile.

'All right, we've got the picture,' Keith said. 'Go on.'

'Mike and Beth Hendrickson were away in Edinburgh, so parricide is out,' Deborah said. Keith glanced at her but she refused to look up. 'A pity. I wouldn't have put it past her. Spoiled and mixed-up,' she explained.

'Next door are the Strathlings. No family. She's an over-dressed snob, for all that she works in the bank, and he's a cold fish.'

'Why do you say that?' Keith asked quickly.

'I don't know. I just get that feeling. And, Dad, that's one of the houses which didn't smell like money. It didn't look like money either, from inside. I mean, there weren't a lot of expensive, personal things around. She was away shopping but, obviously, he could easily have slipped through the hedge.

'Next to them, the Beechers. They're a pair of fusspots, not a weed in the garden nor a speck of dust in the house, but I rather like them. He runs the printing works.'

'Does he own it, or is he a paid manager?' Keith asked. Molly and Deborah looked blank. 'Sam Hendrickson had stirred up trouble there. Beecher's attitude might depend on whether it was his own money that was going down the drain. Never mind.'

'He probably owns it,' Deborah said, 'because their house smells expensive, of cigars and lavender and saddle-soap. They've two sons —'

'Is that why you like them?' Molly asked.

Deborah lifted her nose. 'Please don't be silly, Mum. I like them because they're kind and they treat me as an adult. I was going to say that Garry's away at university. Steven says that he was helping his mother in the garden all morning up to about the time of the shot and that one or the other of them may have gone indoors but never both at the same time. Mr Beecher was away at his fishing. His mum says that Steven had just driven off in that little car of his, but she herself – Mrs Beecher, I mean – was still in the back garden when she heard the bang. So Mrs Beecher could have slipped through the Strathlings' garden, choosing the right moment while there was a race on the box. They all seemed to know that he watched the racing.'

'That's all very well,' Keith said, 'but people can look round from the telly. What makes more sense is that she would have waited until Strathling went over to the Albanys' house. But

151

why would she have waited so long after he went there?'

'I don't know,' Deborah said, 'and I honestly don't care very much. Because I don't think I can see Mrs Beecher doing any such thing. She's very mild and gentle and she jumps at loud noises.'

'Obviously,' Molly said, 'she waited for her son – Steven? – to drive away.'

'I don't think anybody could have slipped through the Beechers' garden from the McLaings', who were on holiday in Italy or somewhere at the time,' Deborah said. 'The Beechers' garden's a bit more open than most.

'That's that side of the road.

'On the other side, the Albanys are next to the Hendricksons. That's another house which smells well-off. Mr Albany's built like a gorilla but he's a good sort if he wouldn't be so patronising.'

'And a hundred years old,' Keith said.

'And that Mrs Albany's the bossy type, which is what usually sets them bickering, and they have a daughter, Aimee, who I can't thole at any price. She thinks she's just beautiful,' Deborah said loftily.

'Any of the Albanys could have slipped through the Hendricksons' garden,' Keith said, again choosing the right moment, but whether they'd have had time to slip back again I rather doubt. I suppose Ian Albany could have hidden round the back of the summerhouse until Mrs Hendrickson and the milkman were inside and then appeared at the door, but he'd have been taking a hell of a risk that somebody else would have come into the garden at that moment.'

'The Albanys have a yappy dog,' Molly said. 'It's always loose in the garden when the weather's dry. They weren't looking out but they say it always barks at strangers —'

'Including the Ortons?' Keith asked.

'Especially them. The Ortons keep cats and chase the dog out of their garden if it gets in. So nobody could have slipped through there from the Ortons or the footpath, but anyway,' Molly said, 'I think that one of the Ortons need only have walked across the street if Grandma Orton was prepared to keep her mouth shut. Their gate's only a few yards from the

Hendricksons', and I don't think that Mr Kechnie could see that far along from his front lawn, there's a clump of holly in the way.'

'They'd have to choose their moment, even more than any of the others, what with the window-cleaner and the milkman,' Keith said.

Molly shrugged. 'So they could have chosen the right moment, while the window-cleaner was at the back of a house. But, again, getting back could have been a problem. They might have had to stay hidden for hours. Jenny didn't go up the garden straight away, but nobody knew that she wouldn't. Perhaps we should go round everybody again and find out who wasn't seen around for the next few hours.'

'If we must,' Keith said.

'The Ortons have one daughter,' Deborah said. 'Pat, who's supposed to be very clever. I get on well enough with them usually, though Pat tries to make me look stupid sometimes. She doesn't try it too often because there are things I can make her look stupid about. Mr Orton's the brainy type, spends his time marketing very high-tech computer programs but he doesn't put on any side about it. Mrs Orton's very neat, but he always looks as if he'd been thrown into his clothes by a giant who couldn't aim very straight.'

'Pat and Mrs Orton were both in their back garden most of the morning,' Molly said, 'which would have prevented the Pollocks or the Kechnies from going that way without being seen, and old Mrs Orton was looking out over the front.' She stopped and cleared her throat. 'Shall I leave the last two families out just now, if they seem to be in the clear?'

'Better finish the list,' Keith said. 'One of you told me that Mrs Orton said that Mrs Pollock came over the bridge and went straight home. Would Mrs Orton tell lies to get Mrs Pollock off the hook?'

'No way!' Deborah said. 'They're friends on the surface but there's a sort of buried cattiness. If one of them could drop the other right in it, she would.'

'That's the best sort of witness to have,' Keith said.

'The Pollocks come next,' Deborah said. 'Mr Pollock's fat and pompous and thinks he ought to have been God only the job had already been taken. He was indoors for the later part of the morning, according to his family. Nobody mentioned seeing him anywhere else.'

'His wife's a poor sort of creature,' Molly said. 'Always ailing with something. I don't know how she managed to produce two great bouncing daughters. But the girls are at boarding school,' she added. 'And that just leaves the Kechnies. You've met him.'

'That I have,' Keith said grimly.

'Well, I haven't,' Molly said. 'He was away at one of his shops when I called in, although he usually takes Saturdays at home. His wife's a pillar of the Red Cross and Meals on Wheels and that sort of thing. She was indoors all morning when Sam Hendrickson died. She says that her husband was out pottering with the cars until lunch.'

Keith frowned. 'Somebody – Strathling it was – told me that Kechnie crossed the road before the shot. It might not be true, of course.'

'He was probably going to see his sister,' Molly said.

Keith nodded and was about to move on when the impact of her words hit him. 'Sister?'

'Yes. Didn't you know? He's Mrs Beecher's brother.'

'Is he, by God! And both the Kechnies and the Beechers had cause to hate Sam Hendrickson. And Beecher tried to scare us off.' Keith stared into space for a full minute and then gave himself a little shake. 'For the moment, it looks as if Kechnie might be the front-runner, with his sister as an accessory – which would please Wal no end –, followed closely by the Albanys and Ben Strathling, then by the Ortons, the window-cleaner and a mysterious lady who might possibly be Mrs Griegson from the union and who seems to have the only real motive which has shown up. And I thought that this was going to be a one-horse or at the most a two-horse race. Any thoughts so far?'

They looked at each other in silence. Molly laughed suddenly. 'Three minds without a single thought,' she said. 'Poor Jenny, she may never know what happened to her Sam. Wouldn't anybody have noticed if the window-cleaner vanished for a minute? Or are window-cleaners sort of invisible, like policemen and posties?'

'I think Mrs Orton Senior would have noticed,' Keith said. 'I'm going to ask her tomorrow.'

'I'll tell you something that's been bothering me all along,' Molly said. 'However shocked she was, Jenny Hendrickson wouldn't have turned off the monitor of the computer if it had shown a message from her Sam. So why would a murderer leave it only showing the menu? The only reason I can think of is that he was afraid that she'd be more likely to switch off the computer if she saw a suicide message, because of the insurance. But that doesn't seem to be good reasoning.'

'I think I can tell you why,' Keith said.

'So can I,' Deborah piped up.

'All right, Toots. You go ahead.'

'No, Dad, you first. I've got a tickle. I'm not used to talking so much without being told to pipe down.' She fetched herself a glass of tonic from Keith's drinks cabinet.

'Very well.' Lightly, Keith touched the ESCAPE key. At each touch, the screen flicked across between the list of functions and the text which they had been preparing. 'I was going to test my theory tomorrow. I'd do it here except that it'll make a mess. It hardly takes a breath to work one of these keys. I'm going to fire a shotgun in the summerhouse, into a bucket of water, and see if the sudden pulse of gas pressure wouldn't be enough to key it. Is that what you were going to say?'

'No, it isn't,' Deborah said. 'I don't think that it would work, not on a key half an inch square. Think about it.'

'Now who's sounding patronising?' Keith said.

'Sorry. But what you said wouldn't explain why the keyboard was one of the first things Mrs Hendrickson cleaned. There's a simpler explanation. A great dollop of blood and brains and chips of bone landed on that part of the keyboard,' she explained cheerfully. 'I noticed it on one of the photographs. Assume that it hit the ESCAPE key. Wiping it off, Mrs Hendrickson would have been keying it to and fro and also putting in all the gibberish. If she'd switched off the monitor, she wouldn't notice anything.'

Keith pointed a finger at her. 'Babes and sucklings,' he said. 'Babes and sucklings! You may be a clype, but you're a clever clype. That's exactly what happened.'

His daughter put her tongue out at him.

155

# ELEVEN

Saturday fishermen quit their beds early, to make the most of the day and in the hope of a dawn rise. Keith slipped out of bed while Molly was still sleeping, scribbled a note, filled a flask with coffee and left home before dawn, re-setting the alarms behind him. He parked the jeep near the entrance to Kenny Stuart's farm and settled down to wait with the patience of the experienced stalker.

The sun was coming up and the flask was almost empty of coffee when a white Volvo estate cruised along the road from Boswell Court and turned towards the town. If he found himself spying on an innocent angler, he told himself, it would only be a few hours of sleep and some petrol lost down life's plug-hole.

In Newton Lauder, the white car turned south. Rather than alert the other driver, Keith tucked in behind a milk-float. A sudden, short crocodile of traffic, probably early golfers, kept him there, and when he managed to get past the milk-float his quarry had vanished.

In a burst of irritation, he uttered a word which Molly had absolutely outlawed and put his foot down. But when the town was behind him and he could see the road for half a mile ahead, there was no white car to be seen. There was no other road to the south and no trout stream within walking distance.

As he turned in a field-gate, he considered. Of course, James Beecher might be picking up a friend. In which case, he might return to the main road and leave the town to the north or go back up the hill to eastward. Or they might take the friend's car. Or the fishing-trips might be no more than an excuse to visit a lady, which would explain the fact that Mr Beecher often purchased cartridges in the shop but never fishing tackle.

Before choosing between trying the impossible or giving up,

156

there was one other cast he could make. He turned off into a side-street which curled uphill round the back of the Post Office and then, after serving some tiny, Victorian houses for a quarter-mile, arrived back at the canal beside a large, blank-faced industrial building of red brick and heavy slates. A sign, much newer than the building, announced that this was the 'Panmure Printing Works. Prop: J.Beecher.' The white Volvo estate stood haughtily apart from two lesser cars, within the mesh-fenced yard. The gate was padlocked.

Keith let the jeep roll back until it was hidden by a rickety wooden garage and parked while he thought again. Jim Beecher might be using his own yard as a secure place to leave his car while going off with a fishing friend, but Keith had not met another car as he came up the hill. If Beecher were merely catching up with a backlog of desk-work, why would he padlock the gate? And if he was in the habit of spending his Saturday mornings in innocent toil, why pretend to go fishing?

Keith got out and locked the jeep. Then he unlocked it again to get out his lightweight binoculars. He began to circle the fence. There was no sign of life in the print-works except for a faint hum of machinery. No other gates were evident, but from the raised canal bank it was an easy vault over the wire on to a stack of crates and pallets.

In the back of the Volvo he could see waders and a rod-case. The most propitious time for fishing would soon be past. But perhaps the fishing tackle was a permanency in the car, just as his own pigeon decoys and hide-nets were never removed from the jeep.

The massive building was flanked by a lower run of what Keith took to be offices, with clerestory windows showing above. Keeping well out of sight from the office windows, Keith fetched three boxes and with their help reached the lower roof. It sloped, but his rubber soles gripped well and he blessed the long-dead builders for their solid slates and heavy timber. He made his way up and crouched against the edge of one of the high windows, keeping very still rather than attract eyes to a moving silhouette.

He was looking down on to the main floor of the print-works. Most of the machinery was idle, but a man was attending to one of the smaller presses and on the other side of a separating

157

partition two women were putting the finishing touches to some bound volumes, while another stowed them in cardboard cartons. A man who, from the bald head and red moustache, Keith took to be James Beecher, came into view, spoke to one of the women and walked out of sight again.

Keith watched for a few minutes longer. It seemed that Beecher, with a small selection of his staff, was attending to some rush job; but, before climbing down, out of no more than idle curiosity as to what work was so urgent as to bring them in at the weekend, he pulled the binoculars from his inner pocket and focussed them on the stacks of pages which awaited binding.

The print was still just too small for him to read, but the one full-page photograph came up sharp and clear. It showed a nearly-nude girl in the hands of three men, and embraced almost the whole spectrum of male fetishes. Before he tore his eyes away, Keith could feel an erection coming.

'I think,' said a voice, 'that it would be better if you came down for a closer look, Mr Calder.'

Keith looked down. The man looking up from the yard was undoubtedly Beecher. Without answering, Keith stowed away his binoculars and climbed down by the way he had gone up. He felt foolish and aggrieved and at the same time much amused. Beecher's emotions seemed not to be dissimilar.

'You'd better come inside,' Beecher said. He led the way through a hall and into a spartan office lined with shelves of files and printing and pointed to a chair. 'Coffee?' he asked.

'I'm already awash with the stuff,' Keith said, 'after waiting an hour for you to leave home. I wanted to know why you tried to warn me off, and where you got to on Saturdays when you said you were going fishing. You never bought any tackle from the shop.'

'I could have been tying my own flies.'

'Nylon line needs replacing every year or two,' Keith said. 'And it's a rare fisherman who doesn't treat himself to a new gadget now and again.'

Beecher smiled wryly. 'Stupid of me,' he said. 'Well, now you know. At least, I take it that you know?'

Keith nodded. 'You've been running off a little porn at the weekends, with a few of your more trusted staff.'

'When we could get the work.' Now that it was out in the open, Beecher had relaxed a little, but although he had settled into his chair Keith could see that his muscles were still taut. 'It's a good earner. It was the only way I could keep the rest of my costs low enough to compete with the bigger firms. We only do the printing, you understand,' Beecher added anxiously. 'We don't write the stuff, or take the photographs.'

Keith, who had been on the point of getting interested, remembered his grievance. 'You phoned up and threatened me,' he said. 'And then you sent a thug to rough me up.'

Beecher nodded slowly. 'I won't admit a thing to anyone else,' he said. 'But, between ourselves, that was a mistake. I only told him to give you a fright.'

'I don't take kindly to threats.'

'Nobody ever threatened me, but I don't suppose I'd take it kindly myself. I just couldn't think of any other course. But there's no harm done,' Beecher said reasonably. 'He didn't frighten you off. All he did was get a dunt over the head from you. I was so damned annoyed I gave him a fiver for his petrol and sent him off without a fee.'

Despite his annoyance, Keith found that he was beginning to like Jim Beecher. 'If you'd paid him off, he might have been a bit more reticent about who'd employed him. After I ignored your phone-call, why did you send him? The damage was already done.'

'If you stopped stirring up the mud, I thought that the police would soon lose interest. Nobody likes working hard to prove that they blew it first time around.' Beecher paused and scratched his ear. 'So what happens now?'

Keith was wondering the same thing. 'Tell me about you and Sam Hendrickson,' he said.

He spoke only to fill a gap and to take advantage of having Beecher at a disadvantage. He expected nothing but a puzzled denial. Beecher surprised him. 'It was several years ago,' he said. 'Hendrickson, representing the union, came after me for a rise for my workers. I refused and had a strike on my hands. I met Hendrickson and took him through the books and showed him that the business couldn't stand it. I thought I was wasting my time; that wasn't the sort of argument Sam Hendrickson was known to accept. But he asked, quite mildly, whether I'd pay the increase if he brought me in some profitable extra work.'

'He introduced you to the porn-publisher?' Keith asked.

'Exactly. And the workers got their rise and Hendrickson took a percentage for one year as we'd agreed. And I'll say one thing for him. He stuck precisely to the letter of our agreement.'

'I ought to tell the police,' Keith said.

'Please don't. It might not come entirely as a surprise to them,' Beecher said. 'As long as there's no complaint, I can stay afloat as a local employer. I don't think they or my workforce would thank you for drawing my activities to their official notice.'

That was probably true. Keith remembered Gowrie's amused dismissal of Beecher as a suspect. For his own part, he had no strong views about pornography and experience had shown him that any form of censorship was counter-productive. 'Well all right,' he said grudgingly. 'I'll keep my mouth shut, unless and until your sideline turns out to have a bearing on Sam Hendrickson's death. But don't you ever try threatening me again.'

The other brightened. 'You're a good sort,' he said. 'I don't know whether you like that sort of thing, but would you like a free copy of what we're working on today?'

On the point of indignant refusal, Keith realised that it would make a perfect Christmas present for his brother-in-law. 'Thank you very much,' he said.

Back in the jeep, with his acquisition safely shrouded in brown paper on the seat beside him, he realised that nothing said that morning need have cleared Jim Beecher as a suspect. Keith would not have put blackmail beyond Sam Hendrickson.

He was home in time for a hasty breakfast. He let his wife and daughter think that his early expedition had failed. He was in no mood for Molly's feminist ire nor for Deborah's curiosity.

Molly took the car and went to open the shop. She would join them if and when Janet and Wallace returned. Keith took Deborah in the jeep.

Most of the cars at Boswell Court were tucked away in large garages or were pulled off the road into broad, well-screened driveways, but there was a glossy Daimler at the kerb outside the Kechnie residence. Mr Kechnie's string of shops, which stretched through the Borders, must be doing better than the old bastard deserved, Keith told himself.

Keith turned the jeep and parked it outside the Hendricksons' gate. He hoped that it would not make the place look too untidy. A small van was already lowering the tone.

'I see the window-cleaner's here,' he said. 'It's the chap who comes out to do our windows. I'll talk to him and then visit Granny Orton. If your fisherman's there—'

'He is,' Deborah said. 'I looked along the canal when we crossed the bridge.'

'See if you can pin him down about the extra wifie. First get hold of Mrs Orton. Ask whether I could visit her mother-in-law a little later. Meet me Chez Pollock.'

'Gotcha,' said his daughter. A blonde teenager, very sexy and well aware of it, came out of a gate, crossed the road and vanished through another. 'That's Aimee Albany,' Deborah said. 'As if anybody cared.'

Keith decided to be careful, but Deborah was waiting for a comment. 'Pretty hair,' he said.

'Yes. Pity the roots are a glorious mud-colour.' Deborah gave her father a sly look. 'Like it, do you?'

'Hoy!' Keith said. 'You're not thinking—?'

'Of course not,' she said. Keith began to relax. 'She'd think I was copying her,' Deborah added. 'When my cheque's cashed, I might consider going redhead. A sort of golden auburn.' She hopped down, gave him a cheerful salute and vanished between the gardens in the direction of the footbridge.

The window-cleaner, a stout and cheerful man known to all the town as Gus, was ready for a break. They took seats in his van while Gus filled a large mug with tea from his vacuum flask. He balanced his mug over the dashboard and the windscreen began to steam up. Gus's memory was good and he loved to talk. Keith could have learned volumes about the bedroom habits of the town's residents, but he limited the discussion to matters bearing on the day Sam Hendrickson died.

'You've always had a helper with you when I've seen you before,' he said.

'Yon was my brother while he was out of work,' Gus explained. 'He got taken on at Selby's Warehouse. The day you

161

want to know about was my first on my own. I found I could manage fine. It's slower that way but the money's all mine and I can do with it. O'er many folk do their own windows these days. But not up here, they'd not want to be seen soiling their hands – except in the garden. Gardening's ladylike, you see, and a gent can polish a car if he feels like it, but cleaning windows is work. Being on my own for the first time is how I can keep that day clear in my mind. It was different, you see, having to handle the ladder by myself.'

'Did you go round the houses in sequence that morning?'

'Sort of,' Gus said. 'Mrs Beecher likes to get away early, some Saturdays, so I aye do her windows first, else I'd likely have to wait a week to get paid. The McLaings was away, but she'd left word to do the windows anyway – she thinks dirty windows is an invite to burglars, the same way she has a man come up and cut the grass – so I did her next. Then I crossed the road and started working back the other side and round to finish at the Strathlings. I was doing the last of their windows when I heard the shot.

While he thought about his next question, Keith wiped clear his side of the windscreen. The girl, Aimee, was crossing the road again. Seeing Keith's eyes reappear, she gave an extra flick of her bottom as she walked. Ian Albany was going to have problems there within a year or two. The thought bothered Keith not at all.

'Did you see much of the comings and goings of that morning?' he asked.

'Aye, I did. I'm an observant sort of chiel and I see a lot from up the ladder, most of it reflected in the glass so's folk don't know they're being seen. There's not much else to think about in this line of work. Mind, I'd be round the back of the houses, half the time.'

And, Keith thought, for half of the other half the glass would be obscured by soapy water. But Gus was the best witness he was likely to get. A person mowing a lawn or washing a car sees much less than he thinks he does. 'Tell me all you can remember,' he said.

Gus sipped his tea while he thought back. 'There wasn't a lot,' he said. 'Mr Pollock drove off while I was doing the Beechers but he was back by the time I got to the Kechnies so I

162

knew I'd get paid. His wife had walked away over the wee bridge, you see, but she came back just as I started on the back of her house. She stopped and spoke to Mrs Orton, so I was finished by the time she reached home. Och, but you can't be wanting all th is!'

'Go on,' Keith said. 'This is all useful stuff.'

'If you say so. Well, then. I mind Mr Albany coming out of the Hendricksons' gate and going in at his own. I took a wee break after that – it's tiring, humping they ladders on your own, and Mrs Orton doesn't like me coming too early in case I give the old body a fright. Next thing, Mr Strathling comes out of his gate and goes into the Albanys'. That was while I waited for Mrs Pollock to arrive home and settle up.'

'Aha!' Keith said. He pencilled the fresh information into a print-out of the timetable. 'Go on.'

'About then,' Gus said, 'Mr Kechnie crossed the road. I thought he went into the McLaing's gate but it could've been the Beechers. The Kechnies and the Beechers are as thick as thieves.'

'They're related,' Keith said. 'What else?'

'Well now, the old mannie Rogers was doing the rounds at the same time, collecting milk-money, but of course he was getting round faster than I was. I did the Ortons next and that's where he passed me, just as I was finishing having a crack with the old body through her window.

'The Hendricksons and the Albanys only take me once every four weeks and that wasn't their week, so I skipped across to the Strathlings just as Mr Strathling came back from the Albanys' and not long before the Beecher laddie went off in his car. Just after that, I heard a bang which must ha' been the sound of the shot.'

'Did you notice anything else around that time?' Keith asked.

Gus looked uncertain. 'Not that I mind. Except that I caught sight, reflected in the glass, of the old lady waving. I looked back over my shoulder, thinking it was maybe me she was waving at, but she was looking between the houses and I guessed that she was waving to Mr Strathling.'

'I think she was waving to Kenny Stuart, the farmer,' Keith said.

'That'd be likely enough. Anyway, I heard the bang just

163

seconds after, and soon aabody was stravaigning around and wondering what to do next. The police arrived and a doctor – although what good he could do beats me.'

'Did you follow the crowd round to the Hendricksons' summerhouse?'

Gus shook his head solemnly. 'What for would I do that? Time's money when you're self-employed. The moment I heard what'd happened I made up my mind I'd not be a witness to anything if I could help it. Not that that's saved me from the police. I gi'ed them the same as I've told you in a tenth of the time.'

Keith took the hint. 'I'll leave you to get on with it in a minute. First, go over that morning in your mind. Can you remember anything else? Anything at all?.

'That's the whole of it,' Gus said, 'but I'll catch you if anything else comes into my mind.'

'Thank you,' Keith said. 'You've been a big help and I'm grateful.'

'I've not landed some poor bugger in the sharn?'

'Mostly,' Keith said, 'you've just borne out what they'd already told me.' He opened his door, admitting the whine of an electric mower, but paused with one foot out of the van. 'From that ladder of yours, you must see most of what goes on around the town. Did the police ask you whether any of the folk up here were having affairs?'

'They did,' Gus said. 'And I'll tell you what I told them. There's yin or two of the men trailing a wing, but none of them's fool enough to shit on his ane doorstane. Ayont that, I'm not telling. I aye think a window-cleaner's like a doctor or a minister and maun steik his gab and no' be blurting his clients' secrets to the whole town.'


The younger Mrs Orton answered her door to Keith. She was a small and cheerful person with a brisk manner. Although she was dressed for gardening she managed to look so clean and fresh that Keith expected her to smell of starch. She pulled off a leather glove to shake Keith's hand.

'Your Deborah will be back soon,' she said. 'But my mother-in-law's expecting you. She's looking forward to an extra visit and I know she'd like to give you coffee. Would that suit you?'

'Very much,' Keith said. 'But you're busy.' He wondered if he dared ask for tea. It would be weeks before he could face a cup of coffee again with any enthusiasm.

'The tray's ready. I'll take you and it up together. She's old but you'll find that she's very much all there.' Mrs Orton paused and looked unhappy. 'I only hope you can clear this up. I've given up hoping for the police to solve anything, and it's got us all on edge. Winnie Pollock next door, and . . . and . . .'

She turned away abruptly and fetched the tray. As she led Keith up the stairs he was able to catch a glimpse of Deborah beyond the canal. The smell of money, to which Deborah had referred, was definitely present, and the paintings which hung on the wall were contemporary originals. A man in glasses with his trousers at half-mast passed them on the landing. He was carrying a large tome and seemed to be quite unaware of their presence. The brainy Mr Orton, Keith presumed.

The senior Mrs Orton occupied a huge bed-sitting room at the front of the house. The furniture was old-fashioned, but because the wallpaper was in keeping there was no suggestion that she had been equipped with cast-offs. It was rather that the furniture, which was well matched, had been chosen carefully to suit the taste of the old lady who was perched in a high wing-chair at the window. Mrs Orton waited only long enough to make introductions before hurrying back to her gardening.

Keith pulled over a light bedroom chair and joined the old lady. Even the smell of the room was old-fashioned, he thought, although just as clean and moneyed as the rest of the house.

Old Mrs Orton was small and frail and when Keith shook her hand he could feel knuckles enlarged by arthritis. Her hearing was failing and he had to wait for her to fumble with a modern hearing-aid. But her eyes were bright and she was indomitably cheerful and blessed with a curiosity as insatiable as that of the Elephant's Child. Before he could turn her attention to Sam Hendrickson's death he had to accept an unwelcome cup of coffee and undergo a catechism about his own and Molly's life and health, the prosperity of the shop and the condition of Briesland House and garden which she had known well as a girl.

In return, Keith filed away some fascinating and mildly scandalous tidbits concerning the early history of his home.

'Of course I remember that day,' she said, when Keith managed to work round to the subject of the late Sam Hendrickson. 'This is a quiet road. I wouldn't want it any other way, you understand, but often there are days when I'm glad to see a leaf blowing along the pavement. Saturdays are usually more interesting, with the men at home. But that Saturday was unusually dull. Reading tires my eyes. I have the television of course, but there was nothing but sport on it. I don't know how you feel, Mr Calder, but I just can't get interested in anything I've never experienced myself. I don't mind the tennis but I've never ridden a racehorse and I've never played Rugby football.' She chuckled at her little joke.

'You prefer something romantic?' Keith said.

'Any day of the week,' she said stoutly. 'Romance is something else I've experienced for myself.'

'I believe you,' Keith said, smiling.

'Happily married for thirty-five years, but before that I'd been engaged six times. My parents were wondering what would become of me.' She chuckled again. 'And I just love a good thriller, although the acting isn't what it was.

'But that's not what you came to hear. I don't know that I can help you, though. You see, I didn't hear the shot. My hearing, you know. It's a curse, especially with the actors on the television gabbling on and mumbling their lines the way they do, and the directors drowning out the most important bits with music or background noise. How do they think a body can follow a complicated plot? Or do they think that we're just unintelligent creatures who'll be satisfied with noises and pictures? I'm rambling again, aren't I?' She grinned mischievously and slapped the back of her wrist gently. 'But I certainly remember the day. It's not every dull Saturday we get a police car and an ambulance up here.'

'Tell me about it,' Keith said.

'I'm afraid I wasn't on duty until close to the time Mr Hendrickson must have shot himself. Or been shot. That's what you're here about, isn't it? Anyway, I can't leap out of bed these days. I have to wait for Jane, my daughter-in-law, to help me get up. She's a good girl. It's not as if she's one of my own,

166

but she looks after me as if I was her own mother. And so does my grand-daughter, when she thinks of it. Anyway, Jane got me up and dressed just in time before the window-cleaner arrived. I like that Gus,' she added. 'Jane says that I like all the men, only joking, but there's a scrap of truth in it. Men don't say as much as women do, but what they do say is often more exciting. Gus always chats to me through the window from the top of his ladder. He's always the joker. Sometimes he pretends that he's trying to persuade me to elope with him. He'd fall off his ladder if I pretended to take him at his word.

'Gus finished here and moved across the street to Mrs Strathling's house. Mr Rogers went by, collecting his money. And Mr Strathling must have been visiting Mr Albany, because I saw him go back across the street. A little later—'

'One moment,' Keith said. 'Exactly where did Mr Strathling go? These details can be important.'

'I didn't watch, not just then. Something distracted me. But a little later I saw him come back through the gap in the hedge from Mr Hendrickson's into his own back garden. Then he went back to the Hendricksons' a few minutes later. And not long after that, the police car arrived.'

'You didn't see Mrs Hendrickson and Mr Rogers go up the garden?'

'How could I?' she said. 'Look for yourself.' She pointed out of the window.

Keith looked and saw that the Hendricksons' house and the trees planted near its gable effectively screened the garden and the summerhouse from that window. The Kechnies' end of the road was also hidden, by a clump of hollies in the Pollocks' garden, although he could see the Beechers' gate. Keith thought hard. Something was evading him.

'I often thought of asking the Hendricksons to get those trees pruned,' she said suddenly. 'It would only have needed a limb or two removed from that last fir tree and I'd have been able to see the summerhouse. With poor Mr Hendrickson stuck in a wheelchair, he was worse off than I am. He might have been glad to exchange a wave now and again.'

That gave Keith the hint that he needed. 'What was it that distracted you from seeing where Mr Strathling went?' he asked.

167

'What was it now?' She looked through Keith with unseeing, very blue eyes. 'I remember! I saw the farmer on his tractor. He seemed to be looking this way, so I waved and he must have seen me because he waved back. The Beechers' son went off about then in that nice little car. He's a good-looking young man. If I were fifty years younger, thirty even, I'd have found some way of going with him. I used to love sports cars, and young men.'

'That's very interesting,' Keith said. 'You didn't see Mr Kechnie cross the road?'

'No. I noticed him coming back from the Beechers' house, but that was later, after the fuss had died down.'

Suddenly, Keith was burning to go. 'I mustn't keep you any longer—'

She gripped his cuff with her frail hand. 'You're not keeping me,' she said. 'I'm keeping you. At least tell me whether I've helped.'

'You've told me where to ask the next question,' Keith said. 'If I get the answer I'm hoping for, then you've helped a lot.'

'You can't give me a hint . . .?'

'I'm not sure of anything yet,' Keith said. 'When I am, I'll come back and tell you all about it.'

'I'll look forward to that.'

He was half-way to the door when he heard her make a sudden exclamation. He turned back. 'Do you need anything?' he asked.

'Bless you, no. It's just that something came back into my mind, suddenly, for no reason. The trouble is that I can't even be sure that it was that same morning. And, if it was, it was much too early to be of any use to you.'

'Tell me anyway,' Keith said.

'It's just that I was woken up very early. You wake easily when you're my age. Of course, I don't sleep with this thing in –' she tapped her hearing-aid and blinked when the sound reverberated in her ear '– but in the stillness of early morning there were no other sounds so I could make out what was happening.'

'What?'

'There was a car, and it had one of those engines which make a sharp knocking sound.'

'A diesel?'

'That's right. A car door slamming had woken me up. That's

168

about all I remember, except a voice. I couldn't make out what it said, although my guess would be that it was doing no more than asking somebody to wait for a few seconds, but I remember that it was one of those very penetrating nasal voices, like Ian Paisley without the Irish accent.'

'And nobody who lives here has a voice like that?'

She laughed like a young girl. 'Certainly not,' she said. 'The residents wouldn't stand for it. I wouldn't have liked living near it myself when I was younger, but now I just wish that everybody had a voice like that. Then I might be able to make out what they were saying.'


Keith walked back towards the entrance road and approached the next house. The garden showed less sign of constant toil than the Ortons', but it had been laid down by somebody with an eye for design and a distaste for hard work. The kidney-shaped lawn was shaped for easy mowing in a single, continuous cut while the beds of shrubs, underplanted with rock-plants guaranteed to strangle all but the hardiest weeds, had been crammed around the edges with a variety of bulbs. Keith guessed that the Pollocks would be blessed with flowers for most of the year, without having to do much more than mow the grass and offer an artificial fertiliser and some extra water to all the competing root systems.

Mr Pollock answered the doorbell, overweight and jowly and with a self-important manner. He frowned when he saw Keith. His displeasure did not seem to be wholly accounted for by his having been caught in a paint-stained sweater and the striped trousers from a cast-off business suit. 'It's Mr Calder, isn't it? Your daughter's with my wife now.'

'I'd like to speak to your wife for a moment, if I may,' Keith said.

'I suppose I can't stop you. But,' Mr Pollock said, standing aside, 'I can't say that I like all this amateur prying. The sheriff decided that Sam killed himself. Why can't it be left at that?'

'The sheriff may not have had all the facts,' Keith said. 'I've only been asked to discover the truth. If I'm a nuisance, I'm sorry.'

'That's all very well. But if Jenny Hendrickson hadn't asked us herself, I'd be telling you to go and bowl your hoop elsewhere.'

'If anybody else had asked me to investigate, I'd have told them the same.'

'Well, all right,' Mr Pollock said grudgingly. 'Can't disoblige the widow, I suppose, and so charming a lady as well. Come on it.' He ushered Keith through a door from the hallway and made himself scarce.

In the Pollocks' living room, Deborah was sitting with Mrs Pollock and nursing a glass of lemonade. It was a room which managed to be gracious without any great expense having been lavished on it. Mrs Pollock was an anxious-looking lady, thin rather than slim. Before offering him a seat, she shook Keith's hand as if afraid that he would break her arm.

Deborah caught her father's eye. 'The extra lady's explained,' she said.

'My cousin,' Mrs Pollock said quickly. 'I'd walked across the bridge to see her. I wanted to borrow a recipe. She couldn't put her hand on it but she gave it to me from memory. After I'd come back here, she found it. So she walked up to give it to me. Simple as that! And quite unnecessary. She just likes to see what we're getting up to. But, anyway, it was after the police and the ambulance had arrived.'

Keith nodded. He had already lost interest in the extra lady. 'Who and what did you see as you came back?' he asked.

Mrs Pollock looked at him as if wondering whether she were under suspicion, but decided to answer the question. 'I stopped to chat with Jane Orton,' she said. 'She was in her garden and the path runs beside it. She keeps the hedge short just so that she can waylay passers-by and see what they're wearing, although what right she has to criticise other people's clothes I don't know, when her husband always seems to have been dressed by Oxfam and about to lose his trousers. She was complaining about the ground-elder and creeping buttercup, but, as I told her, if you want to live near open country that's the price you pay for the peace and the privacy. Seeds blowing around.'

The last was a subject which Keith could have discussed for hours but he held himself in check. 'Did anybody come past you?'

'Not a soul. Not before we'd finished our chat. I could see Gus, the window-cleaner, waiting to be paid. That man hates to

170

have to wait for his money, and my husband gets grumpy if he has to pay something which should go with the housekeeping, so I hurried home.'

'Was anybody else in sight?'

'Just Ben Strathling. As I came out of the footpath from the bridge I was facing into his gateway and I could see up the side of his house. He came through the gap in the hedge from the Hendricksons', hesitated for a moment and then came out and crossed the road. I suppose he was going either to the Ortons' or the Albanys'. I thought at the time that he was looking furtive, but he always does. I didn't notice anybody else,' she added plaintively, as if Keith might blame her for lack of observation or for the failure of others to be on view when required.

'You saw all that mattered,' Keith said comfortingly. 'We'll leave you in peace now.'

She got to her feet quickly, as if glad to be rid of such threatening guests, but then paused. 'It was a terrible thing to happen, wasn't it,' she said. It was hardly a question. 'I don't blame Jenny for not wanting to believe that Sam killed himself, but I'm sure she's got you on a wild goose chase. I knew Sam Hendrickson when we were students together.'

Keith pricked up his ears. 'You knew him well?'

'Not very. He was going out with a friend of mine. We were all left-wingers in those days, I remember, but he never grew out of it. He hated to be fussed over even then, he could get quite nasty about it, and being tied to anybody's apron-strings would have been quite enough to push him over the edge, let alone that wife of his. Such a maternal woman!' She hurried them out before they could comment.

'Meow!' Deborah said, before they were quite out of hearing.

Father and daughter crossed the road together in the midday sunshine, the first sun of the spring to hold any warmth. Keith turned his face upward for a moment. He always liked to feel the first hint of summer to come. The flowers in the gardens already showed brighter tints.

Gus's van had gone, but a plain car was parked outside the Hendricksons' gate with Detective Inspector Gowrie at the wheel. Superintendent Munro sat beside him, unfamiliar in plain clothes of stiff tweed. Gus had somehow been a proper if workaday part of the scene but the two policemen, who were trying to blend in, looked as alien as turnips in a rose-bed.

'They'll be wanting an update,' Keith told Deborah. 'You go and ask Mr Albany – or Mrs Albany, if he's left for his clay pigeons already – one question for me.' He spelled it out for her. 'Then, if we're not in one of the cars, come and find us.'

Deborah's eyes widened. 'You're on to something, are you, Dad?'

'The answer to that's a qualified maybe.'

Deborah strode off, her long legs sweeping her over the ground at almost a running pace. As Keith walked towards the car its door opened and the two policemen got out to meet him.

'Have you anything for us?' Gowrie asked. 'Or can we start our weekend now?'

Keith ducked into the cluttered back seat of the car, forcing Gowrie and Munro to get back in again. 'Not out there,' he said. 'Too many eyes and ears. As it is, I'm afraid I may have said too much. The womenfolk are naturally curious. The men too, some of them. The questions I've asked and the answers I've got must be going the rounds. I'd suggest that we borrowed Mrs Hendrickson's summerhouse, except that I don't think we ought to leave the road unwatched.'

'That's easily fixed,' Gowrie said. He picked up the radio microphone but hesitated before making a call. 'What do you know?'

'I don't know much, but I'm thinking a lot. I know who did it,' Keith said. 'I think I know what he did. But I'm damned if I know why. And I've no proof at all. I need a few seconds longer to think about it.'

The superintendent was looking more than ever like a disgruntled camel. 'Och, I wish now I'd never invited you to meddle,' he said. 'We've had more than our share of crimes around here, and yourself usually on the fringes and interfering. If we announce another murder, my superiors will be wondering what sort of crime prevention we go in for in these parts.'

'You've certainly got a crime,' Keith said. 'But did I say anything about murder?'

Deborah appeared at the door before the superintendent could pursue the subject. Keith had to stack up a briefcase, an

172

orange waistcoat, a blue flasher and two bollards to make room for her beside him. She gave him an affirmative nod.

'Let's get one or two other things out of the way,' Keith said. 'Old Mrs Orton heard a car. She thinks that it was early on the morning Sam Hendrickson died. It was diesel-engined and she heard a penetrating, nasal voice.'

'Means nothing to me,' Gowrie said. 'But it's a combination which shouldn't be difficult to trace. You think the car was dropping off the killer? Where did he hide until the middle of the day, and again afterwards?'

'I don't think anything of the sort,' Keith said. 'Toots, you said you got to know the shotgun users by their voices. You wouldn't know anybody . . .?'

'Only one,' Deborah said. 'There's a Mr McPhail – I've heard them call him Sandy. He farms somewhere out Greenlaw way. He's got a voice like stones dropping into an empty skip. And I'll tell you something else. He has a diesel Land-Rover. Or he had, when they shot for the Joint Council Trophy back in December.'

Munro, who had been slouching despondently, grunted and sat up straight. 'I'm thinking we should maybe go and see this Mr McPhail,' he said. 'There may be others with a voice and a vehicle like that, but one place is as good as another to make a start. If he can account for himself, we'll get Swansea to furnish a list of the diesel-engined vehicles owned hereabouts.'

'Hold on!' Keith said. 'I thought you policemen were renowned for not galloping off in all directions. The name Plod wouldn't have stuck to you if you were always so damned impatient.'

'Mr Calder's right,' Gowrie said with a touch of self-righteousness. 'I've been wondering why I knew the name. It's just come back to me. Mr McPhail's farmhouse burned down overnight, about the time Mr Hendrickson died.'

'I think that's true,' Keith said. 'Was it headlined Greenlaw Farmhouse Fire in the local rag? Because I have a mental picture of that headline next to the report of the suicide.'

'He'll have been putting a letter through Mr Strathling's door about the insurance,' Gowrie said disgustedly. 'Another red herring.'

'I don't think it is,' Keith said.

Superintendent Munro was reluctant to abandon the promising new trail, and he was even more loath to accept correction from his subordinate. 'Why would he do that when the telephone would be quicker? He would telephone for a claim form to be posted to him. That is how it is done. No farmer likes writing letters.'

'He had no phone after the farmhouse burned down,' Gowrie said. 'That's why.'

'A public telephone —' Munro began.

'Near a remote farm?' Gowrie retorted. 'Once he was in the Land-Rover it would be as quick to call in on the way by. And I mind something else. He came into the town to fetch a caravan from the hirers. Our men pulled him in for towing it behind his Land-Rover with some other vehicle's registration number on the back of the caravan. He's living in it now, out at the farm.'

The two policemen scowled at each other. Munro was first to break off the clash of eyes. 'It may be that you are right,' he said. 'We will ask him. Mr Calder, you were going to say something else. What were you about to tell us before we became side-tracked?'

Keith had been toying with an amusing theory which had the farmer killing Sam Hendrickson in reprisal because one of the Hendrickson family had fired the farmhouse. Perhaps Sandy McPhail had despoiled the daughter, Beth. McPhail, of course, had hidden in the garden of the absent McLaings and Kenny Stuart, out of loyalty to a brother of the soil, had kept silent about his movement, beyond the hedges, to the Hendrickson garden and back again and had harrowed over the betraying footprints . . .

Munro's question brought him back to earth where, for the moment, he had no desire to be. 'Did you know that Kechnie crossed the road just before the shot was heard?' He asked.

'We knew that,' Gowrie said. 'But —'

'And did you know that Mrs Beecher is Kechnie's sister? And that Sam Hendrickson and his members harrassed Kechnie almost to the point of ruin?' Keith fell silent and lost himself in thought.

'How is it that folk will tell you things that they do not bother to tell the police?' Munro demanded angrily.

'Perhaps he doesn't look at them as if he suspected them of selling cut flowers on the Sabbath,' Deborah said.

Munro ignored the comment. He swivelled round in his seat to look at Keith. 'So you believe that Mr Kechnie crossed the road, borrowed a leftover cartridge from his sister, Mrs Beecher, slipped through the Strathlings' garden during the races, shot Hendrickson and remained hidden until the fuss was over and he could return home by the same route?' There was no reply. 'Hey?' he added.

'What was that?' Keith said. 'Sorry, I wasn't listening.'

Munro, dusky red in the face, repeated the question.

'No,' Keith said. The digression had gained him time to organise his thoughts. 'I don't think that at all. The persecution of Kechnie must have petered out when Sam Hendrickson fell ill. And revenge was never enough motivation for an intelligent man with a good lifestyle at stake. The only thing that Kechnie told me which I believed was that he hadn't wanted Hendrickson dead. He enjoyed seeing him helpless. Charming gentleman is Mr Kechnie.'

Gowrie had waited, smiling quietly, through this exchange. Now he stirred and looked round. 'Mr Kechnie's phone was out of order,' he said. 'We've checked that with Telecom. He went over to borrow his sister's phone, and he was speaking to one of his shops when the shot was fired.'

Superintendent Munro was in no doubt that his subordinate had stood aside to watch him being fooled. He was ready to explode, but Keith jumped in quickly.

'I was never in much doubt about who might be guilty,' Keith said. 'The man who induced the Hendricksons to come and live next door to him and who, just before the shot was heard, went to visit the one house where he could be sure of a chance to purloin a twelve-bore cartridge. Right, Toots?'

'That's right,' Deborah said. 'I asked Mr Albany. He was a bit snotty about it, but he told me in the end. He keeps his cartridges in a drawer in his study, but his guns live in a cupboard in the hall. So when Mr Strathling came in to ask for the numbers on his guns, Mr Albany had to leave him alone in the study and go to look.'

'What's more,' Keith said, 'Strathling admitted to going as far as the gap in the hedge once, and he only admitted that after he

175

realised that I knew something. But Mrs Pollock saw him coming back from the Hendricksons' garden before he crossed over to the Albanys'. And when he returned home from the Albanys', old Mrs Orton saw him go to the gap again and vanish, and that was at about the time she waved to the farmer. She didn't hear the shot, but she was seen to wave shortly before the shot was heard. So he went through the hedge and towards the summerhouse, not once but twice, the second time just before the shot.'

Gowrie sat up very straight. 'If Strathling killed Sam Hendrickson —' he began.

'I'm not saying that Sam Hendrickson was murdered,' Keith said. 'I never have said that. All I've ever said was that Sam didn't kill himself.'

'Then what?' Gowrie said. 'And why?'

Keith was thinking aloud. 'You don't have to prove a motive in court, but it's a hell of a help.' He stopped. 'That visit from Mr McPhail the farmer. I can't . . .' He stopped again and then burst out, 'Damn it to hell! I've blown it. He must know by now that I'm going to point the finger at him, but I can't do any more until Monday. On Monday, I can fill the biggest gap.'

'Motive?' said Munro.

'Blast motive! I'm talking about good, solid evidence of wrongdoing.'

'Why Monday?' Munro asked plaintively. 'What's so special about a Monday?'

'Because that's when the insurance company will open again,' Keith said reasonably.

'If you mean Mr Strathling's company . . .' Deborah began.

'Which else?'

'Well, there was something on the telly the other night. It was a commercial. A new round-the-week telephone service, evenings and weekends included. A phone-line to somebody at the computer, for quotations, instant cover or reports of claims.'

Keith pulled his daughter to him and kissed her on the cheek, an embrace which she accepted reluctantly but with dignity. 'Then all may not yet be lost,' he said. 'If this works, you can dye your hair any colour you like.'

Munro looked over his shoulder. He seemed about to say that Keith's permission had come too late for him, but Deborah got her oar in first. 'I'll hold you to that,' she said.

'Hang on here for a few minutes,' said Keith. 'If Strathling tries to leave, stop him. Breathalyse him, ask him to produce an alibi for tomorrow morning, anything. But don't let him drive away or you may never see him again.'

'Where are you going?' Gowrie asked.

'Summerhouse.'

'It's sealed.'

'Blast your seal!' Keith erupted from the car and vanished through the Hendricksons' gate.

Gowrie looked at Superintendent Munro. 'He can't treat us – the police – like that, can he?'

'Likely not,' Munro said. 'But he aye does.'

'Anybody else would sit still while we did the running around.'

'It is more restful this way,' Munro said. He slid his long body down again in the seat. 'Were we to understand that the mannie McPhail came into it somewhere?'

'That's what I took him to be saying.'

'He doesn't mean to be obscure,' Deborah said apologetically from the back seat. 'He probably thinks that we know exactly what he's talking about.'

'Well, we do not,' Munro said. 'But we had best wait for him. He has the knack of being on the right track, just now and again.'

# TWELVE

Keith collected the keys of the summerhouse from Mrs Hendrickson, parried her questions and hurried up the garden. He had no interest in the summerhouse as the scene of a crime – what he wanted most in the world at that moment was access to Sam Hendrickson's files and to a telephone where he would not be overheard. He closed the door carefully and looked to see that the windows were shut.

He had finished his calls and was sitting in the wheelchair with the file open on the desk in front of him, mentally sifting the facts in the light of what he had just learned. A breath of air and a soft footfall warned him that he was no longer alone. He span the wheelchair round, half-expecting a furious Ben Strathling.

Beth Hendrickson was in the doorway, fresh-looking in a smart, cotton frock but still showing traces of her rash. She came in the rest of the way. 'Hullo,' she said. 'Have you had German measles? I'm over the worst, but I may still be infectious.'

'I don't remember,' Keith said. 'It doesn't matter. I'm just going.'

'No. I want to talk to you,' she said, as if that settled the matter. 'I'll sit right over here.'

Keith decided that, if he were liable to the infection, Thursday's episode had probably done the damage already. 'All right,' he said. 'But first close the door. I gather that you haven't been telling the police the same tarradiddles you told us.'

She sat down very demurely in one of the armchairs, knees close together. 'About Spike, you mean? I was only being silly. He irritates me sometimes, sucking up to Mother and hanging

178

around that daughter of yours, hoping that she'll let him hold her hand.'

Keith would have liked to pursue this hint at Deborah's innocence but doubted whether he could trust the source. 'So you tell a completely different set of damn lies,' he said. 'Truth isn't something to use or discard as it suits you.'

'I know that,' she said. 'It's just that ... don't you find that the world's full of people who get up your nose?'

This was so close to Keith's own sentiment that he added it to his list of subjects best avoided. 'What did you want to talk about?' he asked.

'About my mother. She's got a bee in her bonnet now about fostering handicapped children. Could you talk to her? She seems to think a lot of your advice.'

Keith blinked at her in amazement. 'I could. But why on earth should I? It seems to be just the thing for her. She desperately wants to help people. She lost your father, and you two will be flying the nest soon. She has a big house.'

'But it's my home,' Beth said as if he were being deliberately obtuse. 'I don't want it filled up with snotty-nosed, half-witted oiks. And she'll be doing it at our expense. Don't forget that she won't have any money of her own.'

'You're wrong there,' Keith said. 'Your father left a lot of investments.'

'But the insurance policies —'

'She won't be broke,' Keith said.

She sat and stared at him. 'You know what happened?' she said. 'All of it?'

'I think so.'

'What, then?'

Keith wanted to promise that she'd be the last to know. Instead, he said, 'I can't tell anybody until the police know and have acted.'

'I have a right to know.'

'Tell me what right,' he said.

'I don't think Mother's so far off the beam after all,' she said after a thoughtful pause. 'You're very clever. And an attractive man. For your age. You could easily persuade her if you wanted to. She's very highly sexed and she's about due for a new man in her life.'

179

Keith's first impression, that he was in for a burst of adolescent hero-worship, faded rapidly at the reference to his age. He came as close as he was capable to being shocked. 'If you're suggesting that I should seduce your mother in order to persuade her not to go in for fostering,' he said, 'put it out of your mind. If she got a little consideration and affection from you, and if you told her, as you've told me, that you value your home, she might not feel the need to try again. Go and tell your mother that I've solved the case. The first and largest insurance policy will pay off, also the union's insurance.'

She looked up at the ceiling but without seeing the damage. It was the gesture of one who is hard pressed. 'Do I have to be the one to tell her? She'll only go on about God and miracles.'

'She could be right. Was it you or your brother who brought home joints for your father?' He awaited her answer with misgivings, not enjoying the prospect of having to be the heavy father.

'That was me,' Beth said to his relief. 'Spike didn't know. He gets a bit virtuous about that sort of thing. But I was sorry for the old boy and I couldn't think of anything else I could do to make it easier for him.'

Keith nodded. He could not show approval. But at least the girl had meant well for once. 'Run along now,' he said.

'If you tell anybody, I'll deny it,' Beth said.

'I expect so. Now, go.' He chased her outside before she could think of any more questions.

They had waited in the car, with some attempt at patience, for nearly an hour before Keith returned, looking pleased with himself, and settled again into the rear seat.

'I was right,' he said. 'I got the key of the summerhouse, broke your seal, dug out Sam Hendrickson's file of insurances and phoned the company. They've got a record of his first policy on the computer but there's no trace of the later two. I phoned the doctor as well, of course. What do you make of that?'

Superintendent Munro began to make a hissing sound.

'I think you'd better explain, Dad,' Deborah said tactfully. 'Go into more detail. Just so that we know we're all talking about the same thing.'

180

Munro, who had been on the point of an outburst, grunted agreement and subsided.

'But it's all quite clear,' Keith said. 'Strathling's a gambler. We've none of us ever found him on a Saturday except in front of the horse-racing on the haunted fishtank, and Sir Peter mentioned bumping into him at the races and in casinos. That would explain his being strapped for cash. Deborah said that the house didn't smell prosperous. You'll likely find that he's in debt for more of a lump sum than he'd have been able to raise on his pension.

'And then, I suppose, while he was facing the prospect of compulsory retirement within a few years and with nothing in the kitty, he realised that he was taking in large sums in premiums and passing them on to his firm. Much of that money would be eaten up by administrative costs, some more was available for investment and in most years, if they'd figured the actuarial risks correctly, only a part of the remainder was paid out in claims.

'He was dealing directly with many of the policy-holders. Why shouldn't he pocket the premiums and fill out policy forms himself? That way, and given a little luck, he could build up a reserve which his creditors never knew about. If he told each policy-holder to deal only directly with himself, why would they do otherwise – especially if he told them that they would save commission that way, or some such nonsense?

'Insurance companies aren't in business for charity. Essentially, they're in the position of bookmakers, taking the premiums and offering odds which can be expected to show them a profit in the longer run. The policy-holder is a punter, betting on his own victimisation by robbers or by the fates. Strathling would only be making the sensible decision to be the bookie rather than the punter. As a gambler, the notion would appeal to him.' Keith slapped his knee as another memory came to him. 'Sir Peter said that the company had been getting very sticky about paying claims. That would be Strathling, not keen to settle claims out of what he'd come to look on as his personal nest-egg.'

Munro gave a low whistle. 'And then Sam Hendrickson fell ill,' he said.

'Exactly. Strathling had underwritten the last two policies

181

himself. Hendrickson, after all, was the younger man and could be expected to outlive him. So, when Hendrickson fell ill, Strathling visited the sick man and saw for himself that his condition was far from good. He suggested that the Hendricksons might move into the house next door to him, where he could keep a weather eye out. At that time he probably intended no more than to get early warning of any worsening of Sam's health, so that he could have funds on hand or be ready to skip out with as much cash as he could lay his hands on.'

'And Hendrickson phoned the company and found him out?' Gowrie suggested. 'Was that the motive for killing him?'

'Mr Hendrickson couldn't speak on the phone,' Deborah pointed out. 'Mrs Hendrickson would have had to do the speaking for him, and she didn't or she'd certainly have told us.'

'The company could have written to him direct, mentioning only one policy,' Gowrie persisted.

'Strathling was manager of the area office,' Keith said. 'He'd have originated, or at least have had to sign, any such letter. Do I have to keep reminding you that I never said that anybody killed anybody else? Strathling took to visiting the invalid – almost every day, Mrs Hendrickson said. And one Saturday, when the television switched to covering basketball or ice-skating or something, he visited him again.'

A moment of silence was broken by a clap which made the superintendent jump. It was Gowrie, slapping his knee. 'And ... found ... him ... dead!' Gowrie said triumphantly. 'Now I think I'm with you.'

'And found him dead,' Keith echoed. 'We should have known from what was on the word-processor. Gibberish, followed by his shorthand for "I'm all right, just tired". Classic symptoms of another stroke on the way, according to the doctor. Remember, Strathling was nearly undone when Mrs Albany kept him talking because she thought that Sam had looked worse than usual.

'And now Sam Hendrickson, a big policy-holder, was dead, immediately after a farmhouse fire. A claim from the widow would spell disaster. Perhaps he simply couldn't meet both claims. Certainly not without blowing his carefully – and riskily – accumulated nest-egg.

'But he had an idea and, beastly and despicable though it

182

was, he had enough nerve to carry it out and nothing whatever to lose. Sam's policies were invalid if he should be found to have committed suicide. Strathling didn't know that there were a couple of twenty-bore cartridges tucked away in Sam's drawer. He crossed the road to Mr Albany's house, asking him some question about the serial numbers of Albany's guns. That entailed his being left alone in the study for a few minutes, and he purloined one twelve-bore cartridge.

'As soon as he could get away —'

'He must have been hopping with impatience when Mrs Albany trapped him for a chat,' Deborah said, 'because Mrs Hendrickson could have decided to visit the invalid at any moment.'

'He was. Albany said so. When he did manage to escape, he crossed the road again and ducked through the hedge back to the summerhouse. Sam Hendrickson's corpse was still undiscovered. So he typed the suicide note on Sam's word-processor. He was hurried, because Mrs Hendrickson might come at any time; but a few typing errors would be typical of Sam.

'And then he took down and loaded the twelve-bore gun, put the muzzles in Sam's mouth and pulled the trigger, effectively destroying any evidence of the stroke, and escaped back home damn quick before the sound of the shot brought Mrs Hendrickson and others to the scene. He'd have checked himself for blood-spots and changed his clothes if necessary, and then gone round to join the horrified group in the summerhouse.'

Silence fell in the car. The radio chattered suddenly with a message for a cruising panda car. 'Damnable,' Munro breathed. 'Just damnable.'

Gowrie stirred at last. 'It fits,' he said. 'And it's the only explanation which fits the known facts perfectly in all respects.'

'You cannot say that yet,' Munro said repressively. 'Not until you have had time to gather every obtainable fact and also to imagine and test every other possible explanation.' He gave a sigh. 'But I think that Mr Calder will probably turn out to be right. At the moment, if Mr Strathling has been defrauding his company or its policy-holders, we have quite enough to hold him on.'

'There'll certainly be evidence to that effect in the house,'

183

Gowrie said, 'if he's been issuing fraudulent policies from there.'

'We'd be the better of a warrant,' Munro said.

'I don't think we have time. I think Mr Calder's right again. Imagine it. First there was a suicide. Mr Calder produced evidence that was not so. They they're asked to co-operate in a fresh investigation. Mr Calder and his lassie ask a hantle of questions and then he comes across the road looking like the cat that swallowed the canary and sits in the car with us under all their windows but right outside Mrs Hendrickson's gate, which means also outside Strathling's gate. He sends the lassie to ask Mr Albany about the cartridge. We should have listened when he suggested the summerhouse. They'll be talking over the fences or phoning each other. "He asked me this, what did he ask you?"'

'And the guilty man will guess that he is found out,' Munro said sadly. 'He will be getting ready to run for it. He may be destroying evidence. We have been less than clever. This would happen at the worst time of the week, for men or magistrates. Well, we will just have to knock at the door and invite him to make a statement. If he refuses, we will have to pull men back from their golf or football and mount a watch right through the weekend.' He took up the radio microphone. 'I'll see if we have got a car to spare.'

Keith nudged his daughter and got out of the car. 'He may have started running already,' he said softly, 'and he didn't go this way. Nip up on to the footbridge and see if there's anybody walking away along the canal side.'

'All right, Dad,' Deborah strode off.

The two officers were out already and walking up the path to the Strathlings' house. As Gowrie rang the front doorbell, Munro continued round the side of the house. Keith followed him. Munro stopped at the gap in the hedge. Now that the gap was no longer in regular use it was already closing up with the new growth of spring. Keith could see old Mrs Orton at her window. He gave her a wave and she waved back. She made signals which he was only too sure that he could interpret.

'Detective Inspector Gowrie does not seem to be getting an answer,' Munro said uneasily. He moved to the back door, Keith again following.

'I think your bird's flown already,' Keith said.

'The house is not silent. Listen.'

A muffled thudding could be heard from the upper floor. It could have been anything. It could have been the heels of a dangling body, drumming against a wall.

'That doesn't sound right,' Keith said. 'We'd better break in.'

Munro looked unhappy. 'They could make trouble, if there's nothing wrong. It could even be a trick, to put us on the wrong footing.'

'And it could be somebody's death-throes.' The windows were double-glazed but the back door was singly glazed in small panes. Keith put his elbow through one of them and reached down to the lock. 'Clumsy me!' he said. 'Look what I've done.'

They followed the thumping sound up the stairs and into a severely furnished bedroom. The house was spacious but Deborah had been correct in commenting on the lack of expensive trivia and the unprosperous smell. The sounds were coming from a built-in wardrobe. Keith turned the key and opened the door.

Mrs Strathling came stumbling out. Two pairs of tights had been used, one pair as a gag and the other to tie her hands behind her back. She looked less than glamorous in tights, a panty-girdle and a longline bra, with her hair flying, make-up smudged and the beginnings of a black eye.

Superintendent Munro made a strangled sound and changed colour. 'Look after the lady,' he said. 'I will let Gowrie in.'

Keith loosened the gag first. He was in no hurry to free her hands. She was as large as he was, probably as muscular and certainly in a sizzling temper, and he was in no doubt that he would be low on her list of favourite people.

As soon as her mouth was free, a pent-up torrent of abuse was released. Her genteel accent had vanished and had been replaced by darkest Glasgow. The target was not himself but the absent Mr Strathling. 'I was meant to gae wi' him,' she said more than once. 'But no. Yon bugger was o'er greedy to share the wee puggie he'd managed to put by.' She faced the two police officers who had arrived, stunned, in the doorway and her voice rose to a screech. 'Near thirty grand he's got in his trammels, and he leaves me wi' a mortgaged house and no' a penny to keep it wi'. Dear God, I'll be slaving at the bank for the rest of my natural life!' Tears were ravaging the remains of her make-up.

'Here.' Keith gave up his half-hearted attempts to undo the knots at her wrists. He pushed her into the arms of the scandalised Munro and shot out of the room. Deborah was at the foot of the stairs.

'I could see a man,' she panted. 'He was miles along the canal bank towards the lock, carrying two suitcases.'

Keith turned back into the bedroom. Mrs Strathling had paused for breath. 'Where's his car?' he asked.

'Ahint Henderson's shop.'

'Tell your men to watch the Square,' he snapped at Munro. He descended the stairs three at a time, grabbed Deborah by the elbow and ran her out of the now open front door.

'Here,' Deborah said. 'Hi! Where's the fire, Dad.'

'I wish you hadn't said that.' He unlocked the jeep and pushed her inside, running round to hurl himself into the driver's seat. The little vehicle jerked into motion as soon as the engine fired. 'Nowhere, please God! Catching him's the police's business now. But who do you think he hates most in all the world?'

'You, I suppose. You rocked his little boat for him all right.'

'Didn't I just! His car's parked behind Henderson's shop, along by the lock, his wife says. He must've made ready to bolt.' Keith hauled the jeep, on yelping tyres, round on to the road into Newton Lauder. 'Maybe he'll only make a run for it, but his chances aren't good. In fact, they're non-existent. Munro should be broadcasting his car number to every force in Scotland by now. Strathling may decide to hit back at me before trying to run. That way, he might have revenge even if he lost everything else. He'll get a stiff term in the nick anyway. Another sentence, probably concurrent, would be neither here nor there. Wallace is supposed to have insured the shop through him but the insurance company knew nothing about it. We're not covered and Strathling knows it.'

'Oh Dad! What about the house?'

'I've got that covered with a different company, so with a bit of luck he'll ignore it. Wal wanted me to transfer my insurance to Strathling. Wait 'til I see him! It's your mother I'm worried about, alone in the shop. We can't beat him to his car, but he's got a longer way round to come.' Keith shot across the Square under the bows of a squealing furniture van and into the side-street beyond. He stopped in the lane behind the shop, blocking it completely. 'I've been burnt out of business twice in my life and I'm not wanting a third time. Come on. You can explain to your mother. Keep her in the back shop and watch out of the window in case he thinks of coming that way.'

'I don't feel very well,' Deborah said, and he saw that she looked as if she might be sick.

They cut through the garden belonging to the upstairs flat and Keith let them in through the back door of the shop. Lunchtime was on them and Molly was alone and on the point of locking up. 'We have an emergency,' Keith said. 'Go into the back shop. Deb will explain.'

Molly hesitated for a second while curiosity fought with caution. The recollection that Keith was never peremptory without good cause prevailed.

Keith was left alone in the shop, far less certain that he was right. Ben Strathling was probably driving furiously towards his chosen airport, probably across the Border, in the hope, almost certainly vain, of outstripping the police net. Word might take longer to reach the English police, but surely not long enough. Perhaps he would dump the car in some city and melt into the crowd.

But, just in case his first hunch had been correct, what would Strathling do? Keith backed in among a rackful of shooting-coats and thought about it. His mouth was dry and he could feel tension in his belly.

He had at first had a vague mental picture of Strathling entering the shop, overpowering Molly and then wandering around with a can of petrol. But somehow the picture was unconvincing. Keith tried desperately to see into Strathling's mind. Such wholesale methods would be unnecessary. Once before, the shop had been burned. He could remember only too well the damage which a small fire had wrought, helped by the boxes of cartridges and the cans of propellant powder. He wondered whether to arm himself and decided against it. The police did not take kindly to a gunsmith who took up arms against a member of the public, however guilty the latter might be.

Another worry hammered at his brain. Suppose he had guessed wrongly and Strathling was headed for the house! He was on the point of calling to Molly to phone somebody, anybody, to get out there when his thoughts were interrupted. Through the shop-window he saw Strathling's Jaguar slide into view and vanish again.

Seconds later, Strathling himself appeared, walking through the traffic as though he were immortal. A furious Mini swerved around him and hooted. Keith's heart skipped a beat when he saw that the man was holding a bottle in his hand and a brick under one arm. Of course! Lobbing a Molotov cocktail through the door would be quicker and safer by far. All that he had needed were a bottle and a rag and the can of petrol that most motorists carry in the boot, plus a brick to open the way.

Without stopping to think, Keith rushed to the door and wrestled with the locks. Through the glass, Strathling saw him and checked in his stride. As Keith got the door open, Strathling let the brick fall and struck a match. Keith paused to pull the door to behind him. The thick glass might stop a bottle but it might not. Flame flowered at the neck of the bottle. On an impulse which he afterwards admitted to have been crazy, Keith hurled himself forward.

Strathling swung his arm, releasing a curl of flame, and threw the bottle at Keith's head. It came straight at his face, roaring like a dragon and trailing smoke, and he felt its breath as he ducked and it went by.

Keith dived under it, rolled once and came up, still moving under his own momentum. He met Strathling, chest to chest, and they both went down, winded.

There was a crashing of glass behind him. The bottle fell short, shattering against the kerb. A roaring hedge of flame spread along the gutter and black smoke was borne up on the heat into the still air above the town. Flame ran and flared under Strathling's car, which was parked askew outside Kechnie's shop. Passers-by, baffled and curious, were approaching. When the heat forced vapour out of the fuel tank . . .

'Get back!' Keith yelled. 'Stay clear!' The message must have got across. He saw feet beginning to withdraw.

Keith realised that he was kneeling on the other's chest and trembling with the effort of not smashing at him.

Strathling had gone limp but his face was working and his eyes were wild. He found a voice at last. 'Why did you have to interfere?' he asked querulously. 'I was only trying to recoup my losses. It wasn't as if I was harming anybody.'

The Jaguar's fuel tank went up. The windows of Kechnie's shop cracked and fell. Keith wondered whether the grocer had been insured through his obliging neighbour.

The Square was full of running feet.

When Keith next had leisure to look around he saw that Molly was beside him. A fire engine was blocking most of his view. 'Where's Deborah?' he asked.

Molly smiled. She was always pleased when Keith remembered to be solicitous. 'She's all right. When we saw that you weren't hurt, I thought it would be better if she didn't hang around. I lent her a few pounds against her earnings. She's gone to the hairdresser.'

A fireman and a policeman were competing for Keith's attention but he shrugged them off. 'You'd better go and get her back,' he said.

'Whatever she gets done, it'll wash off or grow out,' Molly said. 'She wasn't looking too bright and I thought it might cheer her up. Let's not spoil her fun.'

'Let's spoil it straight away before she infects half the girls in the town, and all the preggies,' Keith said. 'I think she's coming down with German measles.'